A PLACE IN THE HEART

Theresa Kelly

CPH.
SAINT LOUIS

In God we live and move and have our being!

For Kerrianne, "Sweet Stuff"—
you have a special place in my heart!

Cover Illustration by Sandy Rabinowitz.

Scripture quotation are taken from the HOLY BIBLE, NEW INTERNATIONAL VERSION®. NIV®. Copyright © 1973, 1978, 1984 by International Bible Society. Used by permission of Zondervan Publishing House. All rights reserved.

Copyright © 1999 Concordia Publishing House
3558 S. Jefferson Avenue, St. Louis, MO 63118-3968
Manufactured in the United States of America

1 2 3 4 5 6 7 8 9 10   08 07 06 05 04 03 02 01 00 99

"Over the river and through the woods, to Grandmother's house we go," Cass Devane sang as she and her stepsister, Tabitha Spencer, biked the short distance between their house and the store.

Tabitha shot her a sour look. "Shouldn't it be, 'Down the street and past the playground, to Surfway we go'? That would be more accurate."

"Yeah, but it's not nearly as catchy." Cass skidded to a stop in front of the island's one grocery store and hopped off her bike. "Did you remember to bring Mom's shopping list? We don't want to forget anything."

Braking and climbing off her bike, Tabitha patted her pocket. "I've got it right here." Following Cass' example, she slid her bike into the rack outside the store entrance. "I'll be glad when Mom can do the shopping again. This is definitely not my favorite activity."

"Really? I kind of like it." Cass pushed open the door and stepped into the frigid building, a welcome change from the tropical heat outside. "Besides, you might as well get used to it. Until Mom has the baby, this is our job. The doctor ordered her to quit riding a bike, and, with how big she is, it would take her half a day to walk from the house to here."

Tabitha grinned. "I'm going to tell her what you said."

"Go ahead." Cass dismissed the threat with an airy wave. "I've already started calling her Shamu. You know, in honor of the whale at SeaWorld."

"I'll bet she loves that," Tabitha said.

"Not really." Cass laughed. "But that's what makes it even more fun."

Cass went to retrieve a shopping cart. They were in charge of shopping for Thanksgiving, a little more than a week away. Mom had heard on Kwajalein's one radio station that morning that a shipment of turkeys had arrived from Hawaii. The minute Cass and Tabitha had got in from school, Mom had sent them to Surfway to pick one up.

"I hope the turkeys aren't all gone," Tabitha said as they headed to the meat section. "It wouldn't be Thanksgiving without turkey. Meat loaf just doesn't cut it."

"Don't worry," Cass reassured her. "If Mom has to swim to Hawaii and back to make sure we have a turkey, she'll do it. She's a very determined woman."

"No joke. If I've learned anything about her since she and Dad got married last year, that's it." Tabitha shook her head in admiration. "When she puts her mind to something, she doesn't let anything stand in her way."

Reaching the meat section, Cass parked the cart off to one side and, together with Tabitha, headed for the turkeys piled in two compartments. They were relieved to see a good selection remained.

"Okay, how big a bird does Mom want?" Cass peered over Tabitha's shoulder at the shopping list in her hand.

"Uh ... let's see. " She pointed to an item about halfway down the paper. "Between 10 and 12 pounds."

Cass frowned. "That doesn't sound very big. We want to make sure we have enough for leftovers." She smacked her lips. "Nothing tastes better than turkey sandwiches the day after Thanksgiving. Then there's turkey soup and turkey casserole."

"Stop." Tabitha elbowed her in the ribs. "You're making me hungry. So what are you saying? We should get a bigger turkey?"

Cass nodded firmly. "Absolutely. I'm sure Mom wasn't thinking when she wrote down only 10 pounds." She peered into the compartment and gestured toward one of the turkeys. "See how scrawny that looks? And it's—" she checked the tag, "13 pounds. I say we go for at least an 18-pounder."

Tabitha shrugged. "Sounds good to me."

Cass dug through the mound of turkeys until she found one that weighed 19 pounds. Triumphantly hefting it out of the freezer, she lowered it into the cart then blew on her hands to restore some warmth.

"The store should provide gloves for a job like this," Cass said darkly, shoving her hands into her shorts pockets.

Tabitha shivered. "Let's hurry up and get the rest of the stuff. I'm about to freeze."

Moving rapidly through the store, they managed to find all the items on Mom's list, plus throw in a few of their own. After paying the cashier, they gave the bagger their address so the groceries could be delivered by taxi.

Exiting Surfway, Cass threw back her head and gratefully soaked up the heat, her red hair glinting with copper highlights in the sunshine. Tabitha glanced over at her and laughed.

"Look at you," she teased. "You're like a cat basking in the sun. Aren't you the one who went around moaning and groaning last year because you missed winter?"

Cass tossed her head and sniffed. "People change, you know. I've discovered being toasty warm is a lot nicer than freezing."

"Does that mean you don't want to go back to the hills

of East Tennessee to go to college?" Tabitha's sidelong look was sly.

"No." Cass grabbed her bike and backed it out of the rack. "It means, since I'm marooned on this miserable little island in the middle of the Pacific Ocean for the next nine months, I intend to do my best to enjoy it."

"Hah! You don't fool me." Tabitha's blue eyes danced with amusement. "You've come to love Kwajalein as much as I do."

"Nobody could love Kwaj as much as you do," Cass retorted good-naturedly. "But I don't hate it like I did when Mom and I first moved here."

"Fortunately, you don't hate me as much, either." Hopping on her bike, Tabitha took off up the street with Cass in laughing pursuit. "That alone proves people can change."

"Maybe it's because you're not as annoying as you used to be." Cass pulled alongside her and stuck out her tongue.

"Maybe," Tabitha conceded. "I have grown up a lot in the past year and a half."

"You and me both, pal." Then laughing and bending over her handlebars, Cass yelled, "Race you home."

Cass wheeled around the side of the house and reached the back patio, or lanai, at the same time as Tabitha. Giggling and out of breath, they slid off their bikes and leaned them against the fence.

"I guess we're not too grown up to enjoy a good race every now and then," Tabitha panted. She lifted her golden curls off her neck and fanned herself. "Whew, that was fun."

Cass' hazel eyes crinkled with laughter. "You're as competetive as I am. I like that in a sister."

"Good thing, since it looks like we're stuck with each other for the rest of our lives." Moving to the porch door, Tabitha opened it and held it for Cass. "Your mom and my dad are going to stay married forever."

"Yup. Isn't it nice?" Cass preceded her through the door. "We'll never have to worry about divorce."

Tabitha made a face. "I've already been through one of those, and it's not an experience I'd like to repeat."

"I know." Cass draped an affectionate arm across her shoulders. "I used to think having my father die when I was a baby was sad, but you had it a hundred times worse."

Tabitha shrugged. "That's all in the past so let's not talk about it. Whatever happened before, our lives now are wonderful. We have parents who love us. Mom's expecting a baby in a couple of weeks. We're seniors in high school. We both have boyfriends. Life hardly gets better than this."

"Well, maybe your life's a little better than mine," Cass pointed out. "After all, your guy's here while mine's 9,000 miles away at West Point."

"Boy, you're never satisfied, are you?" Tabitha's impish smile told Cass she was kidding.

Chapter 2

"Mom, we're home," Tabitha called as she and Cass entered the house. "We got everything you wanted from the store."

"Tabitha added some candy bars and a box of her favorite cereal," Cass added, earning herself a playful shove.

Mom looked up from the couch where she had been reading as they made their way into the living room. "Gee, it was so quiet just a few seconds ago."

"Yeah, wasn't it boring?" Cass plopped down into the recliner with a sigh. "Tell the truth. You like having us around to liven things up."

"I should probably have my head examined, but you're right." Groaning slightly, Mom shifted to a more comfortable position. "Honestly, if this baby isn't born soon, I'm afraid I'm going to wind up having a 20-pounder."

"Speaking of 20-pounders," Tabitha piped up, "we picked out a 19-pound turkey."

"You what?" Mom's eyebrows disappeared under her bangs. "Didn't I specifically ask for one between 10 and 12 pounds?"

"Well ... yes." Cass exchanged an uneasy glance with

Tabitha. "But we decided it wouldn't be big enough so we upped the weight a little bit."

"A little bit?" Mom echoed. "You practically doubled the size I requested." Her eyes narrowing, she scowled at Cass. "This was your idea, wasn't it?"

"Why do you automatically suspect me?" she grumbled.

"Because I know you." A hint of humor crept into Mom's voice. "I don't think Tabitha would have the nerve to change what I asked for unless she was led astray by you."

"Well, I like that." Pouting, Cass flung herself back in the chair and folded her arms. She glared at Tabitha who tried to hide her smug smile. "Why do you always come out smelling like a rose in these situations while Mom pins the blame on me?"

"The same reason Dad usually takes your side, I guess." Tabitha shrugged her unconcern. "Our folks prefer each other's kid over their own."

"What do you suppose will happen when the baby gets here?" Cass asked.

"He or she will be the favorite, and we'll be left out in the cold," Tabitha replied, then added quickly, "Just kidding. I know you and Dad won't love the baby more than you love us."

"Don't bet on it," Cass muttered darkly. "For the first year or so it won't be able to talk back, so of course they'll love it better."

"She has a point." Mom laughed at Tabitha's frown. "Just kidding."

"Gee, I see where you get your sparkling sense of humor from," Tabitha drawled to Cass. "Let's just hope the baby doesn't inherit it too. I'm already surrounded by comedians."

Mom suddenly snapped her fingers. "Oh, Cass, I almost forgot. Alex called. He wants you to call him back."

Cass' eyes widened in surprise. "Alex Johnson?"

"He didn't leave his last name," Mom replied. "Do you

know any other Alex?"

"I don't." Cass turned to Tabitha. "Do you?"

Tabitha shook her head.

Mom frowned at Cass. "Wasn't there some talk that Alex had gotten a girl pregnant?"

Cass nodded. "Her name was Alison Ross. She graduated in May."

"I remember her now. She was quite beautiful." Mom frowned. "I don't want you getting mixed up with a boy like that."

"She won't," Tabitha jumped in, and Cass thought her words were said just as much in warning as in defense. She turned to Cass. "But what do you suppose he wants? You two haven't said more than five words to each other in more than a year."

"There's one way to find out." Pushing down the recliner's footrest, Cass got up. "I'll go call him."

"Don't let him talk you into going out," Tabitha warned as Cass passed the rocking chair where she sat.

Cass snorted. "Yeah, like that's a real possibility. I learned my lesson last year. You couldn't pay me enough to give Alex a second chance."

Cass took the phone out to the porch and perched on the windowsill to dial Alex's number. Although she wouldn't say she was nervous exactly, her finger shook a bit as she pressed the numbers.

"Hello?" a woman answered on the second ring.

"Hello. Mrs. Johnson?"

"Yes."

"This is Cass Devane. Is Alex there?"

"I'm not sure. Let me check."

Mrs. Johnson set down the phone. Cass could hear her calling Alex's name, but couldn't make out a response. Just as she decided he wasn't home, someone picked up the receiver.

"Cass?"

"Hey, Alex." She strove to sound casual. "Long time, no talk. What's up?"

"I was wondering if you'd like to get together this weekend."

Blinking with surprise, Cass held the phone away for a second and stared at it. When she brought it back to her ear, she asked, "Why?"

Instead of taking offense, Alex laughed. "Still as blunt as ever, I see. Do I need a reason to want to spend time with you?"

"After the way we left things last fall, yes." Cass didn't bother hiding her suspicion. "Is this some kind of joke? Or did somebody put you up to it?"

"No, and no. I'm serious about wanting to go out, and it's entirely my idea. So," Alex wheedled, "what do you say?"

"Look, I don't want to hurt your feelings, but we found out last year that we have nothing in common," Cass reminded him. "My faith's the most important thing in the world to me, and you don't believe in God. Life's a big game to you, and I take relationships seriously. I have certain standards when it comes to dating and you ... well ... you know ..." Unable to finish the thought, she let her words trail off.

"You heard about Alison Ross and me?" Alex asked quietly.

"Who didn't?" Instantly regretting her flippancy, Cass apologized, "Sorry. That was uncalled for."

"What if I said that's what I want to talk to you about?"

Cass' mouth puckered with distaste. "I'm not interested in hearing all the gory details about you and Alison. That's sick."

"I'm not talking about going into details. I just ... I don't know ... I get really confused sometimes about what happened."

"Then talk to your parents," Cass advised. "Or make an appointment with Pastor Thompson. He's a good listener."

"No way," Alex objected. "He's a pastor. He'll try to cram God down my throat."

"You see?" Cass sighed her irritation. "That right there is why we can't go out. You have no respect for my beliefs."

"If we can't go out, can we at least be friends?"

"What's the point?" Cass challenged. "We'd only wind up arguing."

"The point is—" Alex spoke so softly that she had to strain to hear him, "I could really use a friend."

Cass hesitated, unsure how to respond. "Look, it's a free country. If you want to talk to me at school tomorrow, I can't stop you."

To her surprise, Alex laughed. "That's the nicest offer I've received in a long time. Be prepared. I'm going to take you up on it."

"Oh, goody. I can hardly wait."

"Good one," Alex approved. "I forgot how sarcastic you are. I've really missed you."

"Don't be silly," Cass shot back. "You can't miss something you never had."

"There you go again. I'll see you in the morning. Oh, and Cass," Alex added, his voice growing serious, "thanks for calling back."

"You're welcome. Consider it my good deed for the day." She hung up on Alex's bark of laughter.

Returning to the living room, she found that neither Mom nor Tabitha had moved. They eagerly watched her as she sat back down in the recliner.

"Well?" Mom prompted when Cass didn't say anything. "Why did he call?"

"I'm not sure." Raising the footrest, she leaned back and crossed her ankles. "He asked me to go out this weekend. When I turned him down, he wanted to know if we could be friends. He said he needed to talk about what happened with Alison."

"I'm not sure I'm comfortable with that," Mom said with a frown.

"Neither am I. I told him that. But there was something—" Cass hesitated, trying to find the right words to express herself, "about the way he sounded. Maybe he does need a friend. What should I do?"

Mom shrugged uncertainly. "My first reaction is to tell you to have nothing to do with Alex. However, if he's truly searching and he's come to you, I don't know how you can turn your back on him. The best thing we can do right now is pray about it."

"Personally, I don't think you should have anything to do with Alex," Tabitha declared. "I don't trust that boy one iota."

"Me neither." Cass shuddered. "He sort of reminds me of something that's crawled out from under a rock."

"That's a terrible thing to say," Mom scolded, trying to stifle a snicker.

"Then why are you laughing?" Cass challenged.

"Because, unfortunately, I still have a long way to go on my Christian walk." Although she tried to sound repentant, Mom couldn't pull it off and wound up laughing.

"You're not a very good role model." Tabitha assumed her sternest expression, which only made Mom laugh harder.

A short while later, a knock sounded at the door to let them know the groceries had been delivered. After helping Tabitha put them away, Cass headed to her room to do homework until it was time for supper.

As much as she tried to concentrate on her assignment, Cass found her thoughts drifting back to her conversation with Alex. *Jesus*, she prayed, *show me how to handle this. I find it hard to believe I'm supposed to have anything to do with Alex, but I've learned You work in mysterious ways. Lead me through Your Word to understand what You would have me do about this.*

CHAPTER 3

The next morning, Sam Steele, Tabitha's boyfriend, arrived to accompany Tabitha to school. Since Cass wasn't quite ready, she told the pair to go on. When she wheeled her bike around to the front of the house, she discovered Alex waiting for her. Stopping, she steadied the bike with one hand and propped the other on her hip.

"What are you doing here?"

"You said we could talk at school."

Cass made a show of looking around. "Does this look like school to you?"

"No," Alex admitted. "I thought we could get a head start on our conversation if I showed up here."

Shaking her head in irritation, Cass climbed on her bike. "That's so typical of you. It doesn't matter what we agreed on. You felt like coming over so you did."

Alex assumed a penitent expression. "Does this mean you're not going to talk to me until we get to school?"

"Yup." Cass headed down the street without a backward glance.

A moment later, Alex pulled alongside her. "Fine. You don't have to say a word. I'll do all the talking."

If Cass could have, she'd have clamped her hands over

her ears to drown him out. Since that wasn't possible, she pedaled as fast as she could, trying to outrun him. Unfortunately, Alex easily kept pace with her.

"I see your sister's dating Sam Steele," he observed. "I don't know him all that well, but he seems like a nice guy. What does Micah think about the two of them going out?"

Cass wanted to keep silent but couldn't. "Why don't you ask him?"

"I would, but I don't know how to get in touch with him," Alex replied pleasantly. "You, on the other hand, appear to have remained true-blue to Logan. I'll bet he appreciates that. How's he doing at West Point, by the way?"

Gritting her teeth, Cass stared straight ahead. One more turn, and she'd be at school.

As if reading her thoughts, Alex commented, "You have to talk to me once we get to school, you know. That's the deal."

Grrr! Cass growled silently. *He really is the most annoying person. How did I get myself into this mess?* Abruptly recalling last night's promise to pray, she grudgingly beseeched God, *Okay, I said I'd ask You what to do about Alex so I'm asking. I'm not happy about it, but I am asking. If You want me to be nice to him, give me a sign. Something, anything.*

"How come you're not being nice?"

Alex's question, using the exact word she'd just used in her prayer, unnerved Cass. She started, and the front wheel of her bike wobbled nearly enough to make her lose control. Righting it, she slowed and stared over at Alex.

"Wh-what did you say?"

"I want to know why you're being so mean," he complained. "You make a huge deal about being a Christian. Aren't you people supposed to be nice to everyone?"

All right, Lord, Cass laughed to herself, *I can take a hint.*

Aloud, she said, "Sort of. A lot of people call it hating the sin but loving the sinner."

Alex's chest expanded with indignation. "Are you calling me a sinner?"

Cass flashed him a humorous look. "I hate to be the one to break it to you, but we're all sinners. Jesus was the only person who never sinned."

"I know a lot of good people," Alex protested.

"So do I." Cass dismissed his assertion with a shrug. "But they're still sinners. Everyone, at some point, sins. Except Jesus," she added. "Which means everyone, including you and I, needs a Savior."

"I'm doing just fine on my own." Alex's jaw thrust forward at a defiant angle.

"No, you're not." Reaching the front of the school, Cass braked and hopped off her bike. "But I'm not going to argue with you. If you want to think you're okay, that's your business."

"I hate it when people act superior." Alex's expression was as resentful as his tone. "Like they know something the rest of us don't."

"I'm sorry if I came across as superior. That wasn't my intention." After parking her bike, Cass turned to level a firm gaze at Alex. "However, I won't apologize for speaking the truth, and the truth is we all need Jesus, whether we want to admit it or not."

Without giving him a chance to respond, she spun around and ran smack into her best friend, Rianne Thayer. Rianne yelped and jumped back. She rubbed her foot, although her eyes remained on Alex.

"Oh, Rianne." Cass clutched her friend's arm and attempted to help rub her foot. "I'm so sorry. I didn't see you standing there."

Wincing, Rianne gingerly set her injured foot back

down. "It's all right. I'm sure the damage isn't permanent. I should be able to walk without crutches in a couple of months."

"I really am sorry," Cass repeated, smoothing Rianne's hair and straightening her clothes in a vain attempt to make it up to her. "I should have looked where I was going."

Rianne's features hardened as she glanced again at Alex. "I can see why you might be in a hurry to escape. What were you doing talking to him anyway?"

"He called last night—" Cass lowered her voice, "then he showed up this morning and rode to school with me."

"He what?" squealed Rianne. "Please tell me you're joking!"

"Ssh! You want the whole school to hear you? Honestly!"

Grabbing Rianne's hand, Cass dragged her into the building. She didn't let go until they reached their lockers.

"What were you thinking, making a spectacle of yourself like that?" Cass demanded.

Rianne pressed a hand to her chest, her brown eyes wide with innocence. "You're accusing me of making a spectacle of myself? I'm not the one who rode up to the school with Alex Johnson, a boy whose reputation is known far and wide."

"Hah!" Cass jeered. "Kwajalein's three miles long by a half-mile wide. How far can his reputation have spread?"

"Obviously you're forgetting Alison left in May," Rianne pointed out with a smirk. "You're not dumb enough to think she hasn't told people what happened, are you? So Alex's reputation has traveled at least as far as she has."

Crossing her arms, Cass leaned against the locker. "Do you really think she would talk about stuff like that?"

A shadow of uncertainty passed across Rianne's face.

"How should I know? If it were me, I'd never tell another soul."

"If it were you, I'd be the most stunned person in the world," Cass quipped. Pushing off from the locker, she turned and began spinning out the combination. "Now, to get back to Alex, it's not what you think with him. He called yesterday while Tabitha and I were shopping for Mom. I called him back when I got in. Reluctantly, I might add. He said he wanted us to be friends, but I couldn't get him to tell me why. He asked if we could get together to talk, but I told him I'd see him at school. Apparently, he took that as an invitation to stop by this morning. End of story."

"Are you going to see him again?" Rianne asked, twirling the combination on her locker.

"I didn't 'see' him this time." Cass' voice held a tinge of impatience. "He showed up. What was I supposed to do? Hide in the house until he left?"

"I guess not." Rianne dug through the locker for her books. "Anyway, when you stepped on me earlier, I was standing right behind you for a reason. I was wondering if you've given college much thought."

Cass blinked at the abrupt shift in subjects. "Uh ... some. Why?"

"I started thinking last night about what a huge decision it is." A frown puckered Rianne's forehead. "I mean, where you go to college determines pretty much the rest of your life. What if you pick the wrong school?"

"Whoa. I think you're going a little overboard here." Grabbing her morning books, Cass shut her locker and turned to face Rianne. "Sure, it's a big deal. But it's not that big. If you find you've chosen the wrong place, you can always transfer. People do it all the time."

"I don't want to transfer. I want to choose right the first time." Rianne raked her fingers through her wheat-colored hair. "But how do you know which school is best for you?"

Cass picked up her backpack and hoisted it onto her shoulder. "You do research. You go to the guidance office and ask Mrs. Stone for college catalogues. You take them home and read them then—voila!—you make your decision. It's easy. Why are you stressing about it?"

"Because graduation's less than six months away." Her eyes darting nervously around the hall, Rianne nibbled on her thumbnail. "Lots of kids have already applied to schools, and some have even been accepted. I'm way behind."

"So am I, but you don't see me agonizing over it." Seeing that Rianne was finished, Cass started for their homeroom. "Talk to your parents. See what their advice is."

Rianne's lips thinned into a discontented line. "I already know what they're going to say."

Surprised by the bitterness in her tone, Cass shot her a questioning look. "What do you mean?"

"They're on record as wanting me to go to school with Randy at UC-Davis." Rianne flipped her hair over her shoulder. "Not that they've asked me what I want."

"So tell them." Cass wove her way through the desks to hers and sat down.

Snorting, Rianne took the seat behind her. "You know what my folks are like. They aren't as open to suggestions as yours are."

Cass frowned. "Fine. I might as well keep my mouth shut if you're going to argue with everything I say."

Rianne sighed. "Sorry. I'm not in the best mood this morning." She hung her head in remorse. "I don't know what's wrong with me."

"Reality is setting in," Cass said with a shrug. "It's dawned on you that you're not going to stay in high school forever. Real life is just around the corner."

"Please—" Rianne gave a delicate shudder, "don't

remind me. Let's talk about something else. I'm depressed enough as it is."

"Thinking about college shouldn't be depressing," Cass protested. "Don't you find it at all exciting to imagine what life is going to be like next year?"

"Nope. I'm dreading it." Rianne raised a hand to forestall more comments. "I'm serious. I don't want to discuss it. Let's talk about Logan. Have you heard from him lately?"

Having no choice but to follow her wishes, Cass launched into an account of Logan's most recent activities at West Point. She soon had Rianne laughing as she detailed his run-ins with upperclassmen. Even as she talked, however, there remained in the back of her mind a nagging concern about Rianne's college fears. Cass vowed to bring the subject up again at the first opportunity that presented itself.

Throughout the rest of the day, she found herself frequently encountering Alex. Instead of ignoring her after her parting remark that morning, he made a point of walking to class with her and even attempted to sit with her at lunch. That idea was quickly voted down, not only by Cass, but also by Tabitha, Rianne, and Tabitha's best friend, Kira Alexander. The four of them sat together everyday and had no intention of allowing any boy to join them. Alex was particularly unwelcome.

"Tabitha said the two of you talked last night," Kira commented to Cass after Alex left. Her dark eyes gleamed with curiosity. "What do you suppose he wants?"

"I have no idea." Cass lifted her hands in a gesture of bewilderment. "He says he wants to be friends, but I don't believe that's all it is."

"Maybe he realizes what a treasure he lost when he blew his chance with you last year, and he's hoping for another chance," Kira joked.

"Uh-huh. Sure." Cass snorted her skepticism. "If I believe that, you have oceanfront property in North Dakota you'd like to sell me, right?"

"Actually, it's in Nebraska," Kira shot back.

"Same difference." Cass bit into her ham sandwich. "If I'm gullible enough to fall for your theory about Alex, I'm gullible enough to fall for anything."

Ignoring the ensuing comments on her gullibility from the others, Cass quickly changed the subject, and thankfully managed to get their minds off Alex.

CHAPTER 4

Near the end of the lunch period, Sam came over to the table and asked Tabitha if she'd like to go outside for the remaining few minutes. She glanced around at the others.

"Are we finished talking?"

"No, but far be it from us to stand in the way of true love," Kira drawled. "Go on—" she flapped a hand at the couple, "enjoy yourselves. We three old maids will just sit in here and wither on the vine."

Accompanying Sam out the door, Tabitha thought about how far Kira had come in her acceptance of her friendship with him. Her ex-boyfriend was Kira's older brother, Micah. Their relationship had fallen apart when Micah left to attend college in Hawaii. Kira had initially blamed Tabitha for the break-up, believing she'd dumped Micah for Sam. Their own friendship had experienced some rocky times, but they'd managed to patch up their differences, and Tabitha was grateful.

"Penny for your thoughts," Sam offered as they exited the cafeteria.

Tabitha smiled up at him. "I was thinking how amazing it is that Kira accepts us enough that she's able to joke about our relationship. She really hated our guts for awhile."

"She was looking out for her brother's interests." Sam led the way to a low wall bordering the courtyard. "I respect that." He laughed wryly. "I didn't like it at the time, but I respected her for it."

Settling herself on the sun-warmed wall next to Sam, Tabitha butted shoulders with him. "You're a good guy. No matter what, you always try to be fair."

"Yeah, I'm a prince," he agreed, grinning. "Which makes you a princess. Of course, I knew that the first moment I laid eyes on you. I said to myself, 'Now there's one very special lady.'"

"At the time, I thought you were interested in Cass," Tabitha reminded him.

Sam dismissed her remark with a disdainful wave. "I only used her to get to you."

Tabitha attempted to muffle her giggle by clamping her hand over her mouth. "Ooh, I'm telling."

Sam's eyes widened with mock alarm. "Please don't. The last thing I want is your sister mad at me. I've seen her when she's angry, and it's not a pretty sight."

"I'll keep my mouth shut on the condition you take me to the movie tomorrow night." Crossing her arms, Tabitha did her best to look threatening.

"Gee, I don't know. You drive a hard bargain." Sam scratched his head, pretending to consider the offer. "Okay, it's a deal." He stuck out his hand, and they shook on it. Before letting go, he leaned over to whisper, "Boy, did you get snookered. I didn't use Cass. I'd never do something like that."

"Duh," Tabitha whispered back. "I know that. Talk about getting snookered. Who just got tricked into taking who out? And who's going to be paying?"

Sam's bark of laughter caused several students to look in their direction. He shook his head in admiration. "Man, you're good. I'm going to have to watch my step around you."

"You mean you haven't figured that out yet?" Sliding off the wall, Tabitha faced him with an impish smile. "You're not nearly as quick as I thought you were. I may have to rethink this relationship."

"While you're rethinking it—" Sam reached for her hands, "I'm just going to enjoy it. Dating you is the most fun I've ever had."

"Boy, have you led a pathetic life." The bell rang, and Tabitha slipped her hands out from Sam's. "We'd better go. I don't like being late for class."

"That's another thing I like about you." Sam held the cafeteria door open for her. "You're punctual. A lot of girls aren't."

Tabitha gave him a teasing look. "What are you talking about? You should know I'm only punctual at school. Have you forgotten about all the times you've had to wait when you've come to pick me up for a date?" As they headed across the lunchroom, she added with mock irritation, "And what's this about a lot of girls not being punctual? You're always hinting around about the girls in your past. Exactly how many are we talking about? More than a hundred?"

"I wish." Sam trailed her to the table where she retrieved her books. "Unfortunately, the number is way— and I mean, *way*—less than that. I talk a good game."

"Between ten and twenty?"

After a stop at Sam's table so he could get his backpack, the couple left the lunchroom and started down the corridor.

"More like two," he admitted. "Believe it or not, I'm basically pretty shy."

"You?" Tabitha's tone was skeptical. "You're the least shy guy I know. You're always talking to people and joking around."

"It's all an act to cover up my shyness." When Tabitha

24

continued to look unconvinced, Sam said earnestly, "Honest. It's hard for me to get close to people. I guess it has something to do with my father being in the army and us having to move around so much. It's not fun leaving friends behind."

Hearing the sincerity in his voice, Tabitha briefly rested her hand on his arm. "Then I'm flattered you decided to take a chance on me."

"Tabs," Sam assured her, "you are definitely worth the risk."

They separated at the end of the hall, each heading for a different class. Tabitha slid into the desk behind Rianne in French class just as the bell rang.

Turning to give her a sly grin, Rianne whispered, "Did you and Sam have a nice walk?"

"Very nice, thank you," Tabitha replied primly.

"Good," Rianne teased. "I wouldn't want you to be depressed for the rest of the afternoon."

The next week passed quickly as Tabitha and Cass helped Mom prepare for Thanksgiving. By the time Thursday rolled around, Tabitha was grateful to be relieved of the cleaning chores to concentrate more on cooking. Ordering Mom and Dad to relax, she and Cass took over setting the table and taking care of the last-minute details.

"Okay, Dad," Tabitha called from the kitchen, "you can carve the turkey now."

Leaving Mom on the sofa, Dad obediently made his way to the kitchen. "Are you sure this is a turkey and not an ostrich?" he quipped, lifting the pan out of the oven and setting it on the counter.

Tabitha rolled her eyes at Cass. "The turkey jokes have gotten really old, Dad. So it's big; get over it. Besides, you'll be thanking us when you're enjoying turkey soup next week."

"And the week after that, and the week after that." When Tabitha threatened him with the turkey baster, he raised his hands in surrender. "Okay, no more jokes. Gee whiz, you don't have to get violent."

After everything had been set out, Dad escorted Mom to the table and seated her, then did the same with Tabitha and Cass. He lit the candles before finally sitting down himself. Looking around the table, his face beamed with happiness.

"Now I truly know what the psalmist meant when he wrote his cup overfloweth," he murmured. "Let's join hands for the blessing."

As she reached for Cass' hand, Tabitha thought back to when she could barely stand to touch her sister during the mealtime blessings and smiled. *Thank You for changing my heart toward her, Lord,* she prayed silently, squeezing Cass' hand.

"Father," Dad prayed, "You are worthy to be praised. Thank You for providing this food to nourish our bodies and for sending Your Son to die for us so that we can live forever. In Jesus' holy name we pray, amen."

Once everyone's plates were heaped with turkey and all the fixings, Mom smiled at Dad. "Steve, you go first. What are you thankful for?"

"My salvation," he promptly replied. "Then you, our beautiful daughters, our unborn baby, our families back home, our friends, my job, this house, this wonderful meal." He stopped and thought a moment. "I believe that about covers it. What about you?"

"Except for the job, my list is the same as yours." Mom turned to Tabitha on her left. "Your turn, Sweetie."

"Let's see." She set down her fork and leaned back in the chair. "Being saved, of course. You and Dad. Cass—" she smirked at her sister, "even though she's a pain most of the time. The baby. Living here. My friends." She shrugged.

"That's it."

"Is Sam included under friends?" Cass asked around a mouthful of mashed potatoes.

Blushing, Tabitha ducked her head in acknowledgment then shoveled turkey into her mouth to avoid answering any more embarrassing questions.

"I guess that leaves you," Dad told Cass.

She pretended to pout. "Well, I like that. Only after you run out of people do you finally ask me." Dropping the pose, she continued, "Anyway, above everything else, I'm grateful that Jesus saved me. Mom, I've always appreciated you, but I appreciate you more than ever since you almost miscarried in September. Dad, you've shown me what having a father is like, and I'll never stop being thankful for that. Tabitha, you're the best sister a girl could have. I can't imagine life without you. And baby brother or sister, I can't wait for you to be born so I can start getting to know you." She crossed her arms and nodded. "There, I'm done."

"My goodness." Mom dabbed at her eyes with her napkin. "I'm overwhelmed. That was quite a speech."

"You probably should have recorded it since you're not likely to hear another one like it for quite awhile." Cass' grin was mischievous. "You know me. I usually don't like things to get mushy."

"Like it or not, you did a bang-up job," Dad observed.

A spurt of jealousy flared in Tabitha, but she tamped it down. *After all, Cass had said some sweet things about her.* "Thanks for saying what you did," she commented out loud, with only a hint of reluctance.

"Aw, don't mention it." Cass shrugged. "I'm nice one day out of the year. How much effort does that take? The rest of you are nice all the time." Switching topics, she asked, "So, is Sam coming over later?"

All remaining traces of jealousy vanished, and Tabitha

nodded happily. "He wants to try the apple pie I made."

"He's a brave boy. Ow!" Cass yelped when Tabitha kicked her under the table. "Is that any way to act on Thanksgiving?"

"What?" Tabitha asked, the picture of innocence. "My foot slipped."

"Yeah, right," muttered Cass, bending to massage her ankle.

"Ah, home sweet home." Mom's expression was equally composed of amusement and exasperation. "Just think. Next year, we'll have a baby to add to this mix."

"Yup," Dad agreed. "Won't it be wonderful?"

Chapter 5

"Tabitha, wake up." Dad shook her shoulder. "Come on, Sweetie. Rise and shine."

Groaning, Tabitha groggily blinked the sleep from her eyes and pried them open. She squinted, barely able to make Dad out in the darkness.

"What time is it? It's not even light yet."

"It's 5:15, and I'm taking Mom to the hospital," Dad explained. "She started having contractions about two hours ago."

"What!" Tabitha bolted upright and scrambled out of bed, grabbing for her robe draped over the footboard. "She's having the baby? Where is she?"

Dad laughed. "She just finished taking a shower and now she's getting dressed. And, no, she's not having the baby right this moment. That's still a few hours away."

"Does Cass know?" Tabitha yanked on her robe.

"Not yet."

"Let me tell her." She headed for the bedroom door. "I want to see the look on her face."

"Be my guest." Dad followed her into the hall and turned left. "While you do that, I'll check on Mom and see how she's doing."

Tabitha crept into Cass' room without knocking. Perching on the edge of the bed, she poked her sister in the ribs. Cass muttered something unintelligible and rolled over, drawing the quilt up around her ears. Tabitha pulled it back and tugged on her hair.

"Knock it off." Cass growled from the depths of her pillow. Flipping onto her back, she glared up at Tabitha. "What are you doing in my room in the middle of the night?"

"Someone's having a baby," Tabitha sang.

Cass looked blank for a second, then comprehension dawned and she squealed. "No way! Mom's not due for another few weeks."

"Tell that to the baby." Tabitha stood and reached down a hand to help Cass up. "According to Dad, he or she has decided to make an early appearance."

"How cool!" Cass felt around the end of the bed until she located her robe. "How's Mom doing? Have you heard her scream or anything?"

"You crack me up." Tabitha helped her into her robe then started out the door. "Can you honestly picture Mom screaming?"

"When it comes to childbirth, absolutely. From what I've read, it's not exactly a fun experience."

"Still, we're talking about Mom here," Tabitha argued. "She's the least hysterical person I know."

"Maybe so," Cass said. "But I've read childbirth can do strange things to a woman."

"Has anyone ever told you that you read too much?" Tabitha drawled.

Once they reached the hall, they hesitated, unsure what to do. The door to their parents' room was closed, and Tabitha didn't feel right knocking. Cass shrugged and gestured toward the living room. They were curled up in the corners of the couch when Mom and Dad emerged from their room a short while later. The moment she spotted their parents, Tabitha jumped up and hurried to them.

"How are you feeling?" Tabitha alternately patted Mom's back and arm.

"You're not walking to the hospital, are you?" Cass asked.

Smiling, Mom responded to them in turn. "I feel fine," she assured Tabitha. "Naturally, I'm anxious to get this over with. But, all things considered, I'm doing very well. As far as walking to the hospital, the answer's no. Even if I wanted to, I probably wouldn't make it. Dad called a taxi, which should be here any minute."

As if on schedule, a horn blared outside. Dad went to the door and waved to let the driver know they'd be right out.

Mom opened her arms to Tabitha and Cass, and they rushed into them. " The next time you see me, I'll have had the baby."

Cass patted her stomach. "It's so weird to think that in a couple of hours the little person in there will be out here with the rest of us."

"Weird," Mom agreed. "And delightful."

Placing her mouth next to Mom's ear, Tabitha murmured, "I love you, and I'll be praying for you."

"I know, Sweetie. Thank you." Mom gave them a final hug and stepped back. "I'd better go. I wouldn't want to traumatize you for life by having the baby in front of you."

"Wow, don't even kid around about something like that." Cass paled at the thought, making her freckles stand out in sharp relief.

After getting Dad's promise to call the second the baby was born, they walked their folks to the door and stood on the front porch to wave until the taxi disappeared from view. Returning to the house, they went back to the couch where they collapsed once again into separate corners.

"I don't suppose this would be considered a valid excuse for skipping school, huh?" Cass asked hopefully.

"Not by anyone else but us." Tabitha didn't bother hiding her yawn. "Which is too bad since it's not like we're going to be able to concentrate on our work." She gazed across the cushions at Cass. "Are you scared something might go wrong?"

Cass hesitated, then nodded. "Sort of. I mean, things happen. It's rare, but bad things do occur."

"Maybe we should pray." Tabitha scooted closer to Cass and grabbed her hand. "You start. My brain's not working too well right now."

Bowing her head, Cass paused for a few moments. Taking a deep breath, she began, "Jesus, we ask You to be with Mom and the baby as they go through labor and delivery. Keep them both safe and healthy. Please don't let there be any complications. Give the doctor and nurses the wisdom to do all the right things for Mom and the baby. We ask this in Your name."

"And please keep Dad calm so he can help Mom through this process," Tabitha added. "Amen."

"Amen," Cass echoed. She squeezed Tabitha's hand before releasing it. "I'm hungry. How about you?"

"Now that you mention it, I could eat something." Unfolding her legs from beneath her, Tabitha stood up. "What would you say if I offered to fix breakfast?"

Cass' mouth dropped open in astonishment. "I'd say, you go, girl. I love having a sister who knows how to cook."

On her way to the kitchen, Tabitha sent a teasing look over her shoulder. "Who said anything about cooking? I figured I'd pour you a bowl of cereal. Just kidding," she added at Cass' crestfallen expression. "I have learned a few things from Mom in the past year and a half. Would you like scrambled eggs or scrambled eggs?"

Tilting her head to the side, Cass pretended to consider

her options. "You know, I believe I'm in the mood for scrambled eggs this morning."

"Excellent choice. Scrambled eggs coming right up. I might even throw in a piece of toast if you set the table." Tabitha opened the refrigerator and began assembling ingredients.

"Make it two pieces of toast, and I'll wash the dishes," Cass counter-offered.

"You've got yourself a deal." Tabitha reached into a cupboard for the frying pan.

They worked in companionable silence for the next several minutes. By the time they sat down at the table, the sun was beginning to peek over the horizon outside the dining room window. After a quick blessing, they took a few moments to admire the view.

"It's going to rain later," Tabitha predicted, noting the crimson steaks interwoven among the gold and lavender of the sunrise. "You know the old saying—'Red sky at night, sailors delight; red sky at morning, sailors take warning.' "

"I don't need some old saying to know it's going to rain," Cass scoffed. "It's the end of November. We're in the middle of the rainy season. Chances are it's going to rain sometime during the day."

"You are the least poetic person I know." Tabitha ladled eggs onto her toast and bit into it. "Why do you always have to be so practical?"

"Somebody has to be. We can't all go around with our heads in the clouds." Cass grinned, taking the sting out of her words. "Not that there's anything wrong with having your head in the clouds. It's just that it takes both kinds to make the world go 'round."

"Like what the Bible says about the body of Christ being made up of lots of different parts," Tabitha observed.

"Exactly." Cass paused to eat a forkful of eggs. "God made us all different for a reason. Take you and Sam, for example. Y'all are about as different as night and day, but you get along really well. I think that's because you fill in the missing pieces for each other."

"I like that idea." Tabitha nodded her agreement then frowned. "But what about you and Logan? You two are a lot alike. What does that do to your theory about opposites attracting?"

"Nothing, because it's a theory, not a hard and fast rule." Warming to her subject, Cass pushed aside her plate and folded her arms along the table edge. "I tend to get annoyed with people who aren't like me."

"No!" Tabitha interjected, feigning surprise. "I never realized that about you."

Ignoring her sarcasm, Cass continued, "Being with someone flighty would drive me nuts. Logan and I do well together because we're both competitive and hard-driving, and we appreciate those qualities in each other. Except for the fact that I don't want to be in the military, I could probably go to West Point and thoroughly enjoy it."

Tabitha shuddered. "While I, on the other hand, wouldn't last more than a couple of hours. I can't imagine a worse place to go to college."

"But that's where Sam's hoping to go," Cass pointed out. "Another example of the differences between you two."

"The problem that Micah and I had is that we got too different." Tabitha made a face, recalling the reasons they broke up. "We didn't believe the same things or share the same values anymore. No matter how far apart Sam and I seem on some things, we have a lot in common when it comes to the important stuff."

"That's what really counts." Cass raised her left hand to display the True Love Waits commitment ring. "If he believes in Jesus and respects your promise to remain pure until marriage, you're way ahead of the game."

Tabitha's expression grew troubled. "Do you think

Micah's still waiting until marriage?"

"I have no idea." Pulling her plate back in front of her, Cass picked up the fork. "It's doubtful, though, with everything else he's gotten into."

"Yuck. Just the possibility gives me the creeps." Tabitha shook her head. "Let's talk about something else. Which kind of person do you think the baby's going to be? Practical or dreamy?"

"Naturally I'm hoping for practical." Cass shrugged. "But who knows? Mom's more the dreamy type, but look how I turned out."

"And Dad's as practical as they come. Hmm." Tabitha nibbled at the edge of her toast. "It looks like it could go either way." Her eyes sparkled with anticipation. "Isn't it going to be fun to see what he or she develops into?"

"It would be, but we're not going to be around much," Cass reminded her. "The baby won't even be a year old when we leave for college."

"That's right." The gleam went out of Tabitha's eyes, and her shoulders drooped. "We'll barely have time to get to know him or her."

"Even worse, the kid won't get to know us." Cass slumped in her chair. "I just realized the timing of this really stinks."

"Yeah." Tabitha began breaking her toast into little pieces and scattering them atop her remaining eggs. "I don't like this one bit."

"What can we do about it though?" As usual, Cass' practical side took over. "Even if we don't go to college, we can't continue to live here with Mom and Dad. The rule is no one over 18 can live on the island unless they work for the government."

"The baby isn't even born yet, and we're depressed about leaving it." Tabitha managed a wan smile. "I guess that means we're already bonded to the little guy."

"Or girl." Cass snapped her fingers. "I have an idea. Let's leave early for school so we can stop by the hospital on the way. Maybe, if we're lucky, Mom will have already had the baby."

"Good idea. I don't feel like eating anyway." Standing, Tabitha stacked her juice glass and utensils on her plate. "I'll get my shower while you clean up."

"Don't take too long though," Cass replied. "I want to get to the hospital as soon as possible."

It wasn't even 7:00 by the time Tabitha and Cass headed out the porch door to retrieve their bikes. As she loaded her backpack into the basket suspended from the handlebars, Tabitha suddenly hit her forehead with the palm of her hand.

"I almost forgot. Sam is coming by to ride to school with me. Should I call him or leave a note on the door?"

Cass glanced up at the clouds looming overhead. A light sprinkling had already darkened the cement lanai. "I don't think the note's a good idea. He's probably up. Why don't you call?"

When Tabitha returned from making the call, the slight drizzle was rapidly developing into a steady downpour. She and Cass pulled on their ponchos, then climbed on their bikes and took off in the direction of the hospital.

"Good morning." With Cass on her heels, Tabitha approached the receptionist at the front desk. "I'm Tabitha Spencer. My—" at Cass' soft cough, she corrected herself, "I mean, our mother went into labor early this morning. Our father brought her in about an hour and a half ago. Her name's Donna Spencer. Can you tell us if she's had the baby yet?"

The woman's fingers flew across the computer keyboard, then she studied the screen. "If she has, we don't have a record of it."

"Would it be possible for us to see her?" Cass asked.

"No, I'm afraid not. Hospital policy forbids allowing anyone but the father in the labor room." The receptionist hesitated, then smiled. "I'll tell you what I'll do though." She picked up the phone. "Let me call her room and see if your father can come out to talk to you." After a brief conversation, she hung up and informed them with a smile, "He'll be right out."

Several moments later, Dad came striding down the hall, a huge grin creasing his face. "Hey, you two," he greeted them. "Mom was thrilled when I told her you were out here."

"I guess there's no way you can sneak us into her room, huh?" Tabitha asked hopefully.

"If I could, I would." Dad ruffled her hair, and, for once, she didn't mind. "She's doing great, by the way. Her contractions are about five minutes apart so the doctor says she still has awhile to go. She's being a real trouper. Her spirits are good, and she's handling the discomfort very well. About the only thing she's complained about is being hungry, but we can't do anything about that until after the baby's born."

"I wish we could see her." Cass gazed longingly down the hall.

"She wishes you could too." Dad took the girls' hands. "Since your mom's going to ask me, did you eat before you left the house?"

"Sort of." Cass flashed her sister a smile. "Tabitha made scrambled eggs, but we wound up throwing most of them away. We didn't feel like eating after we made ourselves sad talking about not being around the baby for very long."

"What do you mean?" Dad swung their hands, his expression curious. "Are you planning on running away to join the circus or something?"

"Hello?" Cass waved to get his attention. "We're going off to college in about nine months. That doesn't give us much time with the baby."

"I've been so busy with everything else that I haven't given it much thought." Dad released their hands. "We'll have to think about that. However, I'm rather occupied at the moment. It'll need to go on the back burner until after the baby's born."

"Oh, absolutely," Cass agreed without hesitation. "I guess you should get back to Mom, huh?"

"In a few minutes. She said to spend as much time with you as I wanted." Dad turned to Tabitha and chucked her under the chin. "So, how do you feel about the imminent arrival of your baby brother or sister?"

"I'm extremely excited. I can't wait to see if we look alike."

Cass rolled her eyes and snickered. "Only you would think of something like that."

"Don't tell me you haven't wondered who the baby will look like," Tabitha retorted.

"Sure I have, but I haven't focused specifically on me." Cass rolled her eyes. "Anyway, it's not important. Uh ... Dad, does this remind you of the day Tabitha was born?"

Blinking in confusion, he stared down at her without responding for several seconds. "Well ... not really. Mom is much calmer than Beth was. As you discovered when you visited her in January, Tabitha, Beth tends to be rather melodramatic. There was a great deal of crying and yelling when she was in labor with you. I much prefer Mom's approach."

"I can imagine," Tabitha drawled.

Cass frowned slightly. "Mom's going to take pain medication if it gets bad, isn't she?"

"She's hoping not to," Dad replied. "She'd rather do it naturally all the way, but we'll see how it goes."

"I don't like the thought of her in pain." Cass swallowed against the sudden lump in her throat.

"I don't either, Sweetie." Dad laid his hand on her back. "Your mom's a strong woman, and she knows what she's doing. I'll go along with whatever she feels is best."

"Okay." Stepping close to him, Cass briefly rested her head against his chest. "Tell her I love her. And I'm really, really looking forward to seeing the baby."

"You and me both, pal. I can't wait to hold that precious little life in my arms." As Cass moved away, Dad pulled Tabitha to him. "Thanks for stopping by. It does my heart good to see your bright and shining face."

"Shining?" Feigning horror, Tabitha covered her face with her hand. "I'd better go powder my nose before I head to school."

"Honestly, do you have to take everything so literally?" Cass muttered.

"Duh. I was joking." Tabitha sniffed, hugged Dad, and walked over to stand beside Cass. "Give me some credit for having a sense of humor, will you?"

"Sounds like you two didn't get enough sleep." Dad wagged a finger in playful warning. "I don't want you talking to each other on the way to school. I know it sounds silly, but it's the best I can do, short of sending you to your rooms."

"You can send us to our rooms." Cass stifled a yawn. "I'm sure I speak for Tabitha when I say we wouldn't mind."

"Nice try." Stepping between them, he slipped their arms through his. "I'll escort you to the door then go back to Mom. I'd hate for her to have the baby without me."

Pedaling as fast as they could, Cass and Tabitha made it to school in record time. They rushed into the building and discovered their friends grouped at their lockers.

"Any news?" Kira asked immediately.

"Not yet. Dad said it's going to be awhile." Tabitha smiled brightly at Sam, who gallantly relieved her of her backpack. "I take it you made like Paul Revere and spread the word to everyone?"

"Guilty as charged." He bowed then held out his arms for Tabitha to pile books into. "I didn't figure you'd mind."

"We don't," Cass assured him. As she bent to pick up her backpack, she noticed Alex loitering in a doorway across the hall. Waving, she turned her attention back to her friends. "We want everyone to know, don't we, Sis?"

"Yup." She stood on tiptoe to examine the locker's top shelf. "Now where's my English book? I was sure I left it here last Wednesday before we let out for Thanksgiving."

"Let me check." Sam waited for her to step aside then lifted two notebooks and a binder. "Here it is." He pulled out the text and handed it to her. "It was pushed up against the back wall."

"My locker's a disaster area," Tabitha apologized. "I keep meaning to clean it out, but I never seem to get around to it."

"I'll do it," Sam volunteered.

"You'd actually clean out her locker for her?" Rianne's eyes widened in amazement. "Wow, where can I find a guy like you?"

"Under the nearest rock?" Cass suggested sweetly.

The others laughed while Sam pretended to sulk. Dropping the act, he and Tabitha left for her homeroom as soon as she finished at the locker.

CHAPTER 6

When they left, so did Kira and Rianne, which left Cass by herself. Alex immediately approached her.

"I came by your house this morning," he informed her. "Where were you?"

Cass stuffed her afternoon books into the locker and shut it. "Good morning to you too. I had a lovely Thanksgiving. Thanks for asking."

Alex grunted something unintelligible.

"What was that?" Cass swung her backpack onto her shoulder.

" 'Morning," Alex grudgingly relented. "Now, where were you? I even rang the doorbell."

"My parents left for the hospital around 5:30 for my mother to have the baby," Cass explained. "Tabitha and I stopped by there on our way to school to see how things were going." She waited for him to ask how Mom was. When he didn't, she continued tartly, "Not that you care, but she hadn't had the baby as of an hour ago."

Alex frowned. "Look, I'm a guy. I'm not into babies and stuff like girls are. I do care about your mother though. She's always been nice to me. I hope everything turns out okay for her."

"Gee, thanks," Cass drawled. "That was really heartfelt. I'll be sure to pass on your best wishes next time I talk to her."

"What do you want from me?" Alex spread his arms in a gesture of exasperation. "I said I care. Why isn't that good enough?"

Suddenly anxious to end the discussion, Cass made a calming motion with her hand. "It's fine. Let's just drop it, okay? I'll tell my mother you asked about her." She turned toward her homeroom.

"In case you're interested, I have my reasons for not wanting to talk about babies." Alex's mutter stopped her.

Cass arched an eyebrow at him. "Such as?"

Alex glanced uneasily around the crowded hallway. "I don't want to talk about it here. How about at lunch?"

"We've already been through this. You know I always eat with my sister and our friends."

"Can't you make an exception this once?" Alex's tone was unexpectedly urgent.

Hesitating, Cass studied her sandals and bit her lower lip. "I'll ... let you know," she finally replied with obvious reluctance.

"Aw, come on," Alex wheedled. "Just say yes."

Cass' eyes narrowed to irritated slits. "That's the best I can do. Take it or leave it."

Alex hesitated, then nodded. "I'll take it." He began to sidle away. "See you at lunch."

Cass stalked into the classroom and sank down at her desk with a sigh. Rianne gave her a sympathetic smile.

"Worried about your mom?"

"Actually, no." Cass glowered at the door as if she expected to find Alex standing there. "Alex has been bugging me again."

Rianne frowned. "What did he want this time?"

"He was put out because I wasn't home when he came

by this morning." Cass' bark of laughter was humorless. "As if I have nothing better to do than to sit around and wait for him to show up. After I told him about Mom going to the hospital, he acted like he couldn't care less. Then he had the nerve to ask me to save some time for him during lunch so we could talk."

"I hope you told him no," Rianne said.

Cass' expression turned sheepish. "Not exactly." When Rianne expressed surprise, she hurried to explain, "I'm still trying to figure out what to do. I said I'd let him know."

"Then that gives me time to work on getting you to say no," Rianne said, sounding like she was only half kidding. "You know how I feel about Alex. I don't trust the boy one iota."

"Yeah." Wondering how she'd gotten herself into this mess, Cass propped her elbow on the desk and leaned her chin on her fist. "I'll confess I'm suspicious about what his game is."

"So why don't you just tell him, once and for all, to leave you alone?"

"Because I keep coming back to one question." Cass drew invisible patterns on the desk. "What if God's brought Alex back into my life for a reason?"

"When it comes to Alex, I'd say it's more likely the devil's calling the shots, not God."

Cass raised troubled eyes to Rianne. "Sometimes it's hard to tell the difference, isn't it?"

"Tell me about it." Rianne's mouth twisted in a bitter smile. "I can't decide which one my parents are listening to when it comes to where I should go to college."

Shock coursed through Cass, and she instantly sat up straight. "Rianne! You're talking about your parents. How can you even think they're being influenced by the devil?"

"All of us are. But don't forget my folks don't go to church," Rianne reminded her. "It's not like they spend any time praying for God's guidance."

"Still—" Cass couldn't imagine ever suspecting her parents' motives, "they're your parents. I know it's hard to believe sometimes, but they do have your best interests at heart."

"Yeah, right." Rianne's serene features contorted with anger. "You're never around when we talk about school. They couldn't care less that I want to go to a Christian college. All they care about is sending me to Randy's school so they can save money and sleep better at night because I'd be close by in case he needed me."

Cass opened her mouth to protest then promptly shut it. Rianne was right. She hadn't been in on any of the discussions with the Thayers. Maybe their first priority really was saving money and providing a guardian for Randy.

"I'm sorry you feel like that's all that matters to them." The remark sounded lame, even to her own ears, so she tried again. "Talk to them again. You might have better success this time. Tell them why your heart is set on a Christian college."

Rianne stubbornly set her jaw. "I'm through talking to them, at least for the time being. I'll wait until Randy comes home for Christmas and see if he'll talk to them. He's the golden child. They usually listen to whatever he has to say."

"Wow, you sound mad."

"That's because I am." Her nostrils flaring, Rianne tossed her head so that her hair flipped behind her shoulders. "I've had it up to here—" she slashed a hand across her neck, "with being overlooked by my folks. I'm as good as Randy is. He got to go to the college he wanted, and I should be given the same right, even if they don't agree with my choice."

The bell rang before Cass could think of a reply. Swiveling in her chair to face forward, she admitted to herself that she was relieved for the break in the conversation. Rianne's fury scared her. It was one thing to disagree with your parents. Everybody did. But this went far beyond a simple disagreement. It was almost like Rianne hated her folks.

The morning passed too slowly for Cass. Through each class, she found herself watching the clock and wondering when Dad would call with news about Mom. When she met Tabitha at their lockers before lunch, she discovered they wore identical expressions of anxiety.

"It's taking too long, isn't it?" Tabitha voiced their unspoken fear.

"How should I know? I've never had a baby." Cass hid her uneasiness behind a mask of impatience.

Tabitha frowned. "When we talked to Dad, he said it'd be a couple of hours. It's been way longer than that."

"I'm sure Dad would have called if there was a problem." Cass knew her voice lacked any conviction.

"Maybe we should call the hospital."

"What—and make pests of ourselves?" Cass closed her locker without having collected her books for the afternoon. Heaving an exasperated sigh, she spun the dial on the lock. "Mom and Dad have better things to do at the moment than talking to us."

"Better to make pests of ourselves and know what's going on," Tabitha reasoned, "than to be in the dark the way we are now."

"So call."

"You call," Tabitha countered.

"It was your idea." Cass' stomach quaked at the thought of calling and hearing bad news.

"You're not chicken, are you?"

Cass recognized her ploy. "No more than you are."

"I know." Tabitha triumphantly snapped her fingers.

"Let's get Kira to call. She'll do it."

Cass briefly considered the suggestion, then shook her head. "We can't. It's our mom. Either we check on her or nobody does."

"I suppose you're right." Tabitha finally started loading books into her backpack. She grabbed her lunch and swung the locker door shut. "Let's wait until after we eat. If Dad hasn't called by then, we'll call him." She paused. "Maybe."

Despite her anxiety, Cass laughed. "We are such wimps. I'm ashamed of us."

"But not ashamed enough to call," Tabitha pointed out.

Cass' smile faded. "You're right. But did you have to make me feel even worse?"

"The comment was meant just as much for me as it was for you." Tabitha suddenly brightened. "Ah, here comes someone to take my mind off things."

"Lucky duck," Cass grumbled, watching Sam move their way. "All I have to look forward to is Alex." She twirled a finger in the air. "Whoopee."

During lunch, Kira and Rianne did their best to bolster their friends' spirits. After Tabitha and Sam left to take advantage of the break in the rain, Rianne informed Cass that she and Kira planned to find a quiet corner where they could pray for Mom.

"Mind if I tag along?" Cass asked, thinking it would give her the perfect excuse for not talking to Alex.

Rianne seemed to read her mind. "What about Alex?"

"What about him?" Cass conducted a less-than-thorough search of the cafeteria. "He hasn't exactly gone out of his way to find me."

"You can't just go off without telling him first." Rianne's expression was stern.

"Who died and left you mother?" Although Cass knew her friend had a point, she hated to admit it. "Besides, you don't even like Alex. Why do you care how I treat him?"

"He deserves to be treated politely, no matter what," Rianne replied firmly.

Kira, who'd been following their discussion like a spectator at a tennis match, suddenly spoke up. "You two are making a mountain out of a molehill. Cass, if you want to come pray with us then come. Rianne, it's none of your business what she does." She held up a hand to forestall Rianne's objection. "Don't say another word. When I'm right, I'm right."

Cass' smirk was cut off when out of the corner of her eye, she spied Alex walking toward her. "Drat."

"What?" Kira and Rianne interrupted their staring contest to ask simultaneously.

"I should have escaped when I had the chance." Cass nodded toward Alex.

"Ooh, busted." Grinning, Kira pushed back her chair and stood. She motioned to Rianne with an exaggerated flourish. "Shall we, old chum?"

"Let's do." Rianne played along with her act. She waggled her fingers at Cass. "Ta-ta, lovey."

"You're not abandoning me, are you?" Cass kept a wary eye on Alex. "How will I know where to find you?"

Kira planted her hands on the table and leaned down so they were eye-to-eye. "It's not that big of a school. You should be able to track us down if you put your mind to it." Straightening, she gestured to Rianne. "Shake a leg. We don't want to find ourselves stuck here with the Don Juan of Kwajalein."

"That's not funny," Cass hissed as her friends walked away, giggling. Assuming a neutral expression, she turned her attention back to Alex. When he was within earshot, she lifted a hand in unenthusiastic greeting. "Hey."

He took the chair Kira had vacated. "Hey, yourself. I didn't mean to run your friends off."

"They were leaving anyway." Cass glanced toward the

exit to see if she could tell what direction they took, but they were gone. "They're going off to pray for my mother."

"Ah." Alex looked uncomfortable with this bit of information. "Have you heard anything?"

"Nope." The corners of Cass' mouth drooped. "Tabitha and I are getting kind of worried."

"She didn't look worried when she left with Sam a few minutes ago," Alex observed. "In fact, she looked like she didn't have a care in the world."

"If you came over here to bash my sister, you can leave right now," Cass ordered hotly. "I won't listen to it."

Alex raised his hands in a calming gesture. "Don't get so worked up. It was just an innocent remark."

"Nothing about you is innocent," Cass retorted.

Alex's expression darkened. "What's that supposed to mean?"

"Whatever you want it to mean." Cass dismissed the question with an airy wave. "Are you going to tell me what you were hinting at this morning or not?"

"Not." Alex shoved back his chair. "You wouldn't understand."

"Okay." Since she didn't want to be having this conversation anyway, Cass wasn't about to argue with him. "Suit yourself."

Jerking to his feet, Alex scowled down at her. "Why do you make such a big deal about being a Christian? You're as phony as they come."

That does it! Cass slammed her hands down on the table. "Look, pal, you're the one who's been after me wanting to talk, not the other way around. If you have something to say then spit it out. Otherwise, leave me alone. I have zero interest in playing games with you."

To her surprise, Alex's face brightened with a huge smile. "Man, I've missed your spunk. I don't know how I ever let you get away."

"What do you mean, you let me—" Sputtering with anger, Cass couldn't complete the sentence. She vented her frustration in a long, low growl. "Honestly! If you're not the most egotistical, annoying, insufferable person I've ever met!" She crumpled her lunch bag into the smallest, most compact ball she could manage. "If you're not out of here in three seconds, I'm throwing this at you."

"Go ahead," Alex taunted, laughing.

"One. Two." A gleam of malicious glee appeared in Cass' eyes. "Thr—"

"I'm going." To prove it, Alex backed up a step. "I'll call you later to find out how things went with your mother."

"I'll hang up." Cass dropped the crumpled bag on the table.

"Then I'll call back." To her utter disgust, Alex blew her a kiss before turning and sauntering away.

Jesus, Cass implored, glaring daggers in his back, *if You brought him back into my life for a reason, would You please hurry up and show me what it is? If this isn't Your doing then would You kindly strike him dead with a bolt of lightning or something? A twinge of guilt tweaked her conscience. Okay, maybe not dead. But couldn't You at least stun him? Anything to get him to leave me alone.*

Neither Cass nor Tabitha had heard from Dad by the time the last bell rang. Resolved to call him the moment they got home, they hurriedly grabbed books out of their lockers and dashed for the exit, their friends right on their heels. So anxious was she to get home, Cass didn't even bother donning her poncho, despite the rain.

They reached the house, Cass dripping wet and not caring a whit. All that mattered was talking to Dad. Tabitha was the first one to see the banner hanging from the refrigerator when she skidded into the kitchen.

"Cass!" she shrieked.

"What?" Her heart pounding, Cass elbowed her way to

the front of the group. She stared at Tabitha, trying to read her expression.

"Look." She pointed a trembling finger at the refrigerator then burst into tears. "We have a sister."

Feeling as if she were moving in slow motion, Cass swung her gaze away from Tabitha toward the refrigerator. A neon pink poster board was taped to the door. In black letters three inches high, Dad had written, "HANNAH ELIZABETH SPENCER! 8 pounds, 1 ounce. 20 inches. Arrival time: 1:38 p.m. GOD IS GOOD!" A Polaroid snapshot occupied the center space.

"There's a picture!" Cass squealed and dragged Tabitha across the floor to the refrigerator.

Leaning close, they carefully inspected the photo of Mom and their new sister. Tabitha gently touched the baby's face.

"She's beautiful," she breathed.

A lump formed in Cass' throat. "Absolutely gorgeous," she agreed and elbowed Tabitha in the ribs. "Congratulations, Sis."

"You too." Tabitha grabbed her in a bear hug. "Yee-hah! I'm officially a big sister!" she yelled. "And you're the oldest of three. Is this cool or what?"

"It's totally, one hundred percent cool." With a last squeeze, Cass released Tabitha and motioned to the others, who hovered in the doorway. "Get over here, y'all. If this doesn't call for a group hug, I don't know what does."

Kira, Rianne, and Sam hurried to them. Her heart filled to bursting, Cass experienced a moment of intensely missing Logan, then thrust it aside. Now was a time for celebrating, not for regrets.

After a short time of hugging and jumping up and down, the group separated. Everyone looked to Cass and Tabitha to see what came next. They silently consulted each other.

"What do you say we get a snack then head over to the

hospital to meet Hannah?" Cass suggested.

Tabitha nodded enthusiastically.

"Wait. I have a better idea. Let's fix something to eat on the way." Cass poked Tabitha. "I'm dying to see our baby sister. How about you?"

"I can't think of anything I'd rather do," she replied with heartfelt sincerity. "In fact, forget the snack. Let's head straight over there."

"Spoken like a true big sister," Cass said in approval. She turned to the others, unable to contain her grin. "Come on, guys, let's go. The Hannah Spencer welcoming committee is leaving the station."

CHAPTER 7

"I can't believe I ever wanted the baby to room with me." Tabitha winced as another wail emanated from behind the closed door of Mom and Dad's room. "How can such a tiny person make so much noise? My eardrums are about to burst."

"Mom says she has my lungs." Cass grinned. "I'm so proud."

Her eyebrows arching, Tabitha sniffed. "You think it's a good thing to be told you have a big mouth? I'd be insulted if I were you."

"Aw, you're just put out because nobody's said Hannah takes after you in any way." Cass smiled fondly at the wall behind her sister. They were sitting on the bed in Tabitha's room, which was next to their parents' bedroom. "I've decided I definitely like having someone related to me. It's neat seeing family resemblances."

"Mom's related to you," Tabitha pointed out. As the crying increased in volume, she gave serious consideration to pulling the pillow over her head.

"Yeah, but we're about as alike as night and day." Cass had to raise her voice to be heard over Hannah's frantic sobs. "You're more like her real daughter than I am. Don't you remember how that used to bug me?"

Unable to concentrate, Tabitha jumped up and headed for the door. "Man, she's on a roll. I can't hear myself think in here. I'm going to the porch until the kid quiets down."

"She is ripping it up pretty good," Cass conceded, following close on her heels. "Give her time though. She's been home less than a week. She isn't even used to her surroundings yet."

"How can you be so calm?" Tabitha breathed a sigh of relief as the weeping faded the farther away they got from it. "I figured you'd be the one climbing the walls from the crying, and I'd be taking it in stride."

"Life's funny sometimes." On her way through the kitchen, Cass paused at the cookie jar to grab a couple of brownies. "We never really know how we're going to react to a situation until we're in the middle of it."

Tabitha collapsed onto the wicker swing and gratefully accepted the foil-wrapped brownie Cass held out to her. "I don't like being crabby about the crying, but it really gets on my nerves. Maybe I'm not cut out to be a big sister."

"Don't make a federal case out of being a little grouchy." Cass sat down on the other end of the swing and unwrapped her brownie. "I'm not crazy about everything that goes along with having a baby in the house either, but you don't hear me getting all melodramatic."

"Oh, yeah?" Tabitha broke off a corner of her brownie, rolled it into a ball, and popped it into her mouth. "What bugs you about Hannah being here?"

"The smell of the diaper pail. Whew-ee." Cass waved a hand in front of her nose. "Does she produce some nasty odors or what?"

"Is that another way she reminds Mom of you?" Tabitha asked sweetly.

Cass kicked her thigh, hard enough to let her know she didn't find her comment funny. "You keep forgetting. I—"

she thumped her chest, "am the comedian. You—" she indicated Tabitha, "are the pretty one. Do I need to make up labels or do you think you'll be able to remember?"

Tabitha rolled her eyes. "That funny one/pretty one routine of yours is getting old. Can't you come up with something new? Besides, if you're funny and I'm pretty, where does that leave Hannah? What role will she fit into?"

"Right now, she seems to have a lock on being the smelly, noisy one. We can always hope she grows out of it though." Cass looked over to where Mom had appeared in the doorway. She held a fussy Hannah in her arms.

"Help." Mom smiled wanly. "Dad and I can't seem to settle her down. Would either of you care to try?"

Cass immediately jumped up. "Give her to me." She took Hannah from Mom, cradling her against her shoulder. "We need some quality sister-to-sister bonding time." She nuzzled her nose against the baby's head. "I'll take her for a walk. Maybe she just needs a change of scenery."

"I'll come," Tabitha volunteered. "We can take turns pushing."

"Thank you." Mom squeezed Cass' arm. "I forgot how exhausting babies can be. I don't think she slept more than an hour at a time last night."

"Tell me about it." Tabitha's tone was as sour as her expression. "I finally went out to the living room and slept on the couch, she was so loud. I don't know how you can stand being in the same room with her."

"It is a challenge," Mom conceded. Her face softened. "But one that your dad and I wouldn't trade for any amount of money." She dropped a kiss on the baby's fuzzy scalp. "She's such a dear. I thank God for blessing us with her every time I look at her."

"Whatever. I guess I'll understand it if and when I ever have a kid." Tabitha turned to Cass. "I'm going inside to get my sandals. You want me to get yours?"

"Would you? Thanks." As Hannah's agitation increased, Cass shifted her so she lay in her arms. "I'll put Stinky here in her stroller."

"Don't call her that," Mom scolded. "You'll give her a complex. Besides, Dad just changed her diaper."

"Aw, Hannah knows I didn't mean it. Don't you, cutey-pie?" Cass made cooing noises at her sister. "Who's the sweetest baby in the world? Who loves you, huh? Who loves you?" Hannah stopped fussing and struggled to focus solemn blue eyes on Cass' face.

"Oh, brother." Tabitha made gagging noises. "I think I'm going to be sick. I hate baby talk."

"Did you hear what your grouchy old sister said?" Cass simpered. "Don't you listen to her. She's just mad because she's not the cutest one in the family anymore. You are." She walked her fingers up the baby's tummy to tickle her chin. "That's right. You, Hannah Elizabeth Spencer, are cuter than anyone on this whole island."

"I'm leaving." Tabitha brushed past Cass and the baby to head into the house. "I'll be back with the sandals and a barf bag."

Returning a few minutes later, she scowled to see Hannah in Cass' arms. "I thought you said you were going to get her settled in the stroller."

"I got distracted. Sue me." Cass held the baby out to her. "Why don't you do it while I put my sandals on?"

"Honestly, do I have to do everything around here?" Despite her complaining, Tabitha took Hannah and positioned her finger so the baby's fist curled around it. "You really are adorable," she informed her little sister, adding to Cass, "Did you hear how I said that? I didn't use a silly baby voice."

"To each her own." Cass shrugged off the implied criticism. "We'll see which approach Hannah prefers as she gets older."

"Hmm." Tabitha frowned. She didn't like the thought of Hannah possibly favoring Cass. "Maybe I'll have to re-think my methods."

Once the baby was laid in the stroller with the hood positioned to keep the sun off her, Cass took over and wheeled her to the door. Tabitha hovered over her shoulder, ready to snatch control at the first opportunity.

"How long do you want us to keep her out?" Cass asked Mom, who leaned wearily against the wall.

She swept a stray lock of hair off her forehead. "She just ate about 30 minutes ago so she should fall asleep on the walk. If she does, Dad and I sure would appreciate time to take a nap. Let's say between 45 minutes and an hour. Of course, if she continues to fuss, bring her back. She may need to eat again."

Snickering, Tabitha elbowed Cass in the ribs. "Gee, she sounds more and more like you everyday."

"Ha-ha." Cass poked Tabitha's shoulder then tapped her own shoulder. "You forgot again. Pretty. Funny."

Muttering under her breath, Tabitha followed her out the door.

"Where do you want to take her?" Cass asked Tabitha when they reached the street.

"I don't know." Tabitha glanced left, in the direction of Kwaj's cluster of stores. "Is she too young to be around crowds? I'd like to show her off, but I don't want her to pick up any germs."

"Good question. We should have checked with Mom." Cass hesitated, not sure what to do. "Just to be on the safe side, I guess we should stay away from people. Let's walk to the lagoon." She peered under the hood of the stroller. "How does that sound, Hannah-Banana?"

Cass took her gurgle as agreement and turned right.

"Kids are going to call her that, you know," Tabitha remarked as they strolled down the road. She squinted at the sky, trying to estimate how long they had before the rain started.

"Call her what?" Cass asked.

"Hannah-Banana." Tabitha made a face. "Poor kid. Nicknames are the pits."

"Oh, I don't know." Cass shot her a sly look. "You don't seem to mind Sam calling you Tabs."

"That's different. He means it in a nice way." Tabitha's nose wrinkled as she recalled childish taunts from years past. "Didn't anybody ever tease you about your name when you were younger? In grade school, the kids used to call me Crabby Tabby."

Cass shrugged. "Sure, I got teased. Everybody does about something." She made a comical face. "You can imagine what I was called. Think about what rhymes with Cass."

Tabitha laughed. "Poor you. That's a hundred times worse than Crabby Tabby."

"You're telling me. I remember the first time a kid called me that. I went home in tears. Mom told me to ignore it, but that was easier said than done. For the longest time, I wanted to change my name to something nobody could rhyme anything with. I finally came up with Lydia."

"Giddy Liddy," Tabitha promptly replied.

Cass stopped walking to glower at her. "Rats! Way to ruin it for me. I never thought about somebody shortening it to Liddy."

"Old Biddy Liddy. Lid the Squid. Get rid of Lid." Tabitha reeled off a list of possibilities.

"Enough." Cass held up her hand. "I get the picture. I guess it's time to start poring over Mom's book of baby names again."

"I'll bet you a candy bar that you won't find one that can't be turned into an insult," Tabitha challenged.

When Cass didn't resume walking fast enough for her, Tabitha took over at the helm of the stroller and began pushing. Cass fell into step with her.

"You're probably right. Kids can be very creative when they put their minds to it."

Tabitha gazed down at Hannah, who, true to Mom's prediction, had fallen asleep. "I hate the thought of anyone picking on her or giving her a hard time. I want her life to be perfect."

"Aha!" Cass crowed. "So you do like our baby sister."

"I never said I didn't," Tabitha defended herself. "I'm not crazy about her crying, but she'll outgrow that. Besides, she's too cute not to like. Look at those fat little cheeks and those chubby legs."

"Mom said it's a good thing she delivered Hannah a couple of weeks early or she might have been over nine pounds." Cass winced. "That's not a pleasant thought. Imagine—"

Shaking her head, Tabitha broke in, "Don't say it. I don't want to imagine anything along those lines. If I ever have kids, I'm going to adopt. Let someone else do all the work."

"That's not a bad idea," Cass agreed.

They walked in silence for several minutes. The wind picked up, setting the palm fronds to clacking and whipping up whitecaps on the waves off to their right.

"Should we cover Hannah or do you think she's okay?" Tabitha asked.

"It's a warm breeze. She's probably okay." Cass glanced at the sky. The clouds had thickened and darkened. "Of course, if it starts to rain, we bundle her up and race home."

Tabitha nodded firmly. "Absolutely." Rounding a curve in the road, she spotted the calmer waters of the lagoon. "I can't wait to see her reaction the first time she takes a dip in the ocean."

"We might not be here," Cass reminded her. "How old do babies have to be before they're allowed to go swimming?"

"Beats me." Tabitha's steps slowed as she thought about the future. "You know, I used to look forward to going off to college. Now I'm not so excited anymore."

"Because you don't want to leave Kwaj?" Cass asked.

"No, silly." Tabitha rolled her eyes. "Because I don't want to leave Hannah."

"That makes two of us." Cass frowned. "We're not the only ones who aren't turning cartwheels about college. Have you talked to Rianne lately?"

"Nope. What's up with her?" Tabitha rolled the stroller over a rock in the path, jolting it. She anxiously checked to make sure Hannah hadn't been disturbed and was relieved to see her sleeping as peacefully as ever.

"She's unbelievably stressed about it," Cass explained. "Her parents are pushing her to go to school with Randy, but that's the last thing Rianne wants to do. She's starting to worry me because she's so uptight. She said she's having trouble sleeping on account of the situation, and she never has anything good to say about her parents anymore."

"Have you suggested to her that she might want to talk to Pastor Thompson?" Tabitha asked.

"I mentioned it, but she said it wouldn't do any good since her parents don't go to church and probably wouldn't listen to anything he had to say. I told her she should talk to him for her own sake, but—" Cass shrugged, "she said she's not the one who needs help. It's her parents who need to be told to get off her back and let her make her own decision about school."

Tabitha looked at her in surprise. "That doesn't sound like Rianne at all. She's normally so easygoing."

"I know." Cass' expression was troubled. "If you remember, though, she got like this awhile ago when her mother talked about the family moving back to California with Randy. When she gets upset about something, she has a tendency to go overboard."

"Is there anything we can do?"

"I've tried, but I can't think of anything." Cass slid her hands in her pocket and hunched a shoulder. "I'll keep listening to her and do my best to talk her out of overreacting. Other than that, I'm clueless."

"It's too bad the youth group meetings have been suspended until after Christmas," Tabitha said. "It might help if she could talk the problem over with the group."

"You see how much trouble you are?" Cass leaned down to complain to Hannah. "Your arrival has disrupted everything."

"You'd better tell her you're kidding so she doesn't develop that complex Mom warned you about," Tabitha pretended to chide her.

"I— uh-oh." The first drops of rain hit Cass' head, and she dove to tuck the blanket around Hannah. "It's too far for us to make a run for it. We'll just have to hole up here in the pavilion and wait it out."

"Let's hope it doesn't last a couple of hours." Tabitha sprinted for the shelter. "We won't be able to feed her if she wakes up hungry."

"We'll figure something out." Cass followed her to the farthest corner of the pavilion, which provided the most protection from the rain and wind. "In the meantime, let's pray it's just a shower and not a full-fledged flood."

Fortunately, the downpour proved to be short-lived. When a break appeared in the clouds 15 minutes later, they immediately wheeled the stroller onto the path and started for home, dodging the dripping palm fronds as best they could. A few yards down the path, they met Sam.

"Hi." Tabitha tried, but couldn't contain her smile. "Where are you going in such a rush?"

Sam braked his bike and hopped off. "I called your house to see if you'd like to go bowling, and your mother said you'd taken Hannah for a walk. I figured you'd head to the lagoon, so when it started to rain, I grabbed a couple of ponchos—" he indicated the parcel lying in the bicycle basket, "and hightailed it over here. I didn't want you and the baby stuck in case the rain kept up."

Tabitha turned shining eyes to Cass. "Is that the sweetest thing you've ever heard or what?"

She nodded solemnly. "It's so sweet my teeth are aching."

"Oh, you." Tabitha gave her a playful swat then directed her attention back to Sam. "Don't listen to her. It was very nice of you to think of us. Since you went to all this trouble, would you like to come back to the house?"

"I thought you'd never ask." Sam lifted a hand to Cass. "Hi, by the way."

"Hi back." She moved next to Tabitha and bumped her with her hip. "Let me push the stroller. The path's too narrow for the three of us to walk side-by-side. You walk with Sam."

"Yeah," he piped up. "You walk with me. Please," he added when Tabitha cocked a brow at him.

"That's better." She scooted ahead and fell in step with him. "I don't respond very well to being ordered around."

"I'll keep that in mind," Sam replied with a smile.

CHAPTER 8

They were less than 50 yards from the house when the first sprinkles hit again. They reached the lanai a few moments before the storm once more unleashed its fury. Hurrying into the porch, they found Dad waiting for them in the swing.

"I was just about to send out a search party." Getting up, he lifted Hannah out of the stroller and snuggled her against his chest. "I was afraid Punkin here would return looking like a drowned rat."

Bristling, Tabitha drew herself up to her full height. "Do you honestly think we'd let anything happen to her?"

"Whoa." Dad waved his hand in a soothing gesture. "It was a joke, although obviously a bad one as far as you're concerned."

"It certainly was." Pointedly ignoring him, Tabitha looked at Sam. "Would you like something to eat? There's brownies in the kitchen if you want."

"Brownies sound good," Sam said, then waved her down when Tabitha started toward the kitchen. "I know where they are. I'll bring you out one if you want."

Tabitha smiled and Sam disappeared into the kitchen.

"Where's Mom?" Cass asked Dad, who'd sat back down.

He gently set the swing in motion. "Catching a few more winks." He smiled down at Hannah. "You're wreaking havoc in Mommy and Daddy's life, aren't you?" The baby stirred and made a mewling sound.

"You don't sound too upset that she's turned your schedule upside down," Cass observed, taking a seat opposite the swing.

"Why have a baby if you're not willing to make a few adjustments?" Dad laughed. "Better make that a truckload of adjustments. Basically, babies come into the house—and your heart—and completely take over."

"You really love her, don't you?" Tabitha asked as she studied Dad's expression and experienced an unfamiliar stab of pain.

"I'm crazy about her."

"Do you think my father was as crazy about me as you are about Hannah?" Cass asked softly. Tabitha could see the pain in her eyes.

Dad smiled gently. "Absolutely. Talk to your mom. She's told me that the way I am with Hannah reminds her of how your father was with you when they first brought you home from the hospital."

"Really?" Cass cleared her throat. "Maybe I will ask her to tell me what it was like. I hardly ever ask about my father because I don't want to make her sad."

"She'll be glad to tell you anything you'd like to know," Dad assured her. "Remembering him doesn't make her sad. Even though they didn't have much time together, the few years she spent with your father were happy ones."

Cass tilted her head to the side, surprised by his comment. "That doesn't make you feel weird? Or jealous?"

"Nope," Dad replied without hesitation. "I'm glad your mom married your father. If she hadn't, you wouldn't be here."

"Wow. That's so ... cool." Cass smiled. "You're a neat person."

Dad inclined his head to accept her compliment. "You're not so bad yourself. I guess that's why we get along so well. We're both neat people."

Tabitha's glance darted from Cass to Dad as they shared a laugh. Seeing him with Cass and Hannah, obviously enjoying himself, made her feel left out. She cleared her throat to get their attention. "I was going to ask if I could go bowling with Sam. But now I'm not so sure I want to."

"Why not?" Cass shot her a puzzled look. "I'd jump at the chance to go out."

Hmm, Tabitha thought. *Here's a way to kill two birds with one stone.*

Aloud, she asked, "Would you like to join us?"

Cass squirmed uncomfortably. "I wasn't angling for an invite. I was just saying what I'd do if I were in your shoes. Besides, what would Sam think about me tagging along?"

"He'd think," Sam called from the kitchen, "he was one lucky dog to have two gorgeous escorts."

"Son—" Dad was laughing almost too much to speak, "you're too smooth for your own good. If I'd had half your brashness—and half your lines—when I was your age, my social calendar would have been full every weekend."

Sam appeared in the doorway, a brownie in one hand and a glass of milk in the other. He assumed his most innocent expression. "That wasn't a line, Mr. S. I meant every word. You have two—wait, make that three—incredibly beautiful daughters."

"Did you hear that?" Dad addressed Hannah. "That's the kind of boy I want you to steer clear of in the future. In fact, by the time you're 10, I'll have built a moat around our house to keep boys like that out. They're nothing but trouble, with a capital T."

An impish smile creased Sam's face. "If I'm so bad, why do you let Tabs go out with me?"

"Yeah," Tabitha chimed in, rounding on Dad. "Don't

you care about me as much as you do Hannah?"

Instead of replying, Dad abruptly stood up. "I think the baby needs changing."

Cass sniffed the air. "I don't think so." She fixed accusing, though dancing, eyes on him. "You're running away, aren't you? Go on, admit it."

"I wouldn't call it running away." Dad crossed the floor to the doorway. Sam stepped aside to let him pass. "I prefer to think of it as retreating with dignity."

"Whatever." Tabitha snorted. "Anyway, before you ... retreat with dignity, am I allowed to go bowling?"

Dad glanced at his watch. "Sure. Just be home by 5:00. You and Cass are fixing supper tonight, remember?" He glanced back at Cass. "Are you going too?"

"I'm not sure." She busied herself smoothing her shorts and avoided Tabitha and Sam's gazes. "I'll let you know."

After he left, Tabitha moved to Cass' chair and perched on the arm. "All kidding aside, we'd really like you to come."

"Yup." Sam puffed out his chest in a comical show of masculine pride. "I'm not afraid to take both of you on. You can combine your scores, and I bet I'll still beat you."

Tabitha rolled her eyes at Cass. "How can you pass up a challenge like that?"

"I can't." She snickered. "Poor boy. He really doesn't know what he's getting himself into, does he?"

"Nope." Tabitha shook her head in mock sympathy. "But he'll know shortly."

"Knock it off, you two." Sam's brow furrowed with concern. "You're scaring me."

"You should be scared." Getting up, Tabitha walked over to stand in front of him. "Be afraid. Be very afraid."

While Cass went in search of Dad to let him know they were leaving, Sam and Tabitha waited for her on the lanai. The rain kept up a steady beat on the tin overhang.

"You're sure it's okay Cass is coming?" Tabitha asked.

Sam grinned. "I'm positive. I like your sister." Leaning closer, he added, "Not as much as I like you, of course."

Tabitha shook her head in mock dismay. "My Dad was right. You are a smoothie. You know just the right thing to say."

"Only when it comes to you." Sam dropped his teasing tone. "Only when it comes to you."

Shivering despite the 85 degree temperature, Tabitha hugged herself. Although she liked it, she didn't know how to respond to Sam's obvious fondness for her. Having made the mistake once of telling Micah she loved him, she wasn't about to commit the same error with Sam. Still, she wanted Sam to know she returned his affection.

"I'm glad you feel that way," she said hesitantly. "I wouldn't want you coming on to other girls."

Surprise and pleasure mingled on Sam's face. "No joke? Are you saying you'd be jealous?"

"I'd be insanely jealous." Seeing his dazzled reaction, Tabitha smiled to herself. "I'd want to scratch the girl's eyes out."

This is fun, she decided. *We can be honest about our feelings without getting all serious the way Micah wanted.*

"Believe me, you have nothing to worry about." Sam's expression and tone oozed sincerity. "I may not be the brightest bulb in the chandelier, but I know when I have a good thing going. I'm not about to mess it up by flirting with other girls."

His declaration warmed Tabitha's heart, and she abandoned her teasing attitude. "Thank you. That means a lot to me. It's like I tell Cass practically every day. You really know how to make me feel special."

"That's because you are special." Sam brushed a stray curl off her cheek. "I'm just the lucky guy who gets to let you know you are."

Before Tabitha could respond, Cass appeared. She eyed the couple with amusement.

"Are you sure you don't want to be alone? The way y'all are looking at each other, you'd think you were the only two people left on earth."

"A guy can dream, can't he?" Sam quipped.

"It all depends on what you're dreaming about," Cass shot back. "As long as your intentions toward my sister are honorable, I have no objections."

"Oh, they're honorable all right." Sam didn't sound like he was joking. "I have nothing but the highest respect for her."

"Stop talking about me as if I weren't here," Tabitha complained, although her stomach flip-flopped at Sam's words. "In fact, let's stop talking, period. I'd like to get to the bowling alley before league play starts and all the lanes are full."

"Your wish is my command." Sam bowed with a flourish. "After you."

CHAPTER 9

Blowing in from the storm into the bowling alley, Cass, Tabitha, and Sam spotted Rianne and Kira at one of the nine lanes. Cass whistled to get their attention, and they came over.

"Hey," Kira greeted them. "What's up?"

"Hopefully my average." Cass elbowed Sam. "I'd like to put 'Mr. I Can Beat You with One Hand Tied behind My Back' in his place." Turning to Rianne with a smile, she was taken aback by the drawn look on her friend's face. "Are you okay? You don't look so good."

"I'm fine." The tightness around Rianne's mouth belied her reply.

Cass decided to wait until they were alone to challenge her response. "The lane next to yours is open. Are you up for some friendly competition?"

"I'm definitely in the mood for competition, friendly or otherwise." With that, Rianne turned and marched back to her lane.

Tabitha shot Kira a quizzical look. "What's with her?"

Kira shrugged. "Beats me. She's been like this ever since she called and asked me to go bowling. She keeps hurling the ball at the pins like a madwoman. When I asked her about it, she said she's taking out her aggression, but she wouldn't say against who. It's kind of spooky."

"I'll talk to her later." Cass hastily pasted on a smile when Rianne turned to glare at the group. "Right now we'd better get over there. We don't want her to think we're talking about her."

"But we are," Tabitha pointed out.

"Duh," Cass retorted. "I didn't say we're not. I just said we don't want her to think we are."

"Girls," Sam muttered, stepping up to the desk to rent shoes. "I'll never understand you people."

"I heard that," Tabitha said darkly.

"Good. You were supposed to." Sam gave the attendant his shoe size then stepped aside so Tabitha could give hers.

Despite Cass' best efforts, Rianne didn't cheer up over the course of the next hour. If anything, her mood darkened and her bowling became more intense. When Sam suggested they take a break to get something to eat, she protested loudly.

"I don't want to. I want to keep playing."

"You've been at it for over two hours," Kira pointed out. "Aren't you tired?"

"I could go another two hours," Rianne declared stoutly. She scowled at each member of the group, in turn. "Who's game?"

One by one, they shook their heads.

"Not me," Sam opted out. "I'm starved."

"Me too." Kira eyed Rianne. "Aren't you? You said you didn't eat breakfast."

"For Pete's sake!" she exploded. "Why don't you just announce my food intake to the entire bowling alley while you're at it?"

The others stared at her in astonishment. Cass' initial surprise quickly changed to concern. *Something definitely isn't right with her*, she thought, and laid a soothing hand on

Rianne's shoulder. "Come on," she coaxed. "Take a breather. We'll get some pizza and gab awhile."

Rianne shrugged off her touch. "What are you? Dense? I'm not hungry. Why should I eat when I don't feel like it?"

"Nobody's trying to force you to eat." Cass raised a placating hand. "Just come and keep us company while we do."

For a few moments, it looked like Rianne would refuse. With an impatient toss of her head, she finally drawled, "Fine. If it'll make you happy, I'll keep you company."

Once they sat down at a table in the snack bar, Cass questioned the wisdom of insisting Rianne accompany them. With her arms crossed and her brow furrowed, she resembled a dark cloud hovering over the table.

While Tabitha and Sam went to order pizza, nachos, and drinks, Cass wracked her brain for a topic of conversation Rianne might respond to. She sent Kira a mute appeal, but the other girl merely rolled her eyes and looked away.

"So," Cass chirped, feeling foolish, but plowing ahead anyway, "how's it going?"

Rianne made a sour face. "How do you think it's going? Do I seem like I'm in a good mood?"

Cass couldn't help snorting. "Hardly."

"So why ask?" Rianne snapped.

Feeling her temper rising, Cass struggled to control it. "Because I'm your friend, and friends are supposed to care how one another is doing."

About to protest, Rianne seemed to abruptly change her mind. Some of the tension drained out of her, and her shoulders sagged. "If you really want to know how I'm doing, the answer is lousy. I'm tired of fighting with my parents about college all the time."

"So don't," Kira advised. "Tell them where you're going, and forget it."

"Yeah, right." Rianne snorted derisively. "You don't

know my folks very well if you think that would fly with them."

"I thought you said you weren't going to talk to them anymore about school," Cass reminded her. "You decided to wait for Randy to come home and then have him talk to them on your behalf."

The corners of her mouth drooping, Rianne leaned her elbow on the table and propped her chin on her fist. "I thought I'd give it one more try last night. I finally told them why I want to go to a Christian college, that it's because I plan to be a missionary. They hit the ceiling. You'd have thought I'd told them I wanted to join a heavy metal band or something with the way they reacted. They flat-out refused to pay for my education if I insist on going to a Christian college. They said a degree from a place like that would be worthless in the real world and that nobody in their right mind wants to be a missionary."

"Wow." Cass' eyes were wide with amazement. She couldn't imagine having a similar discussion with her parents. "Then what happened?"

"I told them the world didn't get any more real than the places I intend to bring the Gospel." Rianne's expression was smug. "They had to think about that for a few minutes. Then they came back at me with wanting to know what would happen if I decided not to go into missionary work. My four years in a Christian college would be wasted."

"And?" Kira prompted when Rianne didn't say anything.

"I assured them I wouldn't be changing my mind. I believe I've been called to be a missionary, and that's what I'm going to do. I don't care what they think." Rianne's jaw thrust out at a defiant angle.

Uneasy with her rebellious attitude, Cass said carefully, "They're your parents. It's natural for them to be concerned about your future."

"They're not concerned." Rianne dismissed the remark with a disdainful wave. "All they care about is controlling me. They act like I'm still 5 years old, and they can tell me what to do." Her lips curved in a disturbing smile. "I'll show them they can't control me."

Cass frowned. "What's that supposed to mean?"

"They think as long as I'm under their roof they have me where they want me." Rianne trilled a scornful laugh. "Boy, are they wrong."

Cass exchanged an unsettled look with Kira. "What are you going to do?"

"Don't worry. I'm not about to do anything stupid." Rianne's expression turned sly. "Actually, it's what I'm not going to do more than what I'm going to do."

Throwing her hands up in exasperation, Cass ordered, "Quit talking in riddles."

"Okay I'll quit." Rianne sat back and crossed her arms once more. "I just won't say anything else."

Cass mimicked her pose. "Fine. Have it your way. I'm tired of playing games. If you—"

"Here we go," Tabitha interrupted. "Cokes for everybody. The pizza and nachos should be ready in a few minutes."

She and Sam began handing out the drinks. Rianne took one look in her cup and pushed it away.

"I asked for water."

"I know. I just thought soda would be more refreshing." Tabitha produced her most winsome smile. "I didn't mean to make you mad."

"Yeah, well, you did." Shoving back her chair, Rianne stood up. "I make one measly request, and you can't even do that for me. I'm out of here."

"Wait!" Cass grabbed the hem of her shirt. "Where are you going?"

"I think I'll take a couple of laps around the island on

my bike." Rianne pulled her shirt out of Cass' grasp. "I need to let off steam."

"It's raining cats and dogs out there," Sam said.

Rianne whirled around to glower at him. "Butt out. I wasn't talking to you."

Too stunned to respond, all the group could do was gape at her as she stalked away. Cass considered going after her, then dismissed the idea. It was clear Rianne wasn't in any mood to listen to reason. No one spoke until the bowling alley door closed behind her.

"Something very weird is going on." Kira's tone was ominous. "I've never seen her act like this."

"That makes two of us." Tabitha looked at Cass. "Do you know—"

Before she could finish her question, Cass shook her head. "I don't have a clue. I'll tell you one thing, though. First chance we get, Rianne and I are going to have ourselves a nice, long chat."

"I hope she opens up to you." Kira frowned at the door through which Rianne had disappeared. "I'm really worried." Her frown deepened as the door opened to admit a familiar face. "Oh, great. Like we don't have enough problems."

The others swiveled in their chairs to see what she was referring to. Alex waved from the doorway and started toward the table.

"Why me?" Cass moaned, wishing the floor would open up and swallow her. The last person she felt like dealing with at the moment was Alex.

"Hi, guys." Reaching the table, he flashed a brilliant smile. "Hello, Cass," he added, singling her out.

She mumbled something that could have passed for a greeting.

"I called, and your father said you were here." Without asking permission, he sat down in the chair Rianne had just vacated. "Naturally, I rushed right over."

"Naturally," Kira muttered. She smiled sweetly when Alex raised his brows at her.

"Are you done bowling?" he asked.

"For the moment." Even though the question was directed at Cass, Sam jumped in and answered for her. "We're taking a food break."

"Can I join you?" Alex continued to focus only on Cass.

To the others' surprise, she smiled. "Sure." Just as Alex's face lit up with pleasure, she pasted on an expression of phony regret. "Unfortunately, I have to leave. I'm fixing supper tonight."

Tabitha opened her mouth to say something, and Cass kicked her under the table. Standing, Cass added, "Sorry you made the trip for nothing, Alex." She fluttered her fingers at the others. "I hate to bowl and run, but duty calls. How about a re-match, Sam?"

He stifled a smile. "You name the time, and I'll be here. You won't beat me again, that's for sure."

"I'll walk you to the door," Alex offered.

Cass pressed him back down when he tried to rise. "That's okay. I know the way. Besides, that looks like the order on the counter now." She moved away, trying not to look like she was hurrying. "See y'all later. Enjoy yourselves."

She waited until she was safely away from the building before bursting into laughter. *God, if that was wrong, I'm sorry. But it sure was fun seeing the look on Alex's face. I don't know what his game is, but I'm not interested in playing it. A twinge of guilt tweaked her conscience. Unless it's what You would have me do. While You're at it, could You also give me some insight about Rianne? I really love her, and I hate to see her so upset. Thanks.*

Finished with her prayer, she ducked her head against the driving rain and raced down the street. In a good mood because of her narrow escape from Alex, she didn't even mind the puddles that splashed up her legs, drenching the hem of her shorts.

CHAPTER 10

"How's it going on the home front?"

It was Tuesday after school, and Tabitha and Kira were at the pool, alternately studying and swimming. Tabitha made a face at Kira's inquiry.

"Hannah's still keeping me up at night with her crying." Her expression softened as she thought about her sister. "I don't really hold it against her though. She's just a baby." She frowned suddenly. "The problem I'm having is with Dad."

"Why? What's he done?" Kira slid the sunglasses down her nose and glanced towards a boy on the diving board. She tapped Tabitha's arm. "Who's that?"

"We're talking about me," Tabitha said darkly. "We can talk about boys later."

"Okay," Kira grudgingly agreed. "But don't forget." She shifted in the lounge chair so she faced Tabitha. "Anyway, what's up with your dad?"

Tired of studying for the moment, Tabitha picked up the history textbook lying in her lap and placed it on the ground beside her chair. "Ever since Hannah was born, Mom talks all the time about how much she reminds her of Cass as a baby. She compares their looks, their eating and sleeping habits. She's gotten out Cass' baby pictures and shown them to Dad and me."

"And that bugs you," Kira said.

"Sort of." Tabitha made a gesture halfway between a nod and a negative shake of her head. "The thing that really bothers me is Dad doesn't do any of that stuff. It's like Hannah's the first baby he's ever had. He hasn't once said that something about her reminds him of me."

"Maybe it's because fathers aren't really into that sort of thing the same way mothers are," Kira suggested. "He was busy with other stuff when you were Hannah's age so he didn't notice as much as a mother would."

"He's not too busy with other stuff now," Tabitha argued. "It's like the sun rises and sets on Hannah. He spends every moment he can with her."

"He's older. I read somewhere that older men make better fathers because they have more time to spend with their children." Kira hesitated, then flashed her a knowing look. "It sounds to me like you're jealous."

Tabitha rejected the possibility with a snort. "Whatever. I'm not jealous of Hannah. I just wish Dad would—" she struggled to find the words to describe her feelings, "try harder to remember what it was like when I was a baby. He must have some memories from that time. Why doesn't he talk about them the way Mom does?"

"It probably hasn't occurred to him." Kira glanced at the sky, where clouds were congregating on the horizon. "Ask him what he remembers."

"No way." Crossing her arms, Tabitha stubbornly set her jaw. "It won't be the same if I have to ask. He should think of doing it himself."

Kira shook her head in disbelief. "You're expecting the man to read your mind."

Tabitha bristled with indignation. "That is so unfair. All I expect is for Dad to remember he has two daughters."

"Uh ... that would be three." Kira made a show of looking around before settling back in the chair. "You don't want to run the risk of having Cass hear you leave her out."

About to argue, Tabitha laughed instead. "True. Just like I wouldn't like it if she didn't include me as one of Mom's kids."

"Have you talked to her about this thing with your father?" Kira asked.

"You mean Cass?" When Kira nodded, Tabitha replied, "Nope. Knowing her, she'd probably tell me to get over it. Plus, I don't want her jumping to the same conclusion you did, that I'm jealous of Hannah. She's like a pit bull when it comes to the baby. She's very protective. I have no doubt she'd rip me up one side of the house and down the other if she thought I was envious of an innocent baby."

"That sounds like our Cass all right." Kira's tone was admiring. "She never hesitates to tell you what she thinks."

"Usually at the top of her lungs." A gust of wind lifted and tangled Tabitha's curls, and she glanced skyward. "They don't call this the rainy season for nothing. Looks like we're in for another deluge."

Kira swung her legs over the side of the chair. "I'm heading home. I've had my share of soakings over the past few days. I feel like I'm starting to mildew."

They exited the pool area together. While Kira retrieved her bike, Tabitha crossed the empty lot to her house. She paused at the front door to wave as Kira took off up the street.

The moment she stepped inside the house, she was greeted by the sound of Hannah crying. Sighing, she turned left toward the bathroom to shower and dress.

"Home, sweet home," she muttered, wondering how long it would be before Hannah began expressing herself in some other manner than wailing. However long it took, she couldn't wait.

By the time she emerged from the bathroom, peace had settled over the house. After calling hello to Cass in her room, Tabitha went in search of Mom. She found her on the porch, stitching, while Hannah slept nearby in her portable crib.

"What are you making?" Tabitha sat down on the other end of the swing and peered into Mom's lap, trying to decipher the pattern lying there.

"I'm cross-stitching a birth sampler for Hannah." Mom studied the chart then selected a skein of lavender floss from the basket beside her. "After I finish this, I want to do one for you and Cass. I didn't know how to cross-stitch when Cass was born so I never made her one."

Touched, Tabitha drew up her legs and clasped her arms around them. "You'd sew one for me? Really?"

"You're my daughter, aren't you?" Mom reached over and patted her leg. "Of course I'll make you one, silly. I love you."

"I love you too." Laying her cheek on her knees, Tabitha gazed down at the baby. "She's so lucky, having a mother like you right from the start. I had to wait until I was 16 before I got a real mom."

A brief frown puckered Mom's forehead. "Is something troubling you? Have you been thinking about your mother?"

"Not really." Tabitha raised her head so she could look at Mom. "Beth pops into my thoughts every now and then, but she never stays long." She laughed shortly. "Sort of like the way it is with her in real life."

Mom nodded. "Does Hannah make you miss your half brother and sister?"

Tabitha took a few seconds to ponder the question then repeated, "Not really. I don't feel connected to Sunshine and Peace. Since I don't ever see them, I have no idea what's going on in their lives or what kind of people they're growing into. They're just faces in the pictures Grandma sends every few months."

"That's sad." Having threaded the needle with the floss, Mom poked it through the cloth. "After all, they are related to you."

"Only physically," Tabitha pointed out. "Not emotionally, the way Hannah is."

"There may come a day when you're able to develop a relationship with them," Mom said.

"Maybe. In the meantime though, I have Cass and Hannah." Tabitha smiled. "They make for a pretty good family."

"I'm glad you think so. I'm rather fond of them myself." Mom worked a row of stitches. "So everything's going well in your life? You and Kira are doing okay?" When Tabitha assured her they were, Mom asked, "And how are things with Sam?"

Tabitha's expression brightened, chasing away the gloom of the storm. "Terrific. He's such a good guy."

"Is he still interested in going to West Point?"

"Yup. He has all his paperwork in. Plus, he's completed all the interviews and tests." Tabitha unfolded her legs and set her feet back on the floor. "Wouldn't it be weird if he winds up at the Academy with Logan?"

Mom gave her a sly smile. "It would sure make it convenient for you and Cass next year. You can drive up to New York together to visit your guys."

A blush crept up Tabitha's neck to stain her cheeks. "Sam will have probably forgotten me by then."

"I don't think so," Mom said with a smile. "He seems quite smitten with you."

"Smitten?" echoed Tabitha in an effort to change the subject. "Who uses the word *smitten* anymore?"

"Obviously I do." Mom began a second row of lavender stitches. "But, to get back to you and Sam, would you like your relationship to continue beyond this year?"

Tabitha's face lost much of its brightness. "Absolutely. But, after what happened with Micah, I'm not getting my hopes up. Sam could go off the deep end like Micah did."

"Sam strikes me as being very different from Micah." Mom grimaced. "He seems much more grounded."

"He seems like he is, but you never really know, do you?" Angling herself sideways in the swing, Tabitha gazed out at the ocean. Instead of its usual brilliant blue, the water reflected the slate-colored sky. "Only time will tell, I guess." A heavy sigh escaped her. "Sometimes I wish I had a crystal ball so I could see into the future."

"That's where faith comes in," Mom reminded her. "Don't ever forget God is in control."

Tabitha gave an impatient twitch. "I don't mind Him being in control. I just wish He'd be more generous about sharing information with us lowly humans."

"I don't know if that desire ever changes." Mom snipped the floss and unthreaded the needle. "With all the decisions facing us concerning college for you girls and how long we should stay here, Dad and I could sure use some clear guidance."

"God tends to take the subtle approach, doesn't He?" Not requiring an answer, Tabitha slid off the swing and started toward the kitchen. "I'd better get back to studying. Kira and I didn't get much done at the pool."

"Why am I not surprised?" Mom teased.

"Are Cass and I doing supper tonight?" Tabitha asked before leaving.

"Nope, you're off the hook. Pastor and Mrs. Thompson sent over a tuna casserole." Mom selected a skein of mint green floss. "All we have to do is reheat it."

"My kind of meal." With a wave, Tabitha disappeared into the house.

During dinner, Dad ate with Hannah cradled in one arm. Mom reminisced about the countless meals she'd consumed that way when Cass was a baby. Tabitha waited for Dad to counter with similar stories. When he didn't, her appetite soured, and she wound up excusing herself early from the table.

In her room, she leaned her forehead against the window and watched as sheets of wind-driven rain pounded the lawn. "Lord," she whispered, "help me not to be so resentful about Dad not bringing up my childhood. I don't like feeling like this. I'm glad he loves Hannah. I just wish he'd say something to let me know he loved me when I was a baby. I'm scared he likes being her Dad more than he liked being mine. Please have him do something to show me I'm wrong."

Over the next few days, Tabitha stayed alert for signs that Dad had enjoyed her infancy. Although she listened carefully to his remarks, she didn't hear what she wanted to hear and eventually gave up hoping she would. Pushing her hurt to the furthest recesses of her heart, she acted as if she hadn't a care in the world and did her best not to let the situation negatively affect her feelings for Hannah. As she kept reminding herself, it wasn't Hannah's fault their dad had such a poor memory.

CHAPTER 11

Saturday afternoon Cass found herself in the rare position of being alone with Hannah. Tabitha had gone to the bowling alley with Sam, and Mom and Dad took advantage of Cass' availability to baby-sit by going to an afternoon movie.

Not one to pass up the break in the weather that resulted in a gloriously warm and sunshiny day, Cass moved Hannah's portable crib onto the lanai for her afternoon nap. After fixing herself a frosty glass of lemonade and a plate of oatmeal cookies, she carried her book and snack out back.

She'd just arranged herself in the hammock when she heard the faint peal of the doorbell. She debated ignoring it before forcing herself to get up. Her displeasure increased when she opened the door and discovered the identity of her visitor.

"Hi." Alex nodded a greeting.

Stifling a sigh, Cass reminded herself to be polite. "Hey."

"What are you doing?"

"I'd just settled in for an afternoon of reading when I heard the doorbell." Cass hoped he'd take the hint that he was disrupting her plans. Maybe he'd have the good manners to leave.

He didn't. "So you're not actually busy." He peered around her into the house. "Where is everybody?"

Cass gave him a terse run-down of her family's various locations, adding, "I'd ask you in, but we're not allowed to have boys in the house when my parents aren't home."

There, she thought smugly, *that ought to send him on his way.*

"We could sit out back and talk," Alex suggested.

Jesus, why do You keep making sure our paths cross?

Aloud, Cass replied gruffly, "Fine. Go around the side of the house, and I'll meet you on the lanai."

Stopping in the kitchen to pour Alex a glass of lemonade, she arrived after he did. She found him standing a few feet from Hannah's crib, staring intently at her.

"Cute, isn't she?" Cass set his lemonade on the patio table.

Alex started and quickly averted his gaze. "All babies look alike to me." He moved to one of the chairs grouped around the table.

"Hannah's not like other babies," Cass bragged. "She's prettier, smarter, and more advanced."

"Whatever." Although Alex pretended disinterest, again and again his eyes were drawn back to Hannah. "How old is she now?"

"Almost two weeks." Cass got up to re-tuck the blanket the breeze had blown off Hannah's shoulders. "A perfect little human being." She laughed. "Of course, I'm prejudiced."

"Do you have to go on and on about her?" Alex complained.

Cass blinked her confusion. "You're the one who asked how old she is."

"Yeah, but a simple answer would have done. I didn't expect you to go into a long lecture about how perfect she is." Alex avoided looking at Cass, concentrating instead on rubbing off the beads of moisture on his glass.

"What long lecture?" she demanded. "I made one measly comment."

"Has it occurred to you that I don't give a rip about your little sister?" Alex jeered.

"Then why did you ask about her?" Cass smirked, sure she'd scored a point.

"I was just being polite." Alex snatched up his glass and gulped half the contents.

"Look, this is a totally pointless discussion." Cass shot him a quizzical look. "Why did you come here if all you planned to do was argue?"

Alex shrugged. "I thought we could talk. I like talking to you."

"You could have fooled me." Cass drummed her fingers on the table, secretly hoping the sound grated on Alex's. "So, what do you want to talk about?"

"Not the baby," was his immediate response.

"There you go, bringing her up again." Cass fixed him with a probing stare. "What is it with you and babies?"

As soon as the words were out of her mouth, she remembered his relationship with Alison Ross and wished she could take them back.

"Nothing. I don't have a problem with babies." Alex's protest was anything but convincing.

Since she'd already broached the subject, Cass figured she didn't have anything to lose by pursuing it. "I don't believe you. Hannah seems to make you uncomfortable."

Alex's eyes narrowed in annoyance. "What are you? Some kind of amateur shrink?"

"Nope." Cass toyed with her glass, shaking it slightly so the ice tinkled. "I just keep my eyes and ears open. It's amazing what you can pick up about people if you pay attention."

"You know—" placing his hands on the table, Alex pushed himself to a standing position, "I've had about enough of this conversation. It's totally lame. I'm going to hit the road."

Eyeing him, Cass noted the uneasiness lurking behind his indifferent attitude. "Why?" she purred. "Because I'm hitting too close to home?"

Alex laughed mockingly. "Don't flatter yourself. You're not nearly as observant as you like to think you are."

"Suit yourself." Cass waved lazily. "Bye. Thanks for stopping by. It was," she paused before finishing pointedly, "interesting."

Alex left without saying a word.

"Good-bye and good riddance," Cass muttered.

After checking Hannah, she eased back into the hammock with a blissful sigh. *Ah! This is the life. As long as pests like Alex stay away, it doesn't get any better than this.* Propping the book on her stomach, she flipped the pages to the first chapter.

"Are you awake?"

Alex's quiet question startled Cass so badly that the book flew out of her hands and landed on the concrete with a smack. Hannah flinched in her crib but, fortunately, slumbered on.

"Didn't your mother teach you not to sneak up on people like that?" Cass muttered crossly. She propped herself on her elbows to glare at Alex.

His smile was apologetic. "Sorry. I thought you heard me coming."

"Well, I didn't." Feeling at a disadvantage lying down, Cass sat up and swung her legs over the side of the hammock. "Why'd you come back?" Having lost track of the time, she added, "And how long have you been gone?"

"About 30 minutes. I started thinking while I was riding, and I realized I needed to tell you something." Alex spread his arms. "So here I am."

"I wonder how long it'll be this time before we're snapping at each other," Cass said. She pushed herself out of the hammock and walked to the table. "I don't know how long this is going to take, but you might as well sit down and make yourself comfortable."

Alex followed her example and sat. "You don't like me very much, do you?"

Cass was momentarily taken aback. "Now that you mention it, no."

"Why not?" he asked calmly, seeming not to take offense.

"Is this what you came back to talk about?" Cass hedged, preferring not to get into a discussion of his faults.

"No. I was just wondering." Alex draped an arm over the back of the chair and stretched out his legs. "If you'd rather not talk about it—"

"I wouldn't," Cass interrupted.

"Fine. I'll say my piece then." Hesitating, Alex glanced around the lanai, his gaze lingering on Hannah. "Do you remember Alison Ross? She graduated in May."

Oh, goodness! He's going to tell me about the baby. A panicky feeling welled up in Cass. *What am I supposed to say if he does? I don't want to hear this.*

She nodded.

"She ... uh ... that is ... we ... well ..." Alex swallowed hard and blurted, "She wound up pregnant."

Cass' face flushed a bright crimson. "I know."

Leaning forward, Alex rested his arms on his thighs and stared down at his clasped hands. "It was my baby."

"That's what I figured."

Cass gazed at the top of his head and thought, *I can't believe we're having this conversation. Lord, help me say the right things.*

"Right after graduation, she and her mother left for the mainland." Alex's voice dropped to a near whisper. "She terminated the pregnancy."

"You mean she had an abortion," Cass stated flatly.

Alex's head shot up. His expression was unreadable. "That's what I said."

"No," Cass disagreed. "You used the nicer, cleaner terminology. Saying she 'terminated the pregnancy' sounds better than saying straight out she had an abortion. Of course, it would be even more accurate to say she killed the baby."

Alex flinched, and his gaze darted briefly to Hannah. "It wasn't a baby."

"Ah." Cass nodded sagely. "What was it then?"

"A ... a ..." Alex searched for the right word. "You know ... a whatchamacallit ... a fetus."

"What exactly is a fetus?" Cass tilted her head to one side, as if truly interested in his response.

Alex opened his mouth then closed it. "You already know the answer," he mumbled.

"Yes, I do." Cass regarded him with a steady gaze. "The question is, do you?"

"It's an unborn baby." Alex flung himself back in his chair and crossed an ankle over a knee, his foot jiggling at an alarming rate. "There! I said it. Are you happy now?"

Cass shook her head sadly. "How can I be happy knowing a baby died before it even had a chance to live?"

Unable to sit still, Alex jumped up and began pacing the length of the lanai. "There wasn't anything else we could do."

"Sure there was. Alison could have had the baby and given it up for adoption," Cass quietly pointed out.

"That would have interfered with college," Alex argued.

Cass snorted, unimpressed with his logic. "At worst, she would've had to postpone starting school until January. Big deal. Isn't a human life worth at least that much?"

"Getting an education is very important. How do you think Alison would have felt if she gave the baby up for adoption? For the rest of her life, she'd have wondered where it was, if it was okay, if it had gone to a good family."

"So you're saying it was better for her to kill the baby? Yeah, I see your point." Cass' voice dripped with sarcasm. "At least this way she knows for sure what happened to it."

Alex agitatedly raked his fingers through his hair. "That's not fair."

"What I said—" Cass arched an eyebrow at him, "or what she did?"

"Cut it out," Alex ordered through clenched teeth. "You're just trying to confuse me."

"No," Cass corrected him. "I'm trying to make you think."

"Maybe I don't want to think." Alex reached the privacy fence bordering the lanai. Shoving his hands in his pockets, he leaned against it and stared up at the sky.

Cass bit back the harsh words poised on the tip of her tongue. "Does the abortion bother you?"

"No!" Alex replied immediately. A second later, he amended that to, "Well ... maybe a little." He pushed off from the fence and returned to the table, looming over Cass. "I don't know."

"What is this? Multiple choice?"

Her unexpected teasing drained some of the tension out of Alex, and he sank back into the chair with a wan smile. "I guess I've been needing to talk to somebody about this for a long time."

"What about your parents?" Cass asked.

Alex's smile abruptly faded. "As far as they're concerned, it never happened. We had one discussion on the subject when Alison first found out she was pregnant. After I told them she'd be having an abortion, they informed me I was never to bring it up again." He shrugged in a vain attempt to act uncaring. "So I never did. You're the only other person I've ever talked to about it."

"My goodness." Cass passed a shaky hand across her eyes. "I don't know what to say."

"Do you hate me?" Alex asked so quietly she wasn't sure she heard right.

Realizing the importance of the question, Cass took her time answering. "No, I don't hate you. I hate that a baby died because of what you and Alison did. I mean, he was the innocent one in all this. He had no choice in what happened to him. You and Alison are going on with your lives because his life was snuffed out."

Alex expelled a shaky breath. "Man, you don't pull any punches, do you?"

"Not when it comes to issues like abortion." Cass gestured toward the crib where Hannah was beginning to stir. "Look at her. She's a tiny human being, a real person. What if my parents had decided they were too old to start over with a baby or having her would be too inconvenient or expensive? Through no fault of her own, she wouldn't be here." Tears pooled in her eyes. "It's just plain wrong that thousands of babies every year never stand a chance because that's how their parents feel. It's also unfair."

"But what about the parents' rights?" Alex argued. "Don't you believe Alison had the right to do whatever she wanted to with her own body?"

"It wasn't her body that was aborted," Cass reminded him. "It was the baby's. Besides, the time to control her body was before she got pregnant. The same goes for you." She held up her left hand. "See this ring?" She pointed to the slim gold band. "It symbolizes how I exercise my right to choose. It stands for my commitment not to have sex before I'm married."

"Oh, come on," drawled Alex. "How can you sit there and say you definitely won't have sex until you're married? Nobody knows what the future holds. What if you meet some guy in college and fall head over heels in love?

What'll you do then?"

"I won't jump into bed with him, that's for sure." Cass didn't let his sarcasm rattle her. "I have my standards, and I'll live up to them."

"But ... but ..." Alex sputtered. "How do you know?"

"I just do. The same way I know I'll never take something that doesn't belong to me or murder my parents." Cass cast an anxious glance at Hannah as she continued to squirm and whimper. "I trust God to give me the strength to resist whatever temptation comes along."

"Oh, it's a God thing." Alex's expression was a cross between disdain and dismissal.

"You bet it's a God thing. You ought to try it. I guarantee you there's no better way to live. It goes a long way toward helping you avoid messing up big time." Cass stood, signaling the end of the discussion. "I hate to cut this short, but duty calls. I need to take care of Hannah."

Alex also rose. Instead of leaving, however, he followed Cass to the crib and watched while she leaned down and picked up the baby. Hannah immediately nuzzled Cass' neck. Alex tentatively reached out a finger to touch the baby's cheek, but let his hand drop to his side before he made contact.

Seeing the gesture gave Cass the boldness to ask, "When was your and Alison's baby supposed to be born?"

For a few seconds, it appeared that Alex wouldn't answer. When he finally did, his voice was low and reluctant. "Sometime in late November or early December."

"So he would've been about Hannah's age if he'd been allowed to live." Cass turned to look directly into Alex's eyes. "Is there any part of you that's sorry about the abortion?"

He stared at her, his face contorted with emotion, then spun on his heels and walked away. Cass watched him leave with a mixture of relief and guilt.

"Maybe I was too hard on him," she murmured against Hannah's sweet-smelling cheek. "What do you think?"

In response, the baby let out a wail designed to alert anyone within a 50-mile radius that she was famished. Wincing, Cass moved her away from her ear and cradled her against her chest.

"Mom will be home in a few minutes," she crooned to the increasingly frantic infant. "In the meantime, let's get you into a fresh diaper. No offense, but you're putting off a really foul odor. It's a good thing I love you. I don't change just anyone's diapers."

CHAPTER 12

By the time Tabitha returned from her bowling date with Sam, Mom and Dad were back and had taken over with Hannah. Cass was enjoying a well-deserved break in the hammock, reading her book and sipping lemonade. That's where Tabitha found her as she wheeled around the side of the house and braked to a stop.

Jumping off the bike, she reached into the basket and waved aloft a fistful of letters. "Look what I have."

Cass set aside her book and snapped her fingers. "If there's anything from Logan, give it here."

"Hmm." Tabitha made a show of flipping through the envelopes. "Would that be a Cadet Russell from West Point, New York?"

"That's the one." Cass eagerly eyed the bundle. "How many do I have?"

"Three. Talk about a treasure trove." Tabitha handed them over then plopped down on the end of the hammock. "Do you want to read them now or can we talk?"

"I don't mind saving them." Tucking the letters into the book to mark her place, Cass closed it. "Is there something on your mind or is this just general conversation?"

Tabitha lifted her legs into the hammock, settling them

alongside Cass'. "First of all, Sam told me he's decided to help out with the Christmas party on Ebeye. You know how he was worried because he thought it would be like going to a Third World country and that made him nervous?" When Cass nodded, she continued, "He said today he was praying about it last night, and he got a strong feeling it was something he should do. That it was time for him to move outside his comfort zone."

"Cool," Cass said. "I like it when a boy talks about turning to God for help in making decisions. It's a good sign that he takes his faith seriously."

Tabitha grinned. "That's what I thought. Who knows? This might lead to us praying at the end of our dates like you and Logan do."

"Not that we've had any dates recently." Cass wistfully patted the edge of the top envelope sticking out of the book. "Logan's been gone over five months now."

"You still pray at the end of your phone conversations," Tabitha reminded her. "I've always thought it would be great to have that kind of relationship with a boy."

"It is," Cass agreed. "It's one of the reasons why I'm not interested in dating anyone else. I figure other guys just wouldn't measure up."

"Logan must love hearing that." Tabitha grinned. "Boys like knowing they're far superior to the competition."

"So do girls." Cass shot her a sly look. "Doesn't it do your ego good when Sam tells you you're the most beautiful girl he's ever seen?"

"Well … yes." Although her response was reluctant, Tabitha's grin stretched from ear to ear. "I have to admit I don't ever get tired of hearing stuff like that."

"Join the club." Cass yawned and stretched. "Did you see anyone at the bowling alley?"

Tabitha slapped her forehead with the palm of her hand. "Thanks for reminding me. I actually meant to tell you first thing. Rianne was there."

"Oh, yeah? Who with?"

"Nobody." Tabitha frowned. "She was by herself, bowling frame after frame like a machine or something. She barely gave the pins time to set up before she rolled the ball. It didn't look like she was having fun. She never smiled. I had to call her name three times before she finally heard me."

"She was probably concentrating," Cass said.

Tabitha shook her head. "No, it was more than that. It was like she was in a zone. Plus, she looked awful."

Cass grew still as her worries for her friend bubbled to the surface. She'd noticed physical changes in Rianne, but had hoped it was her imagination. "What do you mean?"

"I think she's lost weight, and she wasn't heavy to begin with." Tabitha draped a leg over the side of the hammock and pushed her foot against the ground to set it in motion. "Plus, she had dark circles under her eyes like she hadn't slept in a week. I'm worried about her."

"I am too." Cass rolled onto her side and propped her head on her hand. "I'm going over to her house tonight, so I'll talk to her then. Speaking of talking," she added, "Alex came by and we had a very interesting chat."

Tabitha's eyes narrowed with disapproval. "You let him in the house?"

"No, *Mother*," Cass drawled. "Hannah and I were out here." She gestured across the lanai. "Alex and I sat at the table, and he talked to me about Alison's abortion."

"You're kidding!" Tabitha's jaw dropped open. "What did he say?"

"He tried to defend it, and he got frustrated when I wouldn't buy his arguments." Cass merely stated the fact, taking no pleasure in it. "I think it bothers him more than he likes to let on. Otherwise, why would he want to discuss it?"

Tabitha shrugged. "I don't know, but I don't trust him. Maybe he wants to talk you into believing the way he does. Or it could be he's hoping you'll feel sorry enough for him that you'll consider going out."

"I didn't get that impression," Cass said, thinking back to the conversation. "He honestly seemed to be struggling with what happened."

"Don't let him fool you," Tabitha warned. "You know what he's like. I mean, think about his relationship with Alison. As far as I'm concerned, once a lowlife, always a lowlife."

That didn't sit well with Cass. "Don't you think it's possible God's working on him, showing him he was wrong?"

"Anything's possible—" Tabitha sniffed her skepticism, "but, in Alex's case, it's not likely. All I'm saying is be careful. Examine everything he says for hidden meanings."

"Okay," Cass relented for the sake of peace. Picking up the book, she opened it to the page that contained the letters. "Are we through? If so, I'd like to read these now."

Tabitha rolled out of the hammock and headed for the door. "I'll let the folks know I'm home and give them their mail."

The moment she disappeared into the house, Cass tore into the first envelope. For the next several minutes, she savored Logan's letters, alternately laughing and tearing up. When she finished the last one, she refolded it and lay back in the hammock. The soft breeze and warm sunshine soothed her aching heart.

Lord, I miss him so much. But thank You for our relationship. Logan's a great friend and a terrific boyfriend. Please continue to keep him safe. You know how much he means to me. Cass laughed quietly. *Of course You do. You know everything.*

Shortly before 5:00, Cass hopped on her bike and pedaled to Rianne's house. Rianne's younger brother, Robby, answered the door when Cass knocked.

"Come on in," he invited, stepping aside so she could enter. "Rianne's up in her room."

Cass called hello to the Thayers seated in the living room, then headed up the stairs. She didn't bother knocking before barging into the bedroom. Rianne was huddled in a corner of her bed, her eyes swollen and her face splotchy from crying.

"Good grief! What's the matter?" Cass hurried to her side.

"The usual." Rianne's tone was bitter. "My parents and I had another go-round about school right before you got here. They called me a religious fanatic for wanting to go to a Christian college." She punched the pillow scrunched in her lap. "They won't listen to a word I say. It's got to be their way or nothing."

Cass frowned. "How about working out some kind of compromise?" She thought fast, making it up as she went along. "Maybe you could go two years at a regular college and two at a Christian college."

Rianne's mouth twisted with resentment. "Yeah, like they'd go for that. They're not interested in compromise. Either I do what they say, or forget it."

"How do you know if you don't try?" Cass asked. "Wait until y'all calm down, then bring up the possibility."

Rianne brushed aside the suggestion. "I'm to the point where I wouldn't care if I never talked to them again."

Cass shifted uncomfortably. "Don't say that. They're your parents. You know—people you're supposed to honor and respect."

"What if they don't deserve to be honored?" challenged Rianne.

"You're still supposed to do it." Cass picked at pieces of lint clinging to the bedspread. "I know it's hard, but that's the way it is."

Snorting, Rianne jeered, "What do you know about how

hard it can be? It's easy to honor parents like yours."

Recalling the resentment she'd felt during Mom's pregnancy, Cass shook her head in disagreement. "Not always. I've had my struggles too."

"Not like mine." Rianne gave an impatient flounce. "I don't feel like talking about it anymore. I asked you over so we could have some fun. Let's do it."

Eager to go along with whatever she wanted, Cass pasted on a bright, although fake, smile. "You're on. What do you have in mind?"

"Let's go bowling," Rianne immediately replied.

Cass looked at her in surprise. "You want to go again? Tabitha said she saw you at the alley this afternoon."

"Is there some law against going bowling twice in one day?" Rianne said hotly.

Not sure how to handle her friend's rapid mood shifts, Cass decided to answer carefully. "No, but I'm hungry. I thought we were going to eat, then go to the movie."

"I don't feel like eating, especially not here. Being around my parents upsets my stomach. I know—" Rianne uncurled from the corner and scooted to the edge of the bed, "we can bowl a couple of games, get pizza, and still have time to make the movie."

"All right." Cass hoped Rianne didn't pick up on her lack of enthusiasm. "I need to call my parents and tell them the change in plans."

Rianne motioned toward her dresser. "The phone's over there somewhere. I'll go wash my face while you call."

Digging through the clutter on the dresser, Cass finally located the phone under a pair of sweatpants. After informing Dad where she'd be, she clicked off the phone and set the receiver on Rianne's nightstand.

"You all set?"

Rianne bounded back into the room. She'd scrubbed her face and pulled her hair into a ponytail. Cass was shocked at how gaunt she looked. She noticed the smudges beneath her friend's eyes, as well as a new sharpness to her cheekbones. Realizing she was staring, she forced herself to look away.

"Uh ... yeah." She toyed with the hem of her shirt, tucking it in then pulling it out again. "Dad gave the okay about going to the bowling alley."

"I had another idea while I was in the bathroom," Rianne chirped. Her mood had gone from sullen to lighthearted in the space of a couple of minutes. "Let's jog to the alley instead of riding our bikes."

"Why?" Even though she knew she ran the risk of incurring Rianne's wrath, Cass couldn't help the question.

A flash of displeasure tightened Rianne's features, disappearing as quickly as it came. "Because we always ride. Let's do something different," she wheedled.

"I haven't run in ages. I don't know if I could make it." Cass observed the feverish glitter in her friend's eyes and wondered if she was feeling okay.

"We'll alternate running and walking. Come on." Rianne reached out her hand and pulled Cass to her feet. "Time's a-wasting. Let's get this show on the road."

Cass allowed herself to be led down the stairs and across the front hallway. The pair paused at the door.

"I'm leaving," Rianne announced to no one in particular.

Although her parents sat on the couch, they didn't indicate they'd heard her. With a shrug, Rianne opened the door and walked out, pulling Cass behind her.

"You see how it is?" Rianne released Cass' hand and stomped down the steps. "It's like I don't even exist as far as they're concerned."

"I was surprised when they didn't say anything," Cass agreed. "I'd hate it if my parents gave me the silent treatment like that."

"They wouldn't." Rianne took off across the lawn at a rapid pace. "They're much too mature to act so childish."

Uncomfortable with criticizing the Thayers, Cass changed the subject. "What do you hear from Randy? When's he getting in for Christmas?"

"He'll be home the 12th." Rianne rotated her shoulders to loosen them up then jogged in place for several seconds. "I can't wait. I'm counting on him taking my side against the folks. I could use all the help I can get at this point."

"Have you told him what's been going on?" Cass fell into step with Rianne as she trotted out to the road and turned right.

"It's kind of hard to explain over the phone. I thought I'd fill him in after he gets here." Rianne executed a quick jig then resumed running. "I just know he'll understand and go to bat for me."

The pair jogged in silence for awhile. As her own breathing grew labored, Cass glanced over at Rianne to gauge her condition. She was amazed to see that her friend appeared as fresh as a daisy.

"Have you been running on a regular basis?" she panted.

Rianne nodded. "I started a few weeks ago. I try to run a couple of miles every night."

"Why didn't you tell me?" A stitch had developed in Cass' side, but she was determined not to give up until Rianne did.

"I don't know. I didn't think about it."

"I guess that explains your weight loss," Cass remarked. "Tabitha said she thought you'd dropped a few pounds after she saw you at the bowling alley today."

Rianne halted so abruptly that Cass continued on several more feet before she realized her friend was no longer beside her. She circled back to where Rianne stood, glaring.

"Why were you and Tabitha talking about me?" she demanded.

Cass had had enough of Rianne's touchiness. "We weren't talking about you. Tabitha made a simple comment, that's all. But," she went on, "even if we were, what's the big deal? You're our friend. We care about what's going on with you, the same way you care about what's happening to us."

"I don't like being talked about," Rianne said stubbornly.

Cass arched an eyebrow at her. "What do you plan to do about it? Monitor every conversation that takes place on the island?"

Rianne's lower lip curled in a pout. "Why are you being so snotty? You just said you're my friend."

"I am." Deciding she might as well voice the suspicion she'd been harboring for the past week or so, Cass blurted, "Which is why I'm going to ask you something. You probably won't like it, but, in my opinion, that's what friends are for." She took a deep breath. "Do you have an eating disorder?"

Rianne opened and closed her mouth several times before finally speaking. "I don't believe you actually have the nerve to ask me that!" Her eyes flamed with fury. "How dare you?"

"I dare because I care." *Ooh, good one,* Cass congratulated herself.

Unfortunately, Rianne wasn't impressed. "Whatever." She raised a hand in a dismissive gesture. "A real friend wouldn't even think something like that, let alone bring it up."

Cass refused to back down. "I have good reasons for saying what I did. You're showing all the signs of being anorexic. Don't you remember learning about them in health last year?" She ticked them off on her fingers. "You've gone on an exercise kick. You're not eating. I've noticed how often you've thrown your lunch away lately without taking a bite. You're losing weight. You look exhausted all the time." Her hand returned to her side. "What I'm trying to say is I'm worried about you."

"Well, you have a strange way of showing it, accusing me of being anorexic." Rianne scowled her irritation. "You know what's been going on between my folks and me about college. I'm under a lot of stress. Yes, I've lost a few pounds. Yes, I'm not sleeping well. And yes, I've been working off the tension by exercising more. But no, I am not—I repeat, not—anorexic. Honestly—" she shook her head in disgust, "I thought if anyone would understand, it would be you."

Cass, who'd been so sure a few minutes ago that she'd stumbled upon the truth, began to doubt herself. "You're sure that's all it? Stress?"

Rianne nodded. "Yes. You're my best friend. Don't you think I'd tell you if it were something more?"

"I guess." Although she still wasn't entirely convinced, Cass had no choice but to take her word for it.

"You guess?" Rianne emitted a humorless laugh. "I pour my heart out to you, and that's what I get in return?" She flung her arms up in defeat. "I give up. If that's the best you can do, I'm out of here."

"What do you mean?" Cass grabbed her arm before she could leave.

Rianne shook off her grip. "You can find yourself some other sap to hang out with. I have better things to do than spend time with somebody who doesn't trust me."

"But—"

Cass' protest fell on deaf ears as Rianne wheeled around and sprinted away without a backward glance.

Cass waited until Rianne disappeared around a curve in the road then turned to head home. *I'm two for two today when it comes to driving people off,* she mused. *God, if You're looking for a way to minister to Alex and Rianne, maybe You'd better choose someone else. I'm obviously not very good at this.*

Cass slowly made her way back to the house. Even the beauty of the early evening, with its gentle, tropical breeze and lower temperature, could do nothing to raise her spirits. They were further dampened when she let herself into the house and found it empty. A note on the counter informed her that Tabitha was at the Yokwe Yuk with Sam and her parents had taken Hannah with them to visit friends.

After fixing a peanut butter and jelly sandwich for supper, Cass retired to the couch. She refused to turn on the television or radio in case something came on that might cheer her up. Intent on feeling royally sorry for herself, she curled up in the corner of the sofa and reviewed her conversations with Rianne and Alex.

"Cass?"

Cass was so lost in thought, Tabitha's voice an hour later made her jump. She could barely make out her sister's form in the living room's deepening shadows.

"Who else would it be?" came her muffled response.

"What are you doing sitting in the dark?" Tabitha reached over and switched on a lamp.

Cass blinked in the sudden light. "I was thinking."

Tabitha studied her through narrowed eyes. "Are you all right? I thought you and Rianne were going to the movies."

Not wanting to get into a detailed explanation, Cass replied tersely, "Last-minute change of plans. How was your date with Sam?"

"Wonderful, as usual." Tabitha's blissful expression said it all. She walked to the couch and sat down. "Guess who we saw at the Yuk."

Cass didn't feel like guessing. "I have no idea."

"Alex. He was there with Kendra Burleson." Tabitha lowered her voice, as if concerned about eavesdroppers. "You know the kind of reputation she has. Doesn't that tell you Alex hasn't changed as much as he'd like you to believe he has?"

Cass' stomach sank. *This day just keeps getting better and better,* she silently grumbled. *What's next, Lord? I'll get word I upset Rianne so much that she hopped the first plane out of here and ran away to Hawaii?*

Aloud, she said, "It looks like you were right about Alex. What's that old saying? A leopard can't change its spots?"

"Does it bother you that Alex was out with Kendra?" Tabitha peered anxiously at Cass. "You weren't hoping the two of you would start dating again, were you?"

"Believe me, that was the furthest thing from my mind," Cass assured her. "All I hoped was that he'd rethink some of his attitudes and actions." Her laugh was bitter. "Chalk up another failure on my part."

Tabitha hesitated a second before asking, "Is there something you want to talk about?"

Cass flashed her a grateful smile. "Nah. It's just been one of those days."

"Then how about I make you an ice cream sundae?" Tabitha offered. "Would that cheer you up?"

Cass' smile broadened into a grin. "Now you're talking. You're not nearly as bad as I tell people you are."

Tabitha stuck out her tongue as she got up to go to the kitchen. "Gee, I sure wish I could say the same about you."

CHAPTER 13

"Hi."

Cass turned from her locker Monday morning to find Alex standing behind her. "Hey. I didn't think you were still speaking to me."

"I decided Saturday I'd never talk to you again. But I don't know—" he gave her a wry smile, "there's something about you I can't resist."

"Maybe my charm and wit?" Cass suggested.

"No, it's definitely not your charm." Alex laughed at her indignant expression. "Oh, please. Don't tell me you actually think you're charming."

"Of course not. I hoped other people thought I was though. Isn't there an old saying about being able to fool some of the people some of the time? I guess it's not working in this case." Stuffing the last of her books into her backpack, Cass closed the locker and leaned against it. "Did you and Kendra have a nice time Saturday night?"

"How did you—" Alex snapped his fingers. "That's right. Sam and Tabitha were at the Yuk. What did she do? Run straight home and rat on me?"

"No, she biked." Cass looked at him curiously from under

her lashes. "Why do you look at it as being ratted on?"

Alex held up his hand. "I'm not in the mood to be analyzed so don't start."

"What do you mean?" Cass did her best to look innocent. "All I did was ask a simple question."

"Nothing's simple with you," Alex drawled. "Talking to you is like walking through a mine field. I never know when I might say something that'll blow up in my face."

"So why do you keep coming back for more?" Cass pushed off from the locker and started toward her homeroom.

Alex appeared genuinely puzzled. "To tell you the truth, I have no idea."

Shaking her head in mock derision, Cass teased, "Typical male response." She affected a deeper, huskier tone. "I don't know why I do what I do. I'm a guy, which automatically means I'm clueless."

Adopting a falsetto voice, Alex countered with, "And I'm a girl, which means I think I know everything."

"Very good," Cass said, giving him a brief round of applause. "Isn't it comforting to know we understand each other so well?"

"It gives us something to build on," Alex agreed solemnly, his eyes dancing with amusement. He lifted a hand in farewell. "I'll see you in English."

Entering homeroom, Cass thought about the exchange that had just taken place between her and Alex. For some strange reason, they were drawn to each other, not in a romantic way, but in a way that indicated they might be on the road to establishing a friendship. She had no idea if that was where their recent encounters would lead, but she decided to stay open to the possibility.

God sure does work in mysterious ways, she mused. *If Alex and I wind up becoming friends, it will definitely be one of the world's great mysteries.*

Every time someone walked into the classroom, Cass' heart skipped a beat. She hadn't seen, or talked to, Rianne since their disastrous conversation on Saturday. She had contemplated calling her yesterday after Rianne didn't show up at church, then opted to give her more time to cool off. Now she anxiously awaited her arrival, wondering what kind of mood her friend would be in. She hoped Rianne would be as forgiving as Alex, and they'd be able to talk out their differences. The last thing she wanted was a permanent rift with her best friend. When the bell rang signaling the start of the school day, it dawned on Cass that Rianne wasn't coming.

Now what? she wondered, drumming her fingers on the desk and paying no attention to the announcements over the P.A. system. *Should I call her at lunch or wait until I get home? I'll ask Tabitha and see what she thinks.*

Tabitha's advice at lunch was for Cass to call Rianne after school.

"Do you think Rianne's sick?" Tabitha asked Cass, keeping her voice down so as not to disturb Kira, who was cramming for a test she was convinced she was doomed to fail.

Cass shrugged. "Why else would she miss school and church?"

"Maybe she's avoiding you." Tabitha bit into her egg salad sandwich.

Kira's head jerked up. "Rianne's avoiding you? Why?"

Cass shot Tabitha an irritated look before turning her attention to Kira. "Do you have X-ray hearing or something? I thought you were studying."

"I am." Kira tapped the open book as proof. "But I never completely tune out what's going on around me. I don't want to miss out on anything important. So—" her eyes gleaming with interest, she temporarily abandoned her schoolwork, "what's up with you and Rianne?"

"It's no big deal," Cass hedged. "Just a minor difference of opinion."

"What about?" Kira persisted. Her face took on a knowing expression. "Why she's losing weight?"

Cass' mouth dropped open. "You've noticed too?"

"A person would have to be blind not to notice. She wasn't exactly two-ton Annie to begin with, and she looks like she's dropped about five pounds." Kira helped herself to a handful of Tabitha's potato chips. "Is she anorexic or something?"

Cass choked on the milk she'd just swallowed. "What makes you ask that?"

"What else could it be?" Kira asked logically. "She hasn't been sick, and she didn't say anything about going on a diet, at least not to me. The obvious answer is an eating disorder."

"I wouldn't mention that to her, if I were you," Cass warned. "She's a little touchy at the moment, especially if you bring up anorexia."

"Which is precisely why we do need to mention it," Kira insisted. "If she has developed an eating disorder, it's our job to talk some sense into her. She's our friend."

"Then it's your turn." Cass' mouth turned down at the corners as she recalled Saturday's unpleasant episode. "I tried, and all it got me was a royal chewing-out."

"Okay." Kira shrugged agreeably. "I'll stop by her house on my way home from school." She reached for more chips, but Tabitha swatted her hand and pulled them out of the way. "Now quit talking so I can get back to studying. You don't want to be the reason that I fail Spanish."

Since Sam had to stay after school for a meeting with his guidance counselor, Cass and Tabitha rode home together. The wind had picked up and had blown in storm clouds, which all but blocked the sun. Tabitha heaved a resigned sigh.

"It doesn't look like I'll be meeting Sam at the pool for a quick swim."

"Surely you can go one day without doing something with him, can't you?" Cass teased.

"I suppose so," Tabitha pretended to grouse. "But it'll be hard."

"I'm sure you can do it, if you put your mind to it." Cass wheeled around the side of the house, braking as the bike's front tire hit the lanai. "It'll help build your character."

Walking into the house, Tabitha placed a hand on Cass' arm and commanded, "Listen."

Cass frowned. "What? I don't hear anything."

"Exactly. Isn't it great?" Releasing her arm, Tabitha continued through the kitchen. "Hannah isn't wailing up a storm."

"I heard that." Mom looked up from the rocking chair in the living room where she sat cuddling the baby. "And so did your sister. Her feelings are hurt."

"Better her feelings than my ears." Tabitha walked to the far end of the couch and sat down. "Why is she so quiet? She's usually throwing a royal fit when we get in."

Mom gazed fondly at the sleeping infant. "She's growing up, getting more used to her surroundings. Sights and sounds don't set her off as much as they used to."

Cass sank down into the sofa's nearer corner, tucking her legs beneath her. "So you're saying that the sight of us makes her cry?"

It seemed to take Mom a moment to realize she was joking. "Not necessarily. It could be the smell."

Tossing her curls, Tabitha feigned indignation. "How rude. I've never been so insulted in my life."

"Really? Huh." Cass pondered that a few seconds. "I guess I haven't been nearly as nasty as I thought. I'll just have to try harder."

"That's okay," Tabitha hastened to assure her. "You do

fine in the insult department. Hey, is that mail?" she added, glancing at the table.

"Yes, it is. Dad brought it when he came home for lunch, and I completely forgot about it." Mom laughed at herself. "I must be getting old. I haven't even looked through it to see what we got."

"I'll do it." Cass jumped up and hurried to the table. Flipping through the stack of envelopes, she carried them back to the couch. About to sit down, she stopped in mid-movement, her expression unreadable. "Here's one for you." She held a letter out to Tabitha.

"Who's it from?" Checking the return address, Tabitha's mouth pursed as if she'd bitten into a lemon. "Oh, great. What does she want?"

"Who?" Mom looked from Tabitha to Cass, who'd finally sat back down.

When Tabitha didn't say anything, Cass replied, "Her mother."

Mom frowned. "Beth? I thought she wrote Tabitha out of her life once and for all last January."

"So did I." Tabitha slapped the envelope against her palm, as if trying to decide whether or not to open it. "With Beth though, you never know what she's going to do next. She does whatever she wants."

"She is unpredictable," agreed Cass. She eyed Beth's letter. "So, are you going to read it or not?"

"Part of me would prefer throw it away and forget about it." Tabitha slid her thumb under the envelope flap. "But my curiosity won't let me. I want to know what she's up to."

Cass watched Tabitha while she read the single sheet of paper, trying to guess its contents from her expression. Tabitha read the letter again before carefully folding it and sliding it back into the envelope.

"Well?" Cass prompted when her sister's silence went on too long for her liking.

"Basically, she's upset about Hannah being born," Tabitha replied quietly.

Mom's eyebrows shot up. "Excuse me?"

"You remember that I sent Grandma a picture of Hannah?" At Mom's nod, Tabitha explained, "Beth found it when she went through some of Grandma's stuff. She wrote to remind me that Sunshine and Peace are as much related to me as Hannah is. She said it's time I started showing them some consideration too, instead of fawning all over Hannah."

"The nerve of her!" Cass exploded, nearly coming off the couch in her anger. "Who does she think she is?"

Tabitha shot her a wry look. "That's not the best part. She's going to be sending pictures of Sunshine and Peace, and she expects me to put them up someplace—she suggested the refrigerator—where I'll see them everyday and remember I have another sister and brother."

"You're kidding!" Cass turned outraged eyes to Mom. "Do you believe this?"

To Cass' surprise, Mom laughed. "Unfortunately, yes. From what little I know of Beth, it's entirely in keeping with her character for her to react to Hannah's birth this way."

"Because she hates not being the center of attention, right?" Tabitha asked.

Mom nodded. "Exactly. Until Hannah came along, she considered her children your only true siblings. She's put out that Hannah upset the apple cart so—"

"She's trying to lay a guilt trip on me," Tabitha finished for her. "She wants me to feel bad for being more involved with Hannah than with her kids."

"Bingo." Mom shifted Hannah to her other arm. "You're probably going to get more letters from her along the same lines. She might even take to calling and putting Peace and Sunshine on to talk to you."

"I wouldn't mind that. Talking to the kids, I mean," Tabitha quickly added at Cass' questioning murmur. "I don't have anything against them."

"Neither do I," Mom asserted. "In fact, it wouldn't bother me if you wanted to put their pictures up on the refrigerator."

Tabitha arched a brow at her. "What about Dad?"

Mom grinned. "You can put his picture up too."

Tabitha groaned. "You know what I meant."

"Yes, I do." Mom grew serious. "And you're right to be concerned about his feelings. I'll check with him before we do anything drastic."

"I probably won't put their pictures out in the open anyway," Tabitha said. "It's not like they're part of the family."

"Whatever you want to do is fine." Hannah began to fuss, and Mom set the rocker in motion to soothe her. "They're part of your family, and we respect that."

Cass picked up the mail she'd placed in her lap and started sorting through it again. She set aside two letters from Logan then stopped when she came to an envelope near the bottom of the pile.

"Whoa! Talk about a big day for mail." She held up the letter. "It's from Janette." She gauged its thickness. "And it's a fat one. This should be interesting." She hadn't received a letter this thick from her former best friend in Tennessee for a long time.

Hannah chose that moment to wake up with a start. Before she could start crying, Mom carted her off to the bedroom to change her diaper. Tabitha scooted across the cushions to lean against Cass.

"Can I read over your shoulder?" she asked. "I'll bet she wrote something juicy."

"No." Shooting her sister an annoyed glance, Cass elbowed her in the ribs. "Move over. I let you read Beth's letter in peace."

Tabitha edged a scant half-inch away. "When was the last time you heard from Jan?"

"She sent me a birthday card in April." Cass' glower caused Tabitha to put another inch between them. "If I promise to let you read the letter after I'm done, will you quit breathing down my neck?"

In response, Tabitha immediately returned to her end of the sofa. Cass felt her eyes watching her the entire time it took her to open the envelope and read the four-page missive. The moment she was done, Tabitha held out her hand and snapped her fingers. Cass passed the letter to her without comment and waited quietly as Tabitha read it.

"Oh, my. Poor Janette." Her eyes wide, Tabitha returned the letter to Cass.

"What do you mean, poor Janette?" Mom asked as she reappeared with a freshly diapered Hannah.

"Her mother got remarried two weeks ago," Cass said.

"Really?" Mom smoothed the fuzz on Hannah's head. "Whom did she marry?"

Cass consulted the letter. "His name's Billy Clark. The first time Jan met him was the day her mother married him. When she got home from school, she found him sitting in the living room. When Jan asked him who he was, he told her he was her new stepfather. He said he and her Mom had gotten married that afternoon."

"You can't be serious." Mom's exclamation startled Hannah, and she whimpered her displeasure. After calming her down, Mom continued, "This has to be a joke. Are you sure Janette isn't pulling your leg?"

"Tabitha read the letter." Cass turned to her. "Do you think she's kidding?"

"Absolutely not." Tabitha vigorously shook her head. "She's genuinely upset."

"Where did her mother meet this man, and how long has she known him?"

Cass made a face. "According to Jan, she met him in a bar about six weeks ago."

"Does she know why they got married so quickly?"

"Jan's mother told her there wasn't any reason not to. They're in love. They get along well. Waiting made no sense to them." Cass snorted her disdain. "If you ask me, they sound like a couple of teen-agers."

"Hey, I resent that," Tabitha protested. "I'm a teen-ager, and I'd never do something so stupid."

"What does Janette think about her new stepfather?" Mom asked.

Cass grimaced. "She can't stand him. He smokes. He yells a lot. He doesn't lift a finger to help out around the house. She has no idea what her mother sees in him."

Mom frowned. "He has a job, doesn't he?"

"I don't think Jan said, but I sure hope so." Propping her feet on the coffee table, Cass set the letter in her lap. "I can't imagine what this is like for her. I wasn't happy when you announced you were marrying Dad, but it wasn't because I didn't like him."

"I was the one you didn't like," Tabitha said with a smirk.

"What do you mean, didn't?" Cass retorted. "I still don't. Anyway," she continued before Tabitha could think of a comeback, "at least Dad was a Christian, and y'all had known each other a long time. Janette hardly knows anything about Billy. She's not even sure how old he is."

Mom sighed in disapproval. "Someone should have a long talk with Jan's mother. It seems to me she's taking an awful risk. There are some crazy people in the world. She should do a better job of protecting Jan."

Cass' face tightened with concern. "Do you think she's in danger?"

"Probably not, but you know me." Mom attempted to lighten Cass' anxiety with a smile. "I'm a worrywart. I'd rather be safe than sorry. The best thing we can do for Jan is pray that Billy turns out to be a decent man and that she adjusts to her mother's marriage."

"I'll pray for her too," Tabitha promised Cass.

"Thanks." Cass gathered the pages of the letter and, standing, handed them to Mom. "You can read it if you want. I'm going to fix myself a snack. You want something?" she asked Tabitha.

Her sister nodded. "If there's any of Mrs. Simpson's bread pudding left, I'll take that."

"If there's any left, we'll split it," Cass declared firmly.

Other than muttering something under her breath, Tabitha didn't argue.

After delivering Tabitha's pudding to her, Cass took her bowl, and Logan's letters, and retreated to the porch. She would have liked to sit outside on the rocks, but the rain had arrived. It lashed at the windows as she settled herself in the swing and opened the first of the letters. The sight of Logan's familiar handwriting brought a lump to her throat, and she put off reading a few moments to gaze out the window.

Oh, Logan, I miss you so much. I wish you were here so I could talk to you about Alex and Rianne. Cass smiled. *Not that you'd be too thrilled to be discussing Alex. I suppose I should be grateful that it's been nearly six months since you left, and our relationship is still going strong. It sure would be nice to see you though. Next to Tabitha and Rianne, you're my best friend, and half a year is a long time to go without seeing you. Maybe God will work it out so we can get together in January when we come home. Tennessee is a long way from New York, but nothing's impossible with God. If it's His will that we spend time together, He'll open a way.*

With this hopeful thought in mind, Cass turned her attention back to the letters. For the next several minutes, she forgot where she was and allowed Logan's vivid descriptions of life at West Point to whisk her thousands of miles away to the Military Academy.

Chapter 14

When Tabitha came to tell her she had a phone call, she had to say Cass' name twice before Cass jumped and reluctantly made the return trip to reality. Smiling sheepishly, Cass accepted the phone Tabitha held out to her.

"Sorry. My mind was someplace else."

"Oh, gee, let me try to guess where," Tabitha drawled. Lowering her voice, she added as a warning, "Rianne's on the phone, and she sounds mad."

Cass waited until Tabitha left the porch before she put the receiver to her ear. "Hello?"

"Has anyone ever told you that you have a big mouth?" Rianne demanded by way of greeting.

Not about to put up with her sarcasm, Cass shot back, "Hundreds of people. It's what I'm known for. Why do you ask?"

"Kira came by."

"I know. She said she would." Cass decided it was time to put her friend on the defensive. "We were worried about you since you missed church yesterday and didn't show up at school."

"You were worried, huh?" Rianne snorted her skepticism. "So worried that you lied to Kira and told her I have an eating disorder?"

Instead of answering, Cass inquired quietly, "Do you honestly think that's how the conversation went between Kira and me?"

Rianne hesitated. When she finally responded, her tone was sullen. "How should I know? I wasn't there."

"You know me," Cass pointed out, determined not to let her off the hook. "Do I make a habit of spreading lies about people?"

"Well ... no," Rianne was forced to admit. "But where else would Kira get the idea I'm anorexic?"

"Perhaps you haven't noticed, but Kira has two eyes and a functioning brain. She put two and two together—things like your weight loss and your over-exercising—and came to a logical conclusion. If you don't like her conclusion," Cass suggested, "then prove to her—and to me while you're at it—that we're wrong."

"I don't have to prove anything to anybody," Rianne said hotly. "You should just take my word that I don't have a problem."

"I'd like to. I really would." Cass sadly shook her head. "Unfortunately, all the evidence points in the other direction. Believe it or not, I didn't say anything to Kira about what I suspected. She came up with the anorexia thing on her own."

"You talked about me behind my back!" Rianne blazed. "What a sneaky, lowdown thing to do."

"Knock it off," Cass snapped. "We've been down this road before. We're friends, and we're girls. Discussing one another comes with the territory. Quit acting like you've never done it."

"I ... but ... you ..." Rianne's protest died on her lips. "Okay, you're right. But that doesn't mean I have to like being talked about," she asserted.

"Who does? Unless people are saying good things, of course." Pushing her foot against the floor, Cass gently propelled the swing. "Are you still mad at me?"

"Not as much as I was when I first called." It was obvious from Rianne's tone that she'd calmed down considerably. "I just wish you'd get off this anorexia kick you're on."

"I will as soon as you convince me that's not what's going on."

Rianne's exasperated sigh gusted over the line. "So we're back to square one."

"Apparently," Cass agreed cheerfully. "I didn't realize you were this stubborn."

"And I didn't know how unreasonable you could be," Rianne countered.

Instead of taking offense, Cass laughed. "There you go. We're making progress. We're learning new things about each other, which is a good sign in a relationship. Let's build on that."

"Don't make me laugh," Rianne ordered irritably. "I called you up to chew you out."

"Which you did quite well," Cass complimented her. "Now let's move on and talk about something else. Why weren't you in school today?"

"I was too exhausted to get out of bed this morning. My mother was so worried that she took me to the doctor." Rianne's amazement that her mother cared enough to do such a thing was evident in her voice. "After running a bunch of tests, the only thing he could figure was that I'm run-down. He prescribed a multivitamin and sent me on my way."

Alarm bells went off in Cass' head. To her way of thinking, the doctor's diagnosis was further proof of Rianne's anorexic condition. Unwilling to risk more of her friend's wrath, however, she opted to keep her opinion to herself.

"Did he say when you can come back to school?" she asked.

"He left it up to me." Rianne giggled. "I'm thinking I'll stay home another day. I might as well milk this thing for all it's worth."

"It's not a problem being home alone with your mother?" Cass took that to be a hopeful sign.

"It wasn't today. Of course, it helped that we didn't talk about college." At the mere mention of school, the tension returned to Rianne's voice. "She mostly did housework and checked on me every now and then to see if I needed anything."

"Maybe you should go to school tomorrow and not press your luck," Cass suggested.

"You might be right. I'll wait and see how much energy I have in the morning." Rianne emitted a jaw-cracking yawn. "Speaking of energy, I've about used mine up. I think I'll head back to bed."

Relieved they were ending the conversation on an upbeat note, Cass asked, "Do you want me to call you later and see how you're doing?"

"No, thanks. I'll call you if I feel up to it." Rianne yawned again. "Sorry about that. I'd better go. Hopefully I'll see you tomorrow."

"One way or the other, you will," Cass promised. "If you don't make it to school, I'll stop by on my way home."

"Sounds good. See you."

"Bye."

Pressing the off button, Cass set the phone down on the wicker table beside the swing. She spent the next few minutes praying for Rianne before gathering up Logan's letters and the phone, and heading back inside.

CHAPTER 15

Supper that night turned out to be chaotic. Despite Mom's best efforts, Hannah refused to settle down, and her crying made conversation at the table impossible.

"Let me take her." Getting up, Dad came around the table and relieved Mom of the wailing baby. "She'll calm down once she realizes her Daddy's holding her."

Smoldering with resentment, Tabitha watched as Dad settled Hannah in the crook of his arm and began walking from room to room with her. She tuned out Mom and Cass so she could hear what Dad was saying to the baby.

"See this?" He crossed the living room floor and stopped. "It's called a window. Do you know what that is outside the window? It's God's big, beautiful world. Just wait until you're old enough to play in it."

The combination of Dad's crooning and his steady jiggling soon quieted Hannah. After several minutes of quiet, Mom called, "Steve, she seems better now. Why don't you come finish your dinner?"

Dad smiled from his post by the window. "Who needs food for the body when there's nourishment for the soul like this around?" With a look of adoration, he gestured down at Hannah.

Tabitha had about all she could take. "Honestly, Dad," she griped, "you're spoiling her."

"What?" He turned a puzzled face to her. "How?"

"Everybody knows if you pick a baby up every time it cries, the end result is a spoiled brat." Tabitha worked at sounding as superior as possible.

Dad nodded sagely. "I see. Since when did you become such an expert on child-rearing?"

"I read a lot." Since that came across as lame even to her own ears, Tabitha added with a sniff, "Plus, anyone with a lick of sense knows what to do, and not do, when it comes to raising kids."

"I guess I don't have any sense then—" Dad sounded downright cheery at the prospect, "because I'm not about to put Hannah down and let her cry." He flashed Mom a wicked grin. "I leave that to her heartless Mommy."

"Somebody has to be the disciplinarian around here." Mom shrugged her unconcern that it appeared she was elected to the position. "It wouldn't do Hannah any good to have two pushovers for parents."

While Cass seemed to enjoy their bantering, Tabitha seethed. The reason she'd brought up the possibility of Hannah being spoiled was to give Dad the chance to tell her that he used to employ the same methods when she was a baby to soothe her. As usual, he let the opportunity pass, preferring to talk about his precious Hannah.

Tabitha's thoughts shocked her. Even if it was only in her mind, had she really referred to her baby sister with such scorn? She was suddenly struck by the similarity between her musings and what Beth had written in her letter.

Oh, no! I'm just like my mother.

"Tabitha, are you okay?"

Mom's worried voice penetrated the fog of dismay that had settled over her, and she blinked. "Uh ... yes. Why?"

"You had the strangest look on your face." Mom studied her face. "What happened?"

"I ... uh ... I just ... realized something, that's all." She passed a shaky hand across her eyes. "May I be excused? I don't feel like eating right now."

"Yes, of course. Leave your dishes. I'll take care of them," Mom added when Tabitha began to collect them.

Escaping from the table, Tabitha shot Dad a quick glance to see if he was aware of what was happening. She couldn't decide if she was relieved or put out that he was too wrapped up in Hannah to notice anything else. She hurried down the hall, willing herself not to cry until she was safely in her room.

Her tears had mostly subsided when she heard Dad and Cass leave the house 20 minutes later. Soon after that, Mom tapped on her door.

"Sweetie—" Mom opened the door to stick her head in the room, "may I come in?"

Tabitha waved listlessly from where she was sprawled on the bed. "Sure. Join the fun."

Mom pulled out the desk chair and sat down. "What's going on in that lovely head of yours?" she asked, her voice tender.

Tabitha snorted. "It may be lovely on the outside, but it's ugly as sin on the inside."

"That's awfully harsh," Mom gently chided. "Why in the world would you say something like that about yourself?"

Tabitha turned pleading eyes toward her. "If it's all right with you, I don't feel like talking right now. Actually," she corrected herself, "it's more that I can't. I need to think some things through before I can talk about them."

"You're sure talking wouldn't help you think them through?" Mom asked.

Tabitha hesitated a moment, then shook her head. "I'm

positive. I had what my English teacher calls a stunning insight." She smiled slightly. "I've discovered that the problem with stunning insight is it can leave a person in a state of shock."

"I won't push you then." Mom slowly stood up. "If you're not ready to talk, I respect that. You need to know though that I told the others to go for a walk so we could be alone. They probably won't be back for a half-hour or so. You don't want to waste all this quality time, do you?"

"Heaven forbid," Tabitha drawled. "Especially when you arranged it in such a sneaky manner."

"Then what do you say I grill you up a cheese sandwich? You didn't eat much at supper. If you play your cards right, I might even let you talk me into fixing you a chocolate milkshake," Mom offered as added incentive. "In fact, I believe I'll have one myself."

"I'd like that." Tabitha abruptly stood up and threw her arms around Mom. "I love you so much. I hope someday I'll be just like you."

Holding her close, Mom smoothed her curls. "I love you too. But you know what I hope for you? That you'll grow into the person God created you to be. I know you're down on yourself at the moment, but I happen to think you're a pretty terrific person. I'm blessed to have you as my daughter."

"And I'm blessed that you're my mom," came Tabitha's muffled reply.

"This—" grinning, Mom stepped back and cupped Tabitha's face between her hands, "is what's known as a mutual admiration society."

Tabitha uneasily averted her gaze. "You probably wouldn't admire me if you knew the kinds of things I think."

"Don't be so sure." Releasing her face, Mom took one of her hands. "I love you unconditionally. That means no strings attached. When Cass was little and I put her to bed,

I'd tell her, I love you just the way you are, I love you no matter what, and I love you forever. I've started saying that to Hannah when I lay her down in her crib. Maybe you need to hear it as well."

"Even if I don't deserve it?" Tabitha murmured.

"That's when it means the most." Tugging on her hand, Mom pulled her toward the door. "Move it, slowpoke. We don't want the rest of the family walking in on us while we're drinking our milkshakes. Knowing them, they'd expect us to share."

Getting into the spirit, Tabitha heaved an exaggerated sigh. "Some people just don't know their place, do they?"

"You can say that again," Mom agreed, following her out the door. "They actually think they have rights. Imagine that."

Trading jokes, they made their way to the kitchen.

Emerging from the house the following morning to head for school, Tabitha and Cass discovered a group waiting for them. As usual, Sam was there. In addition, Alex and Rianne straddled their bikes, warily eyeing one another.

Spotting the sisters, Sam raised his hand in greeting. "Hey, Tabs, Red." He gestured toward the other two. "Look, your very own welcoming committee."

With Rianne and Alex looking anything but welcoming, Cass muttered so only Tabitha could hear, "Lucky us. Or should I say, lucky me?"

Tabitha snickered softly. "They're not here to see me, that's for sure. What is it about you that attracts so much attention?" Nearing the group, she smiled cheerily. "Good morning, all. I'm glad to see you're feeling better, Rianne." She saved a special smile for Sam. "How are you this fine morning?"

"On top of the world, now that you're here." He glanced at the other three, his expression amused. "What do you say we head on? If two's company and three's a crowd, five must be a thundering herd."

Grateful to escape the tense trio, Tabitha nodded. "I planned to get to school early anyway. I ... uh—" she wracked her brain for a reason before finishing lamely, "just need to."

"Way to think fast on your feet," Sam teased as they took off down the road.

"I'm a terrible liar," Tabitha conceded. "Some people can do it without blinking an eye; but I hem and haw so badly, it's obvious what I'm up to."

"Good." Sam nodded his approval. "I wouldn't be comfortable around a girl who could lie at the drop of a hat." He gave her a sly look. "How would I know if she was telling the truth when she said she liked me?"

"That would be a problem." Tabitha stifled a grin. "So, have I ever told you how much I ... that is ... you know ... uh ... care about you?"

Sam emitted a shout of laughter. "You're good. I thought you said Cass is the funny one."

"She was, until you came along." Tabitha savored Sam's appreciation of her humor. "You bring out the comedian in me."

Sam pretended to frown. "I'm not sure that's a compliment."

"It is," Tabitha assured him. "It most definitely is." She couldn't help sending him a dazzling smile, her depression from the night before almost forgotten.

CHAPTER 16

After Tabitha and Sam left, Cass, Rianne, and Alex continued to mill around in front of the house. Cass decided if Rianne and Alex weren't so busy glaring daggers at each other, the situation would be funny.

"Are you completely recovered from yesterday?" she asked Rianne.

Her friend shrugged. "Enough that the thought of another day in bed didn't appeal to me."

"What was wrong?" Alex asked politely.

"Nothing major," Rianne sidestepped the question. Tilting her head back, she looked down her nose at him. "What are you doing here?"

"Every now and then I come by and ride to school with Cass." Alex returned her stare with an equally scornful expression. "How about you?"

"Me?" Bristling, Rianne pressed a hand to her chest. "I'm Cass' best friend. I have every right to be here."

"She's my friend too," Alex coolly informed her.

"Cut it out," Cass said, breaking in. "I feel like the prize in some silly tug-of-war. As far as I'm concerned, we're all friends."

"Alex and I aren't," Rianne spat out.

"Yeah," Alex chimed in. "How can I be friends with someone who looks at me like I'm something that just crawled out from underneath a rock?"

"If you'd quit acting like a sub-human life form, maybe I wouldn't treat you like one," Rianne suggested sweetly.

"What have I ever done to you?" Alex demanded.

"You haven't done anything to me personally," Rianne admitted. "But Kwaj is a small place. The word's out about your behavior. You've ruined one—no, make that two lives—that I know about. Who knows how many more there are?"

Alex's face suffused with fury as her meaning sunk in. "I don't have to take this. I'm gone." With a curt nod to Cass, he hopped on his bike and left, pedaling as fast as he could.

Her expression reproachful, Cass turned to Rianne. "Why did you do that?"

"Hey—" she shrugged carelessly, "sometimes the truth hurts."

Cass was bewildered by her attitude. "I remember the letter you wrote to Alison after we found out she was pregnant. You were concerned about her and the baby, and offered to do anything you could to help. Why were you so kind to her back then and so mean to Alex just now?"

"Alison wouldn't have been in the predicament she was if it weren't for Alex," Rianne reminded her.

"Their relationship was mutual. Alison was just as much to blame for what happened as Alex." Leaning on the handlebars, Cass gazed at Rianne. "Plus, she was the one who actually had the abortion."

"I'm sure Alex didn't do anything to discourage her." Rianne's jaw had a stubborn set to it.

"Probably not," Cass conceded. "But we should still care for both of them equally."

"Does that mean I'm supposed to pretend everything's

hunky-dory when I'm around Alex?" Rianne snorted her disdain for that idea.

"Of course not. It's like Mom says," explained Cass. " 'We should speak the truth in love every chance we get.' That means we should never shy away from being honest, but we should also remember that God's merciful as well as just."

"Saint Cassandra the holy," Rianne scoffed. She reached over and fussed with an imaginary object above Cass' head. "Here, let me polish your halo for you."

Fed up with her sarcasm, Cass drawled, "You know, I liked you a lot better before you started being anorexic. Not eating is ruining your personality."

The moment the words were out of her mouth, she regretted them. Seeing the look of betrayal on Rianne's face was like being punched in the stomach.

"I'm sorry," she stammered. "I'm really ... really ..."

"Don't bother," Rianne cut her off. "Nothing you say will help."

With a sinking heart, Cass watched her ride away. *First I had too many people to ride to school with. Now I don't have any. It's not even 7:30, and I'm already having a crummy day.* Setting aside her self-pity, she continued, *Father, I know I was wrong to say what I did. First chance I get, I'm going to apologize to Rianne, and I'll keep apologizing until she listens to me.*

Feeling slightly better, she swung up onto her bike and took off in the direction the others had gone. If the way things had started was any indication, Cass figured it was going to be a long day.

Fortunately, her pessimism proved to be incorrect. She cornered Rianne in homeroom and apologized profusely for her remark. In return, Rianne confessed how she was sorry for calling her Saint Cassandra. Although Cass sensed things were still shaky between them, they agreed to put the episode behind them and move on.

During lunch, Cass made a point of seeking out Alex to say hello. He seemed to appreciate the effort and asked her if she'd like to join him at the lagoon on Saturday for snorkeling and a picnic. Uneasy because his suggestion sounded too much like a date, Cass told him she'd let him know.

Riding home that afternoon, Cass decided that, all in all, things had turned out well. Before leaving school, she'd invited Rianne to spend the night Friday, and her friend had agreed without hesitation. Cass' purpose was twofold. She hoped spending that much time together would help patch up any remaining differences between them. She also planned to keep a close eye on Rianne to see what she did and didn't eat.

Boy, am I sneaky or what? she congratulated herself as she parked her bike on the lanai. Coming into the kitchen, Cass found Mom at the stove, stirring a pot of something that smelled wonderful. Hannah was nestled against her chest, securely strapped into a snuggly baby carrier. Cass trailed a finger across her sister's cheek before peering over Mom's shoulder.

"Mmm. What are you making? My mouth started watering the minute I walked in."

"Pot roast." Smiling, Mom used the back of her hand to brush the hair off her forehead. "The little squirt here was considerate enough to sleep most of the morning so I got ambitious and decided to fix a real meal for a change."

"Thank you, little squirt." Cass held her finger against Hannah's fist until the baby curled her miniscule fingers around it. "I owe you one."

Finished with the roast, Mom replaced the lid on the pot and wiped her hands on a towel. "Where's Tabitha?"

"Oh, yeah. She wanted me to tell you she'll be home shortly." Cass withdrew her finger from Hannah's grasp and moved to the refrigerator to see what there was to drink. "She and Kira needed to check the school library to see what's available for some research project they're doing."

"Do you know what class it's for?"

"I'm not—" Before Cass could complete her answer, the phone rang. Setting the pitcher of lemonade she had just pulled out on the counter, she moved to the other end of the kitchen and picked up the receiver.

"Hello?"

"Uh ... Cass," the caller guessed after a brief hesitation. "Right?"

"Yup," she acknowledged.

"Do you know who this is?"

Cass hated questions like that. "Micah," she replied curtly.

"Hey, it's nice to know I haven't been forgotten."

Who could forget you? she thought darkly, thinking of Kira's gorgeous older brother—and Tabitha's ex-boyfriend. He had been a good friend during high school, but then seemed to develop a whole new personality when he went off to college in Hawaii.

When Cass didn't say anything out loud, Micah asked, "So how's it going?"

"Pretty well actually. And you?" she made herself inquire. Even though her loyalty to Tabitha overrode any inclination she had to chat, she had to maintain a semblance of courtesy.

"I can't complain. Look, is Tabitha there?"

"Not yet." Cass explained about her and Kira's trip to the library. "She wasn't planning on taking long. Why don't you wait about 30 minutes and call back?"

"I'll do that. Oh, and Cass?" Micah added with a chuckle.

"Yes?" Her response was wary.

"When she gets there, tie her to a chair or something so

she can't leave. I really want to talk to her."

Cass' spine stiffened at his joking order. "I'm sure that won't be necessary. Bye, Micah." She pressed the off button and, sniffing, replaced the receiver in its holder. "Honestly, some people."

"I take it you didn't care for something he said," Mom observed mildly. She handed Cass the lemonade she'd poured during the brief conversation with Micah.

Cass repeated his remark, adding "Wasn't that rude?"

"I'm sure he meant it as a joke," Mom said.

"I don't care," Cass huffed. "It was still rude."

She was waiting on the porch when Tabitha strolled in about 20 minutes later. Although Kira was with her, Cass immediately told her about Micah's call.

Tabitha's expression was more curious than anything else. "Huh. I wonder what he wants." She glanced at Kira. "Do you know?"

Kira spread her arms in a gesture of ignorance. "I don't have a clue." She frowned slightly. "I hope everything's okay."

"If it wasn't, he'd have called your house, not here," Tabitha said logically. "Oh, well—" she shrugged, "no use guessing. We'll just wait until he calls back and see what he has to say."

The phone rang a short while later. Tabitha answered it and indicated it was Micah. In order to allow her some privacy, Cass and Kira left the porch and walked across the lawn to perch on a couple of rocks overlooking the ocean.

"I love it out here," Kira commented, lowering her feet into the water foaming around the base of her boulder. Again and again, the rising tide slammed against the rocks, sending up spumes of salt spray. "I wish our house were located on this road instead of an inner street." She made a face. "It's so boring where we live."

Instead of sympathizing, Cass laughed. "It's not like you have to drive for miles to get to the ocean," she pointed out. "All you have to do is walk a couple of minutes in any direction, and you're there."

"I know," Kira sulked. "But it's not the same as having the Pacific right in your backyard."

"Look." Cass held up her index finger and thumb, and slowly rubbed them together. "It's the world's smallest CD player, playing 'My Heart Bleeds for You.' "

"Gee, remind me never to come to you when I need compassion and understanding." With a sniff, Kira jerked her head around and stared off at the horizon. Tabitha's arrival a few minutes later instantly thawed her. Motioning to the rock nearest her, she urged, "Sit down, and tell us everything. What did Micah want?"

Tabitha chose a rock midway between Cass and Kira and sat down before replying. She looked confused as she said, "He called to tell me when he'll be in for Christmas, how long he'll be here, and—" she paused to take a deep breath. "to ask if we can get together over the holidays."

Although Cass' first reaction was to advise Tabitha to stay as far away from Micah as possible, out of deference to Kira she refrained. Instead, she asked cautiously, "Get together how? As in a couple of old friends catching up with each other? Or as in a date?"

"I'm not 100 percent sure," Tabitha hedged, "but it sounded to me like he was talking about a date."

"Huh," Kira said. "What are you going to do?"

Tabitha shrugged. "I don't know yet. He won't be here for almost two weeks so I'll use the time to figure out what I should do."

To Cass' surprise, Kira asked, "What about Sam?"

Tabitha frowned. "What about him?"

"How do you think he'll react to Micah asking you out?"

Worry shadowed Kira's dark eyes. "I assume you're going to tell him."

"I have no idea what he'll say." Tabitha folded her arms on her thighs and briefly rested her head on her arms. When she looked up again, her expression was grim. "The only thing I know for sure at the moment is that in another couple of weeks life around here is going to get very interesting."

CHAPTER 17

"I thought the party went even better this year than it did last year." Cass sat in the stern of the boat as the youth group returned from its annual trek to the neighboring island of Ebeye to throw a Christmas party for the Marshallese children. She lifted her ponytail so her neck could catch the breeze kicked up by the boat's speed. "Was it just me, or were the kids even more adorable?"

"They were," Rianne agreed. She rubbed her upper arms as if chilled by the same breeze that just barely cooled off Cass. "They reminded me of why I want to go into missionary work. Just think of all the little children in the world who haven't heard the good news about Jesus yet."

Cass watched Rianne try to warm herself and shook her head. She knew another symptom of anorexia was always being cold because of the loss of body fat. Remembering the way Rianne had hidden food the other night when she stayed at the house to make it look like she'd eaten, Cass sighed to herself. The evidence continued to mount that Rianne had an eating disorder. The problem Cass faced was what to do about it.

"Earth to Cass." Sam jostled her arm. "Hey, Red, I asked you a question."

Blinking, she re-focused her attention on her friends. "I'm sorry. I guess I wandered off for a few seconds."

"As long as you're back safely, there's no harm done," Sam quipped. "Anyway, I was wondering if you'd like to come over after school tomorrow to cram for the economics final. My mother volunteered to fix chili."

"Sounds great. I haven't had chili in ages." Cass yawned, the long day finally catching up with her. "How many will be there?"

"So far I've talked to you, Tabs—" Sam smiled at Tabitha, who was sitting beside him, "Rianne, Greg, and Kira." He paused, thinking. "I plan on asking a bunch more people tomorrow, so we're probably looking at around 15 all together."

"Whoa. Does your mother know what she's getting herself into?" Cass drew her legs up onto the bench and clasped her arms around them.

"She doesn't care how many I ask," Sam assured her. "Don't forget she's an army wife. She's used to cooking for crowds."

"She cooks for you everyday," Tabitha teased. "That's like cooking for a crowd."

"I'd be insulted, except you're right." Sam bumped shoulders with her. "Did you have to point it out in front of everyone though?"

"It's not like we weren't already aware of your appetite," Kira drawled. "We've all seen you eat, and it's not a pretty sight."

The others laughed while Sam pretended to huff with indignation. Greg playfully punched his arm.

"Don't take it personally, buddy. They're girls. To them, a diet soda and six pieces of lettuce are a seven-course meal."

"Hey, good one!" Sam raised his hand so they could high-five each other. "We guys have to stick together."

Cass pulled away as the members of the group continued to tease one another. The party had put everybody in a Christmas mood, but she wasn't quite ready to join in. She moved over to the railing and glanced back at the vast expanse of ocean behind them.

"You okay?" Tabitha asked softly from behind her.

Cass turned and smiled wanly. "Yeah. I was just thinking." She hesitated, hoping Tabitha wouldn't take what she was about to say the wrong way. "I wish Alex had come. It would have been good for him. He talked about it yesterday at the lagoon, but I guess he wasn't serious."

Tabitha frowned. "I'm still not entirely comfortable with you spending time with him. I guess I'm just not sure what he has in mind for your relationship."

Cass sighed. "Sometimes I'm not all that comfortable either. But I made sure he understood yesterday wasn't a date." She lifted one shoulder in a shrug. "I'm pretty sure he understood. I could be wrong, but I think what he really wants and needs is a friend. I think he's really struggling with Alison's abortion, but he's not ready to admit it was wrong."

Tabitha frowned as she leaned up against the boat rail. "It's not just the abortion that was wrong," she said pointedly. "It was the behavior that led up to it, as well."

"Actually, I told him that." Cass laughed, remembering Alex's slight embarrassment with the conversation. "He quickly changed the subject."

Just then, Sam started singing, rather loudly, a rousing rendition of "Let It Snow." Tabitha grinned at Cass. "Come on. We can't let him sing alone."

"You're right. He definitely needs someone to drown him out." Pushing aside thoughts of Alex, Cass let Tabitha lead her back to the group.

With finals every day, the school week passed quickly for Cass and Tabitha. Almost before they knew it, it was Friday evening. They gathered with their friends at the bowling alley to celebrate the end of the semester and the beginning of Christmas vacation.

As the group scooted several tables together to accommodate everyone, Cass happened to glance over her shoulder at the entrance. She paused when she spotted Alex standing just inside the door. He looked like he might be waiting for someone, but she couldn't be sure. Nudging Tabitha, she tilted her chin in his direction.

"I'm going to say hello. If he's not meeting somebody, should I ask him to join us?"

Tabitha made a face. "Why would you want to do that?"

"I keep thinking being around us will help him get his act together." Cass laughed quietly. "I'm not saying we're perfect, but we do have standards, and we're not afraid to stand up for them. Alex needs that kind of influence in his life."

Not wanting to be overheard, Tabitha drew Cass aside to ask, "Is this a personal thing?"

Cass stared into her eyes without flinching. "Are you asking if I consider him potential dating material?" When Tabitha nodded, she vigorously shook her head. "No. I've told you before, and I'll keep saying it until you get it through your thick skull." She smiled when Tabitha bristled. "No offense intended. It's just a figure of speech. Anyway, I care about Alex as a human being. Period. End of story."

"In that case, I suppose it wouldn't hurt to invite him over," Tabitha grudgingly conceded. An impish grin lit up her face. "Of course, I can always hope he has other plans."

"You are so mean." Cass leaned close to add in a whisper, "I like that in a sister."

Alex smiled warmly when he noticed Cass approaching him. "Hi. What's up?"

"Hopefully my grades. That's why I'm here celebrating." Stopping in front of him, she slid her hands into her pockets. "What's going on with you?"

"Not much." Alex glanced around the crowded room, his gaze lingering on the group in the snack bar. "I see you're here with your friends."

"Yeah, we tend to travel in a pack. So—" Cass scuffed the toe of her flip-flop across the floor, "are you meeting somebody?"

Alex snorted. "Yeah, like the people I hang out with are into bowling." He dropped the sarcasm. "No, I was upstairs at the library, and I thought I'd stop in on my way out to see who was here."

"Well—" Cass spread her arms in a gesture meant to include her friends, "we are. We're going to eat, then bowl a few games. Would you like to join us?"

Alex's smile was quickly replaced by a scowl. "I see Rianne's part of your group. I don't think she'd be too thrilled to have me crash the party."

"She'll be fine." Cass dismissed his concern with a wave. "She gave up being mean for Advent."

"Huh?" Alex's puzzled expression told her he had no idea what she was talking about.

"The four weeks leading up to Christmas are called Advent," Cass explained. "During that time, we're supposed to prepare ourselves for the miracle of Jesus' birth. Some people give things up to remind themselves of what God did for us, like they do during Lent. In Rianne's case," she added with a mischievous grin, "I was kidding about her giving anything up. She's still as mean as a snake." At Alex's worried glance in Rianne's direction, she laughed. "I'm joking."

"Maybe you should consider giving up lying," Alex suggested.

"Nah, it wouldn't be worth it. Advent's almost over." Slipping her arm through Alex's, Cass coaxed, "Come join us. I promise Rianne won't bite. If she does try, I'll protect you."

"How can I refuse an invitation like that?" Alex allowed her to propel him toward the snack bar.

"I have been told I'm irresistible," Cass said in a mock-confidential tone. She pretended to frown. "Or was it eerie and resistible? I can never get it right."

Sensing Alex's nervousness, she kept up a line of silly chatter as she guided him to her friends. She was relieved when the majority of them greeted him with welcoming smiles.

Sam pulled out the chair next to him. "Yo, Al, take a load off," he said cheerfully.

"Thanks." Alex dropped gratefully into the seat. He darted Tabitha, who occupied the chair on Sam's other side, a wary glance. "Hi, Tabitha."

She surprised Cass by waving. "Hi. How do you think you did on your finals?"

"Okay, I guess. Calculus was pretty hard."

Tabitha rolled her eyes. "Tell me about it. I chewed three pencils and a ruler practically in half. It's the only grade I'm worried about."

"I wish I could say that." Alex slid a paper cup off the stack in the middle of the table and poured himself some soda from the pitcher. "I'm at the point where I'm wondering if there's a college out there that'll take me."

"Why don't you try an all-girls school?" Rianne suggested sweetly from across the table. "That would be right up your alley."

While Alex squirmed uncomfortably, Cass shot her a scathing look. "Why don't you try remembering what season we're in? You know, peace on earth, goodwill to men?"

Rianne flushed guiltily and turned her attention to someone else.

"Hey, you weren't kidding," Alex murmured to Cass. "You really did stick up for me."

"It's a rotten job, but somebody had to do it." She playfully patted his head. "You looked so pathetic, sitting there like you were about to cry."

"I wasn't—" Alex's protest died on his lips, and he smiled sheepishly. "Sometimes I forget what a joker you are."

"That's me, the court jester." Cass gestured toward the pitcher of soda. "Would you mind passing that?"

"I'll do you one better." With a flourish, Alex selected a cup for her. "I'll pour you a drink."

Affecting an even stronger drawl than usual, Cass fluttered her lashes and fanned herself. "My, my, aren't you being chivalrous tonight? If it's raining when we leave, will you spread your cloak over the puddles for me?"

Instead of responding with a quip, Alex solemnly assured her, "If I had a cloak, I'd do it in a heartbeat."

Aware that he wasn't teasing, Cass dropped the southern belle act. "Thank you. That was a very sweet thing to say."

Alex ducked his head in embarrassment. "I'm starting to think you bring out the best in me."

It was Cass' turn to be touched. "Only God can do that," she softly informed him. "But I'm happy to be His instrument."

"Oh, come on," Alex scoffed. "Give yourself more credit than that."

Cass fixed unblinking hazel eyes on him. "Why?"

"Well ... because ... it's ..." Alex stammered. He finally

threw his hands up in defeat. "Shoot, I don't know. I guess because most people do."

Smiling saucily, Cass retorted, "Haven't you figured out by now that I'm not like most people?"

Before Alex could reply, she turned to Kira on her right and asked her a question, leaving Alex to think about her comment.

CHAPTER 18

The next morning, Tabitha woke up at dawn. Unable to fall back asleep, she slipped into Cass' room. Perched on the edge of her sister's bed, she walked her fingers up Cass' back, pressing harder and harder as she went in order to wake her up. Muttering, Cass reached behind her and swatted at her hand.

"What are you doing? Go away."

"I need to talk." Tabitha pulled the quilt away from Cass' ears. "Micah's due in at about noon today."

Cass flopped onto her back to glare at her through sleepy eyes. "And this affects me how exactly?"

"You're my sister. Whatever affects me affects you. Oh, no, you don't." Tabitha grabbed her to keep her from rolling over onto her stomach. "You have a duty to listen to me."

"Fine." Cass flung her arm over her eyes. "I'm listening. Talk already."

"What should I do if Micah asks me out?" Tabitha nibbled at her thumbnail.

Cass lowered her arm a fraction of an inch to peer up at her. "You want a nice answer or an honest answer?"

Tabitha laughed. "Since when are you ever nice? Give me your honest opinion. I'm a big girl. I can take it."

"Tell him to take a long walk off a short pier. There—" Cass slammed her eyes shut, "can I go back to sleep now?"

Lifting Cass' arm, Tabitha pried open one of her eyes. "I can't say something like that to Micah. It might hurt his feelings."

"All right, then go out with him."

"But what about Sam?" Tabitha persisted.

"I don't think Micah's his type." Cass sighed gustily and struggled to a sitting position. She glanced out the window and sighed again. "Honestly, it isn't even light yet."

Tabitha ignored the remark. "No, really. What should I do about Sam? I'm sure he'll be hurt if I go out with Micah."

"The most important thing is to be honest with him" Cass advised. "If Micah asks you for a date, and for some strange reason you decide to go, tell Sam what's going on. Don't run the risk of having him hear it through the grapevine."

"Okay," Tabitha said slowly. "Now let's say I turn Micah down. How should I handle that?"

Cass shrugged. "I don't know. It depends on why you'd turn him down, I guess."

"Hmm." Tabitha gazed out the window where streaks of gold and violet were spreading across the horizon. "This isn't going to sound very nice, but the first reason I'd turn him down would be to get back at him."

Cass snickered. "Nasty, but honest. In that case, I think a simple, 'No thanks, Micah, I'm not interested,' would do the trick."

"But what if he keeps asking?" Tabitha scooted across the bed to lean against the wall.

"Say it louder. He's reasonably intelligent. Eventually he'll catch on." Crossing her arms over her midsection,

Cass gazed at her. "Is that the only reason you wouldn't go out with him?"

Tabitha picked at a loose thread on the quilt. "No. Maybe even more importantly, I don't want to ruin things with Sam." The face she raised to Cass was soft with tenderness. "I really like Sam. He's probably the nicest guy I've ever met. He's also the most polite and respectful. Did you know that it took him two months to kiss me goodnight? Even now, he never kisses me more than once or twice at the end of a date. I feel so ... so—" she fumbled for the right word, "*cherished* when I'm with him."

To her surprise, Cass' eyes misted with tears. She reached for Tabitha's hand. "I'm glad. Take my advice. You don't want to lose a guy like that."

"Exactly." Tabitha squeezed Cass' hand before releasing it. "The problem is there's a part of me that wants to go out with Micah. I'm curious about what it would be like to spend time with him again. I can't help wondering if the spark's still there."

"What if it is?" Cass asked quietly. "What would that do to your relationship with Sam?"

Tabitha lowered her head, passing her hand across her eyes in a weary gesture. "End it, I suppose." She looked up again, her expression anguished. "Wouldn't it be better to find that out sooner rather than later though?"

Cass lifted her hands in a helpless gesture. "I don't know. I guess so. I mean, if Micah's changed and would treat you like you deserve to be treated, I suppose I wouldn't object to y'all starting up again. I'd miss Sam, but if Micah's who you wanted, I could live with that. On the other hand—" her eyes narrowed, "if he's the same Micah who left here in July, I'd have to kill you."

Tabitha produced a wobbly smile. "You're not kidding, are you?"

"I've never been more serious." Cass yawned, not bothering to cover her mouth. "Are we done? I wouldn't mind catching a few more hours of sleep." She slid down, tucking her arms under the quilt. A sudden thought bolted her upright again. "You're not going to the airport to meet Micah's plane, are you?"

"No," Tabitha assured her. "I'll wait and see if he calls me. There's a part of me that hopes he doesn't. That way I don't have to worry about what to say if he asks me out."

"Then there's another part that's hoping like crazy he will call." It was a statement, not a question.

Hanging her head again, Tabitha nodded. "You must think I'm nuts."

Cass gave her an affectionate kick. "No, just human like the rest of us. You may look like an angel, but you're as real as they come."

"Thanks." Tabitha made a comical face. "I think." Pushing herself to the edge of the bed, she stood up. "I'll get out of your hair and let you get back to sleep. I hope the crying machine co-operates."

"She's getting better," Cass said in Hannah's defense.

"Define better." Tabitha walked to the door and paused, her hand on the knob. "Would you pray that I make the right decision if Micah calls?"

"Absolutely." Yawning, Cass snuggled back under the covers. "The moment I wake up again, that'll be the first thing I do."

Quietly closing the door behind her, Tabitha turned right and headed to the living room. She went to the Christmas tree standing in the front window and plugged in the lights. Their soft glow soothed her jangled nerves as she nestled into a corner of the couch. Pulling the afghan over her legs, she leaned her head back against the cushions.

"Jesus," she whispered, "I know I always need You. But I really, really need You this time. I want to do the right thing by both Sam and Micah. I'm just not sure what that is. If You would see fit to, through Your Word, give me some direction on the matter, I'd greatly appreciate it." She hesitated. "There's something else I could use Your help with too. Could You help me not be so jealous of Dad and Hannah? I'm glad he loves her, but I wish there were some way to know he loved me just as much when I was a baby. Thanks for listening. I pray for Your will to be done in both these situations. In Jesus' name, amen."

Feeling calmer, Tabitha slid farther down on the cushion, rested her head on the sofa arm, and tugged the afghan up over her shoulders. She didn't bother fighting the wave of sleepiness that soon took over.

The pealing of the telephone jarred Tabitha awake, and she shot upright, blinking and trying to recall where she was. She relaxed when she heard Mom answer the phone. As she lay back down, Mom came across the floor, holding the receiver out to her.

"It's for you. Are you awake enough to talk?"

Her stomach turning cartwheels, Tabitha reached for the phone. She placed her hand over the mouthpiece and asked, "Who is it?" Since she had no idea what time it was, she didn't know if Micah's plane had landed.

Mom's mouth pursed. "Beth."

"Beth?" Tabitha echoed. "As in my mother? That Beth?" Mom nodded curtly.

"Great," Tabitha grumbled. "I wonder what she wants."

Bringing the phone up to her ear, she said coolly, "Hello, Beth."

Her mother's tinkly laugh grated on her nerves. "Tabby-Cat! How wonderful to hear your voice. How are you?"

"I'm swell," Tabitha replied, sounding anything but. "And you?"

"Other than missing you something awful, I'm terrific."

Tabitha rolled her eyes, but made no comment.

"Look, the reason I'm calling," Beth continued in her breathy voice, "is to see if you got the pictures I sent of Sunshine and Peace."

"They arrived a couple of days ago." Although Tabitha realized where the conversation was going, she couldn't think of a way to head it off.

"Wonderful!" Beth gushed. "Aren't my babies the most precious children you've ever seen?"

Careful not to be disloyal to Hannah, Tabitha acknowledged, "They're very cute."

"Oh, come on," Beth pouted. "They're better than cute. They're downright fabulous. After all, they take after me." She emitted another trill of laughter. "So, where did you wind up putting the pictures? On the refrigerator like I suggested?"

I guess it would be wrong to lie, huh, Lord? Tabitha sighed. *It sure is tempting though, because she's going to go ballistic when I tell her the truth.*

Aloud, she said, "I haven't put them anywhere yet. They're still in the envelope."

Beth's sharp intake of breath told Tabitha how displeased she was with her response. "I suppose your father and his wife object to you openly displaying them," she sniffed.

"Actually, no," Tabitha was happy to report. "Dad is less comfortable with the idea than Mom, but neither of them told me I couldn't put them out."

"How many times do I have to tell you that woman isn't your mother?" Beth demanded. "I'm your mother. Why do you persist in pretending I'm not?"

For one of the few times in her life, Tabitha found the courage to speak her mind. "It's not a pretense. Other than you giving birth to me, you and I have no connection. I told you back in January that Mom's been more of a mother to me in the short time I've known her than you ever have. She deserves to be called Mom, and that's exactly what I'm going to do. It's not a slap against you. It's a way I can honor her, and I'm not going to stop."

Instead of arguing, Beth took another tack. "Now, Tabby-Cat, let's not fight, especially over something so silly."

"I'm not the one who brought it up," Tabitha reminded her. "And please don't call me Tabby-Cat. You know I hate it."

"We're even then since I hate you calling that woman, Mom." Before Tabitha could reply, Beth continued, "But, like I said, that's neither here nor there. The important thing is that you got the kids' pictures, and you're going to put them out where you can see them every day and remember how much we all love and miss you. Peace still asks about you. He wants to know where his Tabby is."

"That's ... nice." Tabitha couldn't think of anything else to say. "Uh ... look ... I hate to cut this short, but I'm expecting a call. Wish Sunshine and Peace a merry Christmas for me."

"We don't celebrate Christmas," Beth informed her. "We celebrate the winter solstice."

"Oh. Well ... okay." Tabitha was not about to buy into Beth's New Age beliefs and wish her a happy winter solstice, whatever that was. "Like I said, I'd better get off."

"All right, precious. I'll be in touch. I know things didn't go well when you were here in January, but I've worked through the experience. I forgive you for the things you said, and I'd like for us to try again to have a relationship." Beth made several kissing sounds. "I love you, Baby. Bye. Talk to you soon."

After Beth hung up, Tabitha sat for several seconds, staring at the phone. *You forgive me?* She wasn't sure she'd heard right. *What planet are you from? I didn't do anything wrong. You're the one who lied about Dad and tried to place a humongous guilt trip on me.* Growling, she tossed the phone across the couch.

"Are you okay?" Mom immediately appeared from the kitchen.

"Talking with Beth totally frustrates me, but other than that, I'm fine." Tabitha produced a wan smile. "I can't believe I'm actually related to someone like her."

"She is … different." Mom suddenly laughed. "Oh, who am I kidding? She's borderline loony, with a generous helping of self-centeredness thrown in just to make things even more interesting."

Tabitha, who rarely heard Mom criticize anybody, blinked in surprise. "You never talk about people like that."

Leaning down, Mom ruffled Tabitha's hair, still tousled from her nap. "Beth is a special case. I pray for her and her children every day, but try as I might, I can't find anything to like about her."

"That makes two of us. Three, if you count Dad." Tabitha stretched, easing the kinks out of her back. "She's decided she wants us to resume a relationship. It took her awhile, but she finally forgave me for what happened when I visited."

Mom nodded sagely. "I see. How generous of her. And what do you think of her proposal?"

"Am I allowed to say it stinks?" When Mom assured her she was, Tabitha grinned. "In that case, it not only stinks. It positively reeks."

"Now don't hold back," Mom teased. "Tell me what you really think."

After a quick laugh, Tabitha sobered. "I love you. You always know just what to say to make me feel better."

"I love you too, Sweetie." Mom bent down to give her a hug and kiss. Straightening, she added, "What would you say to pancakes and sausage?"

Tabitha's stomach rumbled at the mere mention of food. "I'd say, amen and hallelujah." Throwing off the afghan, she scrambled to her feet. "I'll set the table while you cook. The sooner you get those pancakes coming, the happier I'll be."

CHAPTER 19

Cass shuffled into the dining room a short while later. Tabitha saw her bleary eyes light up when she saw the stack of pancakes sitting on a platter in the middle of the table.

"Ooh, pancakes! Great." Cass pulled out a chair at one of the places that Tabitha had set and made a move toward the pancakes.

Smacking her hand, Tabitha slid them out of reach. "Uh-uh-uh. I get first pick."

"Why?" Cass' lower lip protruded in a pout.

"Because she set the table," Mom explained from the kitchen.

"Okay," Cass said with a sigh. "So, did you ever go back to sleep?" she asked Tabitha. "You were pretty wound up when we talked earlier."

Tabitha speared three pancakes, leaving two for Cass. "I napped for a little while. The phone woke me up."

In the process of transferring the pancakes from the platter to her plate, Cass glanced up sharply. "Micah didn't come in early, did he?"

Tabitha shook her head. "Beth called."

Cass frowned for a moment, then understanding spread across her face. "Poor you," she murmured sympathetically.

"What's she harassing you about now?"

"She had two items on her agenda this morning." Tabitha uncapped the syrup bottle and poured a hearty helping over her buttered pancakes. "She wanted to know what I'd done with the pictures of Peace and Sunshine. After that, she wanted to talk about us picking up where we left off in January."

Cass' eyes rounded into saucers. "Are you serious?" When Tabitha nodded, she snorted. "The woman obviously isn't playing with a full deck. Doesn't she remember telling you that she never wanted to see, or hear from, you again?"

Tabitha cut a wedge out of the stacked pancakes. "That was then. This is now. Beth isn't the most consistent person in the world."

"No joke." Cass swirled a piece of sausage in a puddle of syrup and popped it in her mouth. "What did you tell her?"

"She didn't give me a chance to say anything. She hung up right afterwards." Tabitha shrugged. "I'm not going to worry about it. Knowing Beth, she's probably changed her mind already about wanting to be friends. I'll wait and see if I hear from her again."

"Boy, I'm glad I have a normal mother." Cass smiled impishly. "Or at least more normal than Beth."

Mom instantly turned to Tabitha. "Have I told you lately that you're my favorite child?"

Tabitha laughed. "Thanks, but look at the choice you have. It's not like I have stiff competition."

Tabitha and Cass were out back, relaxing on lounge chairs they'd carried down to the sand, when Dad brought the phone out to Tabitha. He told her it was Micah as he handed it to her.

Tabitha's face paled, and she waited until he turned to go back to the house to bring the receiver up to her ear.

Before she spoke, Cass snapped her fingers to get her attention.

"Do you want me to leave?" she whispered.

Tabitha shook her head and motioned for her to stay put. Once Cass had settled back in the chair, she took a deep breath and said into the phone, "Hello, Micah."

"Oh, man, is it ever good to hear your voice and know you're just a bike ride away," came his enthusiastic response. "How are you, gorgeous?"

Tabitha rolled her eyes at Cass, wishing there were some way her sister could eavesdrop on the conversation. "Great, now that school's out for 10 days. How was your flight?"

"Long and boring. I wanted the pilot to speed it up so we could get here faster. I can't wait to see you." Micah's voice dropped to a husky murmur. "Are you as excited to see me as I am to see you?"

What is this? Tabitha wondered. *Why is he giving me the rush all of a sudden? He practically forgot I even existed while he was up in Hono.*

Aloud, she replied coolly, "Since I don't know how excited you are, I really can't say."

"Then how about I hop on my bike and head over there so I can show you?"

Tabitha's stomach went through a series of roller coaster movements. "I ... uh ... okay. Just give me a few minutes to freshen up," she added hastily in an attempt to stall for a little more time.

"You've got 15 minutes," Micah informed her. "Then, ready or not, I'm coming over."

His bossiness rankled Tabitha. Feeling rebellious, she countered, "Make it 20."

"Any particular reason why?" Micah's voice held a hint of irritation.

To her surprise, Tabitha realized she didn't give a rip if he was annoyed. "Because I said so."

A silent battle of wills waged for several seconds before Micah gave in. "Fine. I'll see you in 20 minutes." He hung up without saying good-bye.

Pressing the off button, Tabitha laid the phone on her stomach. She glanced over at Cass and smiled weakly.

"That went well," Cass teased. "He's not back five minutes, and you've already had your first disagreement. This is going to be an interesting visit."

Tabitha nibbled on her lower lip as she stared out at the Pacific. Although the tide was coming in, the waves were still 20 or so yards out, keeping the pounding roar to a minimum. "He did his ordering me around routine. Sam never does that. I'm not used to being treated like that anymore, and I wasn't going to take it."

"Good for you," Cass approved. She too, gazed at the ocean. "I liked that 'because I said so' remark. I'm always glad when you stand up for yourself."

"Thanks." Now that the conversation was over, reaction was beginning to set in. Tabitha's hand shook as she brushed wind-blown hair off her face. "Micah didn't much care for it."

Cass' snort revealed how little she cared what Micah thought. "Is he coming over so the two of you can talk, or are you going out?"

Tabitha lifted a shoulder in a shrug. "I don't know. We didn't get that far." With a gusty sigh, she eased her legs over the side of the chair. "I guess I'd better get ready."

Cass smiled. "Are you going to put on a special 'welcome home' outfit?"

"Is this special enough?" Tabitha gestured down at her cut-offs and white shirt. "If not, too bad. I'm not changing."

"That's the spirit." Cass gave her a thumbs-up. She abruptly sobered. "All kidding aside, I'll be praying for you. I know you're nervous."

Tabitha pressed a hand to her midsection. "I'm way

beyond nervous. I believe I'm heading straight into pan-icky."

"Oh, come on." Cass dismissed her anxiety with a wave. "It's only Micah. There's no reason for you to be scared of him."

"I didn't say I was—" Tabitha's protest was interrupted by the phone, and she snatched it up off the chaise lounge. "Hello?"

"Tabitha, it's me," Kira replied softly.

"Kira?" Tabitha frowned. "Why are you talking like that? Do you have a cold?"

"No, I don't want Micah to hear me." If possible, her voice grew even quieter. "He said he's going over to see you in a little while. You know about that, right?"

"Uh-huh. We talked a few minutes ago." Tabitha's eyes narrowed suspiciously. "Why?"

"I wanted to warn you that I think he's planning to real-ly turn on the charm. He's in the bathroom right now, dousing himself in cologne." Kira snorted her disgust. "He's acting like he's heading out on a big date."

"If it makes you feel any better, he didn't say anything about us going out." Tabitha dug her toe into the sand. "It was kind of weird though, the way he went on and on about how excited he was to see me."

"Be careful, okay?" Kira sounded worried. "I'm not sure what's going on in his head. He might mean it when he says he missed you. But then again, it could be nothing but a game to him."

Tabitha brought her hand up to her mouth to chew on her thumbnail. It was highly unusual for Kira to say any-thing negative about her brother. The fact that she had gave Tabitha pause. She wondered if Micah had told Kira how he really felt about her and their relationship.

"Did he say something to make you think it's just a game?"

Kira hesitated. "Not exactly. It's just a ... a feeling I have. I'm scared he's going to use you while he's here, then dump you again once he goes back to school. I hate to say something like that about my own brother, but, for some reason, I'm afraid that's what he has in mind. I don't want to see you hurt."

Touched by her concern, Tabitha murmured, "Thanks. I know it's not easy for you to criticize Micah. I promise I'll do my best not to let him snow me into thinking I'm the love of his life."

"Okay. Oops, I think Micah's coming down the stairs. Gotta go."

Tabitha held the receiver to her ear for another moment or two to make sure Kira was gone, then she hung up. She smiled wryly at Cass.

"The plot thickens. That was Kira, warning me not to be taken in by Micah." She appealed to heaven. "Why can't life ever be simple?"

"Simple is boring." Cass got up and tucked the magazine she'd been leafing through under her arm. "Complicated, on the other hand—" she winked, "gets the old heart pumping. Think of it as emotional aerobics."

"My heart wouldn't mind a rest every now and then." Tabitha folded the lounge chair and, carrying it, started for the house. "At this rate, I'll probably have a heart attack before I'm 20."

"Just think, though—" Cass followed her, toting her chair, "you'll have led a short, but extremely eventful, life."

"You know, there isn't always a bright side." Tabitha grinned over her shoulder to show she was kidding.

Cass just grinned. "Like I always say—there's way too much pessimism in the world. We need more optimists."

"And it's just my luck to live under the same roof with one," Tabitha pretended to gripe.

"Yup. God sure did you a favor when He brought us

together. Otherwise, you'd have gone through life with a really sour attitude."

Tabitha's only response was a loud groan.

Tabitha was still in her room when Micah arrived, so she cracked open her door to listen as Cass greeted him.

"Aren't you going to say hello?"

Tabitha frowned as his familiar voice sent a shiver down her back.

"Of course," Cass responded dryly. "Hi."

"Where is everybody? I've been looking forward to seeing the baby."

"Mom and Dad took her to a cook-out at the Nishiharas'. Tabitha's in her room." Cass' voice hardly sounded welcome. "Why don't you sit down while I get her?"

"Let me. It'll be like old times."

Tabitha's heart started pounding and she almost slammed the bedroom door. Thankfully, Cass jumped in. "No. Don't you remember what sticklers my parents are about boys being in the house when they're not home? What do you think they'd do if I told them you went and knocked on Tabitha's door?"

"Hey, no problem," Micah responded cheerfully, although Tabitha thought she heard a note of irritation. "I've lived in a dorm so long I forgot what it's like to have to deal with parents. College students don't sweat the small stuff when it comes to silly rules and regulations," he added.

"Are you saying my parents' rule is silly?" Cass' voice raised a notch, and Tabitha decided maybe it was time to rescue her. She slipped out her door and padded softly down the hall.

"You know I think the world of your folks. What's keeping Tabitha? She must have heard the doorbell. Oh, that's right. She doesn't know the meaning of being on time."

"Sure I do. I also know the meaning of making a grand entrance."

Tabitha came around the corner, and her heart slammed against her chest at the first sight of him. Despite her best intentions, and the frown she half-noticed on Cass' face, she couldn't keep herself from smiling up at him.

Micah quickly stepped toward her and grabbed her in a bear hug. He swung her around twice before setting her back on her feet. She reached a hand out to the wall to steady herself, pressing the other one to her throat.

"My, that was quite the hello," she managed to remark after several deep breaths.

"Looking at you—" Micah took his time examining her from head to toe and back again, "is like coming across an oasis after stumbling around in the desert for a few weeks."

Tabitha decided to ignore Cass' snort of disgust, and her disapproving stare at her outfit. She had, after much debate with herself, changed into a blue sundress that had been one of Micah's favorites.

"Micah, what do you say we sit on the lanai and catch up on what's been happening in each other's lives?" she suggested. She began to squirm under Cass' withering stare.

"I've been sitting all morning, and plane seats aren't very comfortable." Micah ruefully rubbed his backside. "How about we go for a walk instead?"

"If that's what you'd prefer." Tabitha forced herself to look at Cass. "We'll be back in ...what?" She glanced at Micah.

He shrugged. "An hour? Hour and a half?" Sending Tabitha a conspiratorial wink, he murmured, "However long it takes us to—how did you put it?—catch up."

Tabitha blushed. Cass equally divided her scowl between the two of them before spinning on her heels.

"Enjoy yourselves," she spat out, stalking down the hall to her room. She slammed the door with an earsplitting bang.

"What was that all about?" Taking Tabitha's hand, Micah laced his fingers through hers.

Her expression was troubled as she gazed up at him. "Why did you have to imply we're going to ... you know—" she bent her head, "kiss and stuff?"

Micah lifted her chin with a gentle finger. "Aren't we? I don't know about you, but I was about to go nuts from missing you."

Tabitha pulled away from his touch, although she left her hand where it was. "How can I believe you when you all but dumped me? We haven't called or written each other in months."

"So we went through a rocky period." Micah shrugged. "Lots of couples do." Tugging on her hand, he pulled her close and slipped his arm around her waist. "We're back together now, and that's all that matters." He brought his head down to whisper against her ear, "I can't believe I forgot how beautiful you are."

"Stop." Tabitha used both hands to push him away. Her knees wobbly, she headed for the door. "Let's go for that walk. Dad and Mom really wouldn't be happy to hear how much time we've already spent in the house."

Micah's features hardened with annoyance. He made no comment, however. Instead, he opened the front door for Tabitha, then followed her through it. Out on the lawn, he took her hand again.

"Which way, fair lady?"

It took Tabitha a few seconds to reply because she was concerned about Sam unexpectedly showing up and finding her holding hands with Micah. Realizing he was waiting patiently for a response, she shook herself and focused on his question. Since there was less likelihood of running into Sam there, she would have preferred walking on the beach. Unfortunately, the tide was nearly in, and climbing over rocks wasn't any fun.

"Let's head to the lagoon," she decided reluctantly.

"Good choice," Micah approved. "There's nothing I like better than being in one of my favorite places in the world with one of my favorite people in the world."

A passing breeze tumbled Tabitha's curls around her face. She immediately used fixing her hair as an excuse to release Micah's hand. Once she anchored the hair behind her ears, she slid her hands into the pockets of the dress. If Micah noticed, he didn't say anything.

"So ... uh—" Tabitha wracked her brain for something to talk about, "how'd you finish out the semester grade-wise?"

"I don't know." Micah pulled a pair of sunglasses out of his shirt pocket and slipped them on. "The school won't be sending out the grades for another couple of weeks."

"How do you think you did?" Tabitha persisted.

For a few seconds, it appeared Micah wouldn't answer. When he did, it was with obvious reluctance. "Not too well. I goofed off a lot, especially early on in the semester." At Tabitha's tut of disapproval, he defended himself, "From what I understand, it happens to most freshmen. Sooner or later, the novelty of being away from home wears off, and everybody settles down. I'll do better next semester."

"I hope so. Your parents are spending a lot of money to send you to school." Tabitha waited for him to ask how she was. Quite a few seconds passed before it dawned on her that he wasn't going to. Sighing inwardly, she urged, "Tell me about the people you've met and the activities you're into."

Micah launched into a description of his life at the university that lasted all the way to Eamon Beach. As they rounded the curve in the path that brought the lagoon into view, he stopped and made a face.

"Great—just my luck. Every little kid on the island is here."

Tabitha shot him a curious glance. "What's the matter? They're all playing in the water. We can sit in the pavilion and talk. They won't bother us."

"You are such an innocent." Laughing, Micah took her by the shoulders and turned her to face him. "Do you really think I brought you here to talk?"

Tabitha's gaze slid uneasily away from his to focus on a pair of toddlers gleefully splashing one another. "It's the middle of the day. Even if the place was deserted, I wouldn't feel right carrying on in broad daylight."

Releasing her shoulders, Micah picked up her left hand and rubbed his thumb over her promise ring. "I see you're still taking your commitment seriously. I'm glad. I got a little worried, what with Sam in the picture and all."

"That's a terrible— You actually thought Sam and I might—" Tabitha sputtered.

"Chill." Micah made a calming motion with his hands. "I was kidding. What I am serious about is the two of us getting reacquainted." He waved disdainfully at the beach. "Preferably somewhere with a little more privacy. Not that there's much privacy on this rinky-dink island." Turning his attention back to Tabitha, he murmured, "So how does a romantic dinner for two at the Yuk, followed by a moonlight stroll on the beach, sound?"

Although Tabitha thought it sounded scary, she pasted on a bright smile. "Wonderful. What time?"

"Let's head back so I can call and see if I can get reservations for 8:00." Micah briefly removed his sunglasses so he could wink. "I've learned that's considered a fashionable hour to eat."

"Okay." Tabitha hoped she didn't sound as doubtful as she felt. She figured she'd be fainting from hunger by 8:00. "We can wait and catch up tonight then."

"You bet we will."

Was it her imagination or did Micah's smile have a certain wolfish quality to it? Shivering despite the heat, Tabitha allowed him to take her hand and lead her back to the house. She hoped Cass hadn't left because she desperately needed to talk to her before going out with Micah tonight. She had a really bad feeling about their date.

CHAPTER 20

It was shortly after 11:00 when Tabitha, having said good-night to Micah, slipped in the back door. She half-expected to find Cass waiting for her on the porch and couldn't decide if she was disappointed or relieved that she wasn't there. Arranging her features into a carefree expression, she went in search of her parents to let them know she was home. She discovered Cass stretched out in the recliner with a book propped up on her stomach.

"Hey." Cass immediately closed the book and pushed down the footrest to sit up straight. "How'd it go?"

"And a pleasant good evening to you too," Tabitha teased. Crossing the floor, she turned down the music lilting from the stereo.

"Yeah, yeah. Whatever." Cass waved impatiently. Her eyes alight with curiosity, she gazed at Tabitha. "I've been dying for you to get home. What happened?"

Tabitha collapsed on the couch and plunked her feet on the coffee table without removing her sandals. "Before I start, where are the folks?"

Cass gestured over her shoulder toward the hall. "Hannah went down about 20 minutes ago so they decided to go to sleep early. They asked me to wait up for you."

"They appointed you curfew police for the night?" Tabitha arched an eyebrow.

"It's a rotten job, but somebody has to do it. Anyway, enough of the small talk." Cass tucked her legs beneath her. "Tell me everything, and don't leave out a single, gory detail."

Tabitha's mouth twisted in a grimace of distaste. "Gory's a good word to use to describe at least part of the evening."

Cass' eyes widened to saucers. "Did Micah get ugly with you?"

"Oh, no, nothing like that," Tabitha hastened to assure her. "He didn't step over any lines or anything. The problem was he kept pressuring me to prove how happy I am that he's back. No matter how many times I told him I wasn't comfortable enough yet to ... you know ... kiss and hug and stuff, he wouldn't let up. He told me he loves me, then put on his sad puppy-dog face when I wouldn't say it back."

"Yuck." Cass' expression was as sour as her tone. "It sounds like the evening was a real bust."

"That's the weird part. It wasn't." At Cass' murmur of surprise, Tabitha explained, "When Micah wasn't acting like a jerk, things were okay. We talked." Laughing, she corrected herself, "Actually, he did most of the talking. He had a ton of funny stories about his roommate. The guy sounds like he should be locked up, but he's a riot."

Cass made a face. "Did he bother to ask about what's been going on in your life since he left?"

Tabitha shifted uncomfortably. "He wanted to know what the deal is with Sam."

"That's it?" Cass demanded. "He's been gone almost five months, and all he cares about is what's going on between you and Sam? He didn't ask about school or the youth group or how you're adjusting to the baby?"

Tabitha avoided Cass' glare by pretending great interest

in her nails. "You know how Micah is. He has a tendency to be self-absorbed."

"A tendency?" Cass snorted her derision. "You mean, like a charging elephant has a tendency to knock down everything in its path?"

Tabitha's eyes flew up to meet Cass', and she bristled in Micah's defense. "That's not fair. He had a lot to talk about. After all, he's been living in Hono. That's way more exciting than living here."

"Why are you sticking up for him?" Cass threw her hands up in exasperation. "Does he have some sort of magical power over you? The boy's not even back 12 hours, and he has you eating out of his hand. Where does Sam fit into the scenario?"

"Micah doesn't have me—" Tabitha's protest died on her lips, and she slumped against the sofa cushion. "Oh, who am I kidding? You're right. I'm so used to doing things his way, I just automatically fell back into the habit."

"No, you're not used to it," Cass argued. "Don't forget you've spent the last few months dating Sam, who treats you like a queen. That's what you should be used to."

"I know." Sighing, Tabitha pulled a pillow onto her lap and began poking at the stuffing. "It's just ... it was so familiar being with Micah. We reminisced about all the years we've known each other and about the year we dated. We go back a long way. Compared to Micah, I hardly know Sam at all."

Cass leaned back, folded her arms, and sniffed. "If you ask me, it sounds like a case of quality versus quantity. You've been having a blast with Sam. Are you saying you're willing to throw away the great relationship you have with him, now that Micah's back in town?"

"No." Tabitha's response was instantaneous and fervent, and she smiled sheepishly. "Obviously that's a no-brainer since I didn't have to think about it. The problem isn't what to do about Sam. It's what to do about Micah." She laid the pillow on the arm of the couch then rested her head on it. "He made it clear he wants to spend as much time as possible with me."

"And?" Cass prompted when she didn't continue. "How do you feel about that?"

"I'm not giving up Sam to spend all my time with Micah." Tabitha wearily passed a hand across her eyes. "But I would like to see him some while he's home."

Cass' features tightened with suspicion. "This doesn't have anything to do with the fact that Micah's better looking than Sam, does it?"

"I— that's—" Tabitha sputtered, straightening to glower at Cass. "No way! I'm insulted you'd even ask me a question like that. Give me a little more credit for being a decent human being."

Motioning for her to calm down, Cass laughed. "I'm sorry, okay? I just needed to make sure. I can sort of understand you being torn between Sam and Micah, but you weren't going to get any support from me if it was based on something as shallow as looks."

Tabitha's eyebrows slammed together in a ferocious scowl. "And, what may I ask, is wrong with Sam's looks? I happen to think he's very attractive."

"Hey, you won't get any argument from me about that," Cass assured her. "When you first started going out with him, it was an issue, especially where Kira was concerned. I thought it might still be lurking in the back of your mind."

"Aren't you forgetting Kira called earlier to warn me to be careful around Micah?" Tabitha reminded her in a snide voice. "Doesn't that tell you neither of us is judging by appearances?"

"This conversation is going nowhere so let's drop it." Placing her feet on the floor, Cass stood up. "I'm sorry I said anything about Sam's looks. He's a terrific-looking guy. You're a beautiful girl. I hope the two of you marry and have a litter of gorgeous kids. There, are you happy now?"

Tabitha grinned up at her. "You really think we'd have cute kids?"

"Grr! I give up." Cass ground her teeth in frustration. "One minute you're talking about going out with Micah. The next minute you're wondering what kind of kids you and Sam would have. You're too much for me to deal with. I'm going to bed." She headed for the hall, calling over her shoulder, "Don't forget to lock up."

Tabitha waited until Cass disappeared into the bathroom before getting up and going out to the porch to lock the door. She paused on her way back into the house to lean her forehead against the window and gaze out at the moon-dappled ocean.

Breathing on the cool glass, she drew a heart in the condensation and wrote her initials. She hesitated, her finger poised over the bottom half of the heart. With a frustrated sigh, she erased the heart and turned back toward the house, switching off lights and locking up as she went.

The following morning, Tabitha and Cass arrived at church at the same time as Rianne and Kira. Since Mom and Dad had opted to sleep in after a long night with a fussy Hannah, the four friends decided to sit together.

"You might as well save a seat for Sam," Kira advised Tabitha as they parked their bikes. "Micah won't be here."

"Oh." Tabitha strove for a casual tone. "Why not?"

"He didn't say. He just told me to leave him alone when I woke him up to see if he was coming to church." Kira's mouth pursed. "My guess is he stayed up pretty late. After he got in from your date, he asked Mom if he could call some friend in Hawaii. He was still on the phone when I went to bed around midnight."

Tabitha fiddled with the buttons on her skirt. "Do you know if the friend was a guy or a girl?"

"I didn't ask, but I hung around long enough to get a feel for the conversation." Kira leveled Tabitha a pitying look. "I'm 99 percent certain he was talking to a girl."

"I see." Her expression bleak, Tabitha placed her hand over her stomach as if she'd been punched and took a deep breath. "I wish I could say I'm surprised, but I'm not."

"Neither am I." Crossing her arms, Kira shook her head. "I never thought my own brother would turn into a player, but it sure looks like he has. Which means—" she gently poked Tabitha's shoulder, "I don't want you going any-where near him, at least not without me along for protec-tion. That way, if he makes a move on you, he'll have me to contend with."

Despite her misery, Tabitha smiled. "I can take care of myself."

"Right," scoffed Kira. "You're one tough chick. You spent a measly couple of hours with him last night, and this morning you look like you've lost your best friend."

"I do not," Tabitha protested weakly. She grinned sheep-ishly when Kira snorted. "Okay, maybe it would be in my best interest to sign you up as my personal bodyguard."

"Not when it comes to him." Kira tilted her chin in the direction of the boy approaching on his bicycle.

Spotting Sam, Tabitha's smile became genuinely pleased. "Since when did you become such a fan of Sam's?"

"Since I was forced to admit he was treating you better than Micah." Lifting her hand in a wave, Kira headed across the lawn to join Cass and Rianne by the church entrance. "I'll see you inside. We'll be in our usual spot."

Tabitha walked to the bike rack where Sam had stopped. His face lit up when he saw her.

"Man, I now know what they mean by the phrase, 'a sight for sore eyes,' " he greeted her.

Tabitha laughed. "Why are your eyes sore?"

"I just spent 10 minutes staring into the bathroom mirror while I shaved." Sam shuddered. "If that's not enough to hurt a person's eyes, I don't know what is."

"Don't say things like that," Tabitha scolded with a frown. "I like the way you look."

"And I like," Sam leaned close to confide, "the fact that you lie so convincingly."

"Samuel John Steele—" Tabitha shook her finger under his nose, "knock it off, or you'll find yourself sitting alone in church."

"There's always the other kids in the youth group," Sam pointed out with a grin.

"Oh, really?" Propping a hand on her hip, Tabitha tossed her hair. "Who would you rather sit with? Them or me?"

"Man, that's a tough one." When Tabitha pretended to flounce away, Sam caught her by the wrist. "Just kidding. I'd have to be nuts to turn down the chance to sit with the prettiest girl on the island."

"That's better." Tabitha fell into step with him as they turned toward the entrance.

"So," Sam observed in an offhand tone, "how come I'm not vying for your attention with Micah this morning?"

"Kira said he decided to skip church," Tabitha replied.

"Did you two go out last night?" Sam shoved his hands into his pockets and bent his head, staring at his feet.

"We had a late supper at the Yuk, then took a long walk." Uncomfortable with the discussion, Tabitha's face flushed. She wracked her brain for some way to change the subject.

"Ah." Sam nodded sagely. "Are you and Micah getting together today?"

"We didn't make any plans," Tabitha was happy to report.

"In that case—" Sam's head jerked up, and he turned to

her with a hopeful expression, "would you like to do something with me?"

"I'd love to." Tabitha laid a detaining hand on his arm. "I want to make sure you know you're not second choice. I'm not going out with you just because I don't have anything better to do."

Sam expelled a whoosh of relief. "Thanks. I appreciate that. My stomach's been tied in knots since noon yesterday when Micah's plane landed. I figured you'd probably want me out of the picture while he's here. I usually don't like being wrong, but this time I don't mind a bit."

Tabitha surprised him by slipping her arm through his. "As far as I'm concerned, Micah's being back doesn't change a thing. If you want to let it keep us from spending time together, that's up to you. But unless I'm busy, I'll go out with you any time you ask. Same as always."

Puffing out his chest, Sam beamed. "Lady, you sure know how to boost a guy's ego." He dropped the act before continuing, "Seriously though, I've seen pictures of Micah and heard all the stories about his baseball ability and stuff. I knew there wasn't any way I could compete with someone like him."

"There you go, putting yourself down again." Tabitha flung up her arms in disgust. "What do I have to do to convince you that I think you're every bit as good as Micah?"

Sam shot her a sly look out of the corner of his eye. "I don't know. How about agreeing to go to the Valentine's dance with me?"

"Aren't you jumping the gun a tad? The dance is two months away," Tabitha pointed out with a giggle.

"When it comes to a girl like you, a guy shouldn't take any chances." Sam turned serious. "So, what do you say? Will you be my date?"

"It would be my pleasure." Tabitha briefly rested her head on his shoulder. "Wait'll I tell Cass I'm already spoken for. She'll be thrilled. She can be such a mother hen, fussing about my social life and making sure I'm having a good time."

"She loves you." Sam stepped aside to allow Tabitha to precede him into the church.

"Believe me, the feeling's mutual," she whispered as she passed him.

CHAPTER 21

Following church, Sam and Tabitha headed to the Yokwe Yuk for lunch. After stopping to speak with Logan's family, Cass hurried to catch up with Rianne and Kira at the bike rack.

"I just invited Kira to the house to eat," Rianne informed Cass. "Then she can tag along when we go to the airport to meet Randy's plane. Would you like to come too?"

"I'd love to, but I can't," Cass regretfully declined. "I need to go home and see if Mom wants help with Hannah. She was a real wild child last night. She must have cried every hour on the hour."

"Tabitha was probably ready to run away." Kira snickered. "She still hasn't adjusted too well to Hannah's presence."

"She's getting there," Cass defended her sister. "It's not easy having a baby in the house."

"You seem to be doing okay," Rianne observed.

"Everybody reacts differently. I don't take things as hard as Tabitha does." Wheeling her bike out of the rack, Cass straddled it. "I'd better go. Call me as soon as you get back from the airport," she told Rianne. "I can't wait to talk to Randy."

"Will do," Rianne promised.

With a wave, Cass took off for home. Keeping an eye on a fast-approaching storm system, she just barely managed to reach the safety of the lanai before it unleashed its fury. She parked her bike and blew into the house on a gust of wind that slammed the porch door shut behind her. Mom and Dad looked up from the swing where they were sitting.

"It looks like you brought the rain home with you." Mom patted the cushion between her and Dad.

Instead of taking her up on her unspoken invitation, Cass opted for the chair opposite the swing. "Don't say I never bring you anything." She glanced around the room, looking for the bassinet. "Where's Hannah-Banana? Did you decide to give her away after her little performance last night?"

Dad laughed. "No, but I won't make any guarantees if she tries it again. She was a corker, all right." He paused to yawn. "She's in her crib, sleeping like a little angel. You'd never know she kept us up half the night."

"What's that quote from the American Revolution?" Wrinkling her brow, Cass tried to recall. "Something like, 'These are the times that try men's souls'? Anyway, these are the times that try parents' souls."

"Tell me about it." It was Mom's turn to yawn. "Babies are lucky they're so cute. Otherwise, parents wouldn't put up with their shenanigans."

"You talk a good game," Cass scoffed. "But everyone knows how crazy you are about Hannah. You—"

The ringing of the phone interrupted her. Since she was the closest to the kitchen, she got up to answer it.

"Hello?"

"Cass? It's Alex."

"Oh. Hi." She still wasn't sure of her feelings where he was concerned.

"Hi, yourself," he replied. "What are you doing?"

"I just got in from church, and I'm talking with my parents. What about you?"

"Nothing much." Alex hesitated. "Uh ... I was wondering if you'd like to go to a movie this afternoon."

"I would, but Randy Thayer's coming home from college today. You remember Randy," Cass prompted when Alex didn't say anything. "Rianne's brother."

"I remember him." Alex's tone was flat. "You passed up the chance to go to the fall formal with me last year so you could go with him."

Cass' temper flared. "If you'll recall, he asked me first. Unfortunately," she couldn't resist adding, "you got pretty nasty about the situation. You didn't like the fact that I'd chosen a cripple—that's an exact quote, by the way—over you." Randy had been seriously injured in a diving accident when he was younger, leaving him in a wheelchair. Cass was always quick to defend him against people who refused to look past the chair to see Randy for the wonderful guy he was.

Alex sighed. "Ouch. Did you have to remind me what a louse I was?"

"What do you mean, *was*?" Cass retorted, only partially in jest.

"Sometimes I wonder why I keep calling you," Alex mock-complained. "All you ever do is abuse me."

"It's a rotten job, but somebody has to do it. Anyway," Cass went on before Alex could respond, "how about I take a rain-check on the movie?"

"You mean it?" He sounded surprised.

"Of course I mean it. You're not the worst person to spend time with."

"Gee, you really know how to build a guy up," Alex drawled. "I'll call you tomorrow about getting together."

"Sounds good."

After saying good-bye, Cass replaced the phone and returned to the porch. Sitting down, she stretched out her legs.

"That was Alex. He asked me to a movie, but I told him I'm going over to the Thayers' later to see Randy." She snapped her fingers. "That reminds me. Tabitha and Sam went to the Yuk for lunch."

Mom raised her eyebrows. "Hmm. Interesting. How did Micah react to the two of them going off together?"

Cass' lips twisted into a smirk. "He wasn't at church. According to Kira, he stayed up late talking to a girl in Hawaii."

"I see." Mom exchanged a look with Dad. "Did Kira's report upset Tabitha?"

"I don't know. I wasn't there when she told her." Shrugging, Cass got up. "I'm going to get something to eat. Would y'all like me to make you lunch?"

Pressing a hand to his heart, Dad made a show of turning to Mom. "You see why she's my favorite daughter?"

"Boy, what they say is right," Cass quipped as she headed inside. "The way to a man's heart really is through his stomach."

Her parents joined her in the kitchen while she fried three egg sandwiches for lunch. While she ate, she listened for the phone, sure Rianne would be calling any minute. The phone jingled at the same moment that Hannah emitted a howl from the bedroom.

Cass grinned across the table at Mom. "Sounds like you're being paged."

"You stay and finish eating," Dad ordered her. "I'll get our daughter."

Pushing back her chair, Cass stood up. "And I'll get the phone. Of the two, I'll bet the phone smells a whole lot better."

Picking it up on the third ring, she chirped hopefully,

"Rianne?"

"Close, but you have the wrong gender," teased a male voice.

"Randy!" Cass squealed. "You're home!"

"Gee, nothing gets past you," he quipped. "So, how long are you going to make me wait to see you? I figured you'd be part of the welcoming committee when I got off the plane."

"I would have been, except for the new arrival. Can you hear her?" Cass held out the phone so it could pick up the wails echoing down the hallway.

"She has your lungs," Randy commented when Cass got back on the phone. Ignoring her protest, he continued, "Bring pictures when you come. I can't wait to see her."

"I'll be there in—wait a sec, let me check." Peering around the counter, she consulted Mom. "Do you need me here or can I go over to the Thayers' for awhile?"

Mom smiled. "Go on and visit. I'd like you and Tabitha to take care of supper tonight though. I'm still whipped from last night's marathon session with Hannah."

Cass brought the receiver back up to her ear. "Randy? I'll be there as soon as I clean up the lunch dishes."

"Great," he said. "You have no idea how much I'm looking forward to seeing you."

"Sure I do," Cass countered. "Because I know how much I'm looking forward to seeing you."

In less than 10 minutes, she was draped in a poncho and on her way to the Thayer house. She found herself grinning as she splashed through puddles, she was that eager to see Randy. The moment she parked her bike and started across the lawn, Randy flung open the door and motioned for her to hurry. Cass took off at a run, skidding to a breathless halt in the front hall.

Grabbing her hands, Randy beamed up at her from his wheelchair. "Look at you! I can't believe how great it is to see you again."

Cass removed one of her hands from his so she could push down her hood. Trying not to drip on the floor, she bent and gave Randy a resounding kiss on the cheek. "Not half as great as it is to see you, pal."

"Wow." Randy rubbed his cheek and pretended to look dazzled. "If I'd known this was the kind of welcome I'd get, I'd have left sooner."

Blowing on her knuckles, Cass polished them on her chest. "Yeah, I've been told my kisses are pretty potent."

Randy's bark of laughter brought Rianne and Kira from the kitchen. They waved to Cass before demanding what was so funny.

Randy winked at Cass. "Sorry, ladies. Private joke."

"Hey!" Rianne playfully punched his arm. "I'm your sister. You shouldn't have any secrets from me."

"Boy, do you have a lot to learn." Randy backed up his wheelchair then turned to head into the living room. "If you think I'm going to let you in on everything that's gone on the last several months, you're nuts."

Kira's smile instantly became a frown. "Oh, great," she muttered. "Don't tell me you're another Micah."

Randy shot her a startled look over his shoulder. "What's that supposed to mean?"

"Have you talked to my brother recently?" Kira passed his chair to plop down on the sofa.

"No, we haven't kept in touch much." Randy parked the wheelchair in the middle of the room. "Why?"

"He's pretty much gone hog-wild since going off to college." Kira's lip curled up in a sneer. "He's really into the party scene, which means his grades have taken a nosedive. It sounded like you were hinting at a similar situation."

"Not me. No way." Randy assumed his most innocent expression. "I was kidding about having deep, dark secrets. You can ask my roommate. About all I do is go to class, then come back to the room and study. A big evening is when I go to the library."

Kira mopped her brow in mock relief. "It's nice to know not everyone who goes away to college cuts loose like Micah. You've restored my faith in mankind."

"Man, talk about an awesome responsibility." Puffing out his chest, Randy sat up straighter. "It's a good thing I'm up to it."

From her place on the other end of the couch, Rianne laughed. "That's one thing I didn't miss about you. Your massive ego."

"My ego isn't massive," argued Randy. "If anything, it's not nearly as big as it should be for someone of my incredible abilities. Speaking of not being as big," he went on when Rianne opened her mouth to protest, "have you lost weight, Sis? You look like a shadow of your former self."

An awkward silence descended on the group. Cass and Kira exchanged startled glances while Rianne avoided everyone's gaze by studying the hands folded in her lap.

"What did I say?" Randy looked at each person in turn. "Did I stumble on a touchy subject?"

Rianne raised her eyes to glare at Cass. "What did you do, rat on me?"

"Hey, I just got here," Cass defended herself. "When would I have had a chance to say anything?"

"You could have called or written Randy before he left California," Rianne pointed out with a scowl. "The two of you might have concocted a plan about how he could pretend to casually mention my weight."

"You're really losing it." Cass returned Rianne's scowl with an even fiercer one. "For your information, I've never said a word to Randy about your weight loss. Although, to be honest," she continued, "I did intend to say something to him while he's here. He just beat me to it by noticing all on his own how skinny you've gotten. Doesn't that tell you something?"

"Excuse me." Randy waved to get their attention. "Would somebody mind telling me what's going on?"

Cass motioned to Rianne. "Be my guest. I'm curious to hear your explanation."

Sniffing, Rianne tossed her head before focusing on Randy. "You're right. I have lost a few pounds. It's nothing more than a typical case of senior year stress. But Cass is convinced I have an eating disorder. Have you ever heard anything so ridiculous in your life? You know how much I like to eat. I couldn't give up food, even if I wanted to."

While Cass debated with herself about whether or not to contradict her, Kira spoke up. "You're not being entirely truthful, Rianne. We've all seen you pretend to eat when what you were really doing was hiding your food under a napkin or pushing it around the plate to make it look like some of it was gone."

"So what?" Rianne dismissed her comment with a derisive snort. "Why are you making a federal case out of me skipping a couple of meals? Aren't there times when you're not hungry and you play with your food?"

"Not for days—even weeks—at a time." Although she didn't raise her voice, Kira's tone was firm.

"You see what I'm talking about?" Rianne appealed to Randy. "Cass has turned everyone against me. Everybody thinks I'm anorexic. All my so-called friends watch me like hawks to see if, and what, I eat. It's enough to ruin a person's appetite. Can you blame me for losing a few pounds, having to deal with this kind of attitude on a daily basis?"

Randy's expression was troubled. "Are you sure that's all it is? Stress?"

Rianne hesitated a fraction of a second before nodding. "Yes. Don't you think I'd tell you if it were something else? You're my big bro. We don't keep secrets from each other."

"We never used to." Randy stared at her for several

moments, and she returned his look without flinching. "Okay, I guess I believe you. I'd sure feel better if I saw you eat something though. You didn't eat lunch with the rest of us."

"That's because Kira and I ate before we went to the airport," Rianne explained.

"No, we didn't," Kira said, stressing the *we*. "I had a sandwich and chips. You ate one of my potato chips then said you'd have lunch with the family when Randy got here."

"Who are you? The food police?" Rianne said, throwing up her hands in exasperation. "I forgot I said that, okay? Am I supposed to remember every conversation I have during the day?"

"You should be able to recall something that happened a half hour ago," Cass put in quietly, earning herself a scathing look from her friend.

"That's it!" Rianne jumped up and stalked across the floor to the stairs. "I'm not going to sit around while you lecture me about my memory and my food intake. I have better things to do with my time. I'll be up in my room if anybody cares."

Nobody said anything until after she stomped up the steps and the door to her bedroom slammed shut. Randy expelled a rush of air.

"Man, how long has she been like this?" He agitatedly raked his fingers through his hair.

Cass glanced at Kira, who shrugged. "Six weeks?" she guessed. "It started around the first time she and your parents talked about college. She got upset because they don't want her to go to a Christian college."

"I know." Randy's lips thinned with annoyance. "They want her to enroll at UC-Davis with me. I've tried to talk to them about it, but their minds seem to be made up." He directed his gaze at Cass. "Is Rianne trying to get back at them by not eating?"

"That could be part of it." Cass lowered her voice, in case Rianne was eavesdropping from the top of the stairs. She also checked to make sure Mr. and Mrs. Thayer hadn't come in from the porch. "I've been reading everything I can get my hands on about anorexia. There are lots of reasons why people—particularly girls—develop it. In Rianne's case, I think it's a combination of stress and feeling that if she can't control where she goes to school, at least she can control her body and how much she puts into it."

"How much weight has she lost?" Randy asked.

"I'm guessing maybe 10 pounds at this point." Cass looked at Kira, who nodded her agreement. "It doesn't sound like a lot, but she was pretty much skin and bones to begin with. In addition to not eating, she's also taken to exercising like a fiend. She runs a couple of miles everyday and swims laps as often as she can. She tries to hide the weight loss by wearing baggy clothes, but you can see how knobby her knees are. Plus, she's cold a lot. That's another sign of anorexia. The loss of body fat is the problem."

"People—" Randy swallowed hard before continuing, "have been known to die from eating disorders, haven't they?"

"Sometimes," Cass reluctantly admitted. "Rianne's still in the early stages though. If enough of us tell her how concerned we are, I'll bet we'll be able to get through to her."

"You can count on me," Randy declared stoutly. "I'll be in her face so much, she'll start eating just to get me to leave her alone."

"We can't push her too hard," Cass cautioned. "The trick is to let her know we care without making her mad. I also think it would help if she talked to somebody. Of course, my first suggestion is always Pastor Thompson, but a teacher might be better. It would have to be someone she trusts."

Randy rolled his chair closer to Cass in order to ask softly, "Do you think my folks are aware of what's happening?"

She lifted her hands in a helpless gesture. "Who knows? As far as I can tell, Rianne's hardly ever here anymore. She's either out exercising or holed up at the library. When she is here, she stays in her room as much as she can."

"What a mess." Randy thumped the arms of his chair. "Before I say anything to Rianne, I'm going to have a long talk with my parents. They need to know what's going on. It might make them more willing to compromise about college."

"Not to blame your parents, but I think it would help if they did," Kira said. "Rianne's been really bummed about not going to a Christian college. All she's ever dreamed about is being a missionary."

Randy gave them a sour smile. "My folks don't consider missionary work a real profession. The pay's crummy, and nobody ever gets promoted."

Cass blinked her surprise. She'd never heard Randy criticize his parents before.

"Aren't you being a little harsh?" she ventured to ask.

He shook his head. "If anything, I'm sugarcoating the truth. They tolerate Rianne and me going to church and being involved in Christian groups, but they don't approve. I'm lucky because I want to be a lawyer. Rianne, on the other hand, is in for it because of the missionary thing. I've been hoping they'll come around and respect her wishes, but it doesn't look like that's going to happen. I guess the time has come for me to stand up for my sister and her beliefs."

"You're a good brother." Cass leaned forward to pat his knee. "She'll appreciate having you in her corner on this."

Randy ducked his head in embarrassed acknowledgment of the compliment. "Better late than never, I suppose."

"I wish I had a brother like you," Kira muttered.

"That's the second time you've busted on Micah," Randy said. "What's up with you two?"

Slumping back against the sofa cushions, Kira made a face. "Ever since Micah got in yesterday, he's been putting the rush on Tabitha. I'm afraid he just wants somebody to hang out with while he's here and that he'll give her the old heave-ho the minute he steps on the plane to go back to school."

"Have you asked him if that's what he's planning to do?" Randy asked.

"Yeah, right." Kira sounded as disdainful as she looked. "Like he'd tell me if it was. We're not exactly on the best of terms right now. College has really changed him."

"You want me to talk to him?" Randy offered.

"Would you?" Kira sat up straight and peered earnestly at him. "I'd be forever in your debt. He might listen to you."

"I'll call in a little bit and see if he's interested in a round of golf." Randy glanced out the window at the rain that continued to pour. "As soon as it clears up, that is." He heaved a sigh. "If only Logan were here, it'd be like old times, the three of us hitting the links together." He shot Cass a rueful smile. "Oops. Sorry."

She brushed aside his apology. "It's okay. I like hearing people talk about Logan almost as much as I like talking about him. I'd forgotten how much y'all liked to play golf. The poor boy doesn't get a chance to play anymore. The last time he did anything fun was about three months ago."

"I know. We usually write each other a couple of times a month." Randy's mouth curved in a mischievous smile. "Of course, all he ever writes about is how much he misses you.

Talk about boring."

"That depends on your definition of boring," Cass shot back, grinning to let Randy know she was teasing. "I happen to find the subject of myself extremely interesting."

"Which may explain why you talk about yourself all the time," Randy replied.

"You two are good." Kira's tone was admiring. "Sitting here listening to you hit shots back and forth is like being at a tennis match."

"We are a good team, aren't we?" Cass flashed Randy a thumbs-up. "I've missed trading insults with you."

"Same here," he acknowledged then cast a worried glance at the stairs. "Maybe I should go up and see how Rianne is. I don't want her thinking we're down here talking about her."

Cass took that as her cue to leave and stood up. She beckoned to Kira.

"I can take a hint. What about you? The boy wants us to scram, but he doesn't know how to come right out and say it."

"Well, I never," Kira pretended to huff as she scrambled to her feet. Laughing, she added, "Actually, I have. People are always hinting around for me to leave. I'm beginning to get a complex."

"Thanks, you two." Randy accompanied them to the door. "I'll call you later. I want us to spend as much time together as we can. I'm afraid the three weeks I'll be here are going to fly by."

"I know." Cass leaned down to hug him before stepping out onto the front stoop. "Good luck talking to Rianne."

"And your parents," Kira put in. "We'll be praying for you."

"Thanks." Randy lifted a hand in farewell. "I have a feeling I'm going to need it."

CHAPTER 22

Leaving the Thayer's house, Cass and Kira decided to head back to Cass' house for the afternoon. After slipping on their ponchos and removing their sandals, they raced across the yard to retrieve their bikes.

The ride home was fast and wet, and they arrived thoroughly drenched. Parking their bikes next to Tabitha's, they hurried into the house. Mom looked up from the book she was reading as she lazed on the porch swing.

"Isn't the rainy season fun?" she chirped.

Cass pushed down her hood and raked her fingers through the bangs plastered to her forehead. "Yeah, I rank it right up there with having my teeth pulled." She peered into the kitchen. "I take it Tabitha's back from lunch?"

"She's probably in the living room. She said something about watching a movie." Sighing, Mom pursed her lips. "She's had an exciting afternoon."

On her way into the house, Cass paused in the kitchen doorway. "What do you mean?"

"I'll let her tell you about it." Mom angled herself sideways and stretched her legs the length of the swing. "Life isn't a bowl of cherries for her at the moment."

"Oh, boy." Cass tugged on Kira's sleeve. "Let's go see

what's going on. Things sure don't settle down for long, do they?"

As Mom had predicted, they found Tabitha lying on the sofa, staring blankly at a movie unfolding on the television screen. Since the sound was turned off, Cass figured she and Kira wouldn't be interrupting anything if they struck up a conversation. She settled in the rocking chair while Kira chose the recliner. Tabitha acknowledged their presence with a nod before turning her attention back to the television.

"What's with the silent movie routine?" Cass finally asked after several moments of silence.

"A couple of minutes into the video, I realized I didn't have the energy to follow the dialogue, so I muted it." Tabitha rolled onto her side and propped her head on her hand. "That way I can think while I watch. I'm not distracted by any sounds."

"What are you thinking about?" Before Tabitha could reply, Cass went on, "Just so you know, Mom told us something happened this afternoon."

Tabitha made a face. "Two somethings." She glanced uneasily at Kira. "Sam and I ran into Micah on our way home from the Yuk. And my mother called."

"Whoa." Cass emitted a soft whistle. "Two major somethings. Which one do you want to talk about first?"

Kira raised her hand as if in school. "I vote for hearing about what happened with Micah. You don't have to worry about my reaction," she assured Tabitha. "I'm not the blindly loyal kid sister I used to be."

"Then Micah it is." Sitting up, Tabitha folded her legs beneath her. "Sam and I stopped at the Ten-Ten after lunch. Lo and behold, who's there, but Micah? You can imagine how awkward the encounter was."

"I can, but I'd much rather you told us about it." Kira's eyes gleamed with anticipation.

"The moment he saw us, Micah went into his swagger mode. You know how he gets, when he seems to grow a couple of inches and puffs out his chest." Tabitha giggled. "He reminds me of a rooster whenever he does it. Anyway, he strolled over to us, put his arm around my waist, and said, real snotty like, 'So, Tabitha, who's your little friend?' I could have slugged him."

Groaning, Kira rolled her eyes at the ceiling. "Oh, brother. I thought he'd show more class than that when he finally met up with Sam. Speaking of which, how did Sam react?"

Tabitha's face lit up in a genuine smile. "He was great. I was so proud of him. He stuck out his hand to shake Micah's and said, 'Sam Steele. Pleased to meet you. And you're Micah, of course. I'd know you anywhere. Tabitha's told me all about you.' Micah just stood there for a couple of seconds with his mouth hanging open. I think he expected Sam to be intimidated by him."

"Good for Sam." Kira vigorously nodded her approval. "It's about time somebody put my brother in his place." She frowned. "How long did he keep his arm around you?"

"No more than a second or two. I moved out of reach first chance I got." Tabitha's expression darkened at the memory. "I could tell by the look on his face he didn't like that. He made a big deal out of saying he'd call me so we could get together again since last night was so much fun. Sam—bless his heart—just stood there smiling and acting all friendly. I don't know how he did it. I couldn't wait to get out of there."

"Did Sam say anything after Micah left?" Cass pushed her feet against the floor to set the rocker in motion.

"That's the part that really upset me." Tabitha gazed at the action on the screen for a few moments before continuing, "He was quiet the rest of the time we were in the store. On the way home, though, he said it was easy to see how I could fall for someone like Micah. He repeated what he's said before, that he could never even hope to compete with a guy like him. Then he said—" she paused to take a deep breath, "he'd understand if I didn't want to get together while Micah was here. He left before I had a chance to argue with him." Her face crumpled. "He didn't even say he'd call me."

"Then you call him," Cass ordered without hesitation. "Let him know how wrong he is about you not wanting to see him."

"Yeah," Kira chimed in. "The sooner you set him straight about how you really feel, the better off you'll both be." She growled low in her throat. "Honestly, my brother and his superior attitude are really starting to bug me," she fumed. "Who does he think he is, treating Sam like a second-rate nobody?"

Cass and Tabitha exchanged amused glances, and laughed. Kira's brows drew together in a scowl.

"What?" she demanded suspiciously.

"Who'd have thought, a few months back, that the day would come when you'd take Sam's side over Micah's?" Cass pressed a hand to her chest. "Not me, that's for sure."

Kira grudgingly joined in the laughter. "It is a switch, isn't it? But fair is fair. I don't like people picking on other people, even if it is my own brother doing the picking."

"Then it's settled," Cass declared. "You're to call Sam as soon as possible. Let's move on to Beth. Why did she call this time?"

"Wait until you get a load of her latest harebrained scheme." Tabitha pulled a pillow into her lap to play with the fringe. "She wants me to spend the summer with her. She said we could check out colleges in Oregon, and I could earn money for school by helping in her tie-dyed T-shirt business."

Cass yelped her amazement. "You've got to be kidding! Where does she come up with these nutty ideas?"

"As far as I can tell, she dreams them up in her little pea-brain. I'm sorry," Tabitha hastily apologized. "I guess I shouldn't talk about her like that. I mean, she did give birth to me."

"And that's about all she ever did for you," Kira reminded her. "What was your response to spending the summer with her?"

Tabitha assumed a sheepish expression. "You know me. I have a hard time being direct. I hemmed and hawed, and told her I'd get back to her."

"You chicken," Cass jeered good-naturedly. "Do you want me to call her?" She gleefully rubbed her hands together. "I'd love to have a little chat with your dear, sweet mother."

"As tempting as your offer is, I'll do it." Ducking her head, Tabitha ruefully peered up at Cass. "As soon as I get up the nerve, that is."

"Timing is everything in life." A sudden wail from the bedroom had Cass turning to look over her shoulder. "It sounds like it's time for someone to eat. I think I'll give Mom a break and go get Hannah for her."

"Don't bother," Tabitha advised sourly. "Dad's in the room, napping. He'll bring her to Mom." She drummed her fingers on the arm of the sofa. "I wonder how much time he spent with me when I was a baby, compared to how much time he spends with Hannah."

Cass shrugged as if the answer should be obvious. "Ask him."

"No way." Tabitha vehemently shook her head. "What if he says it wasn't as much? Or even worse, that he can't remember?"

"You're just bound and determined to be miserable, aren't you?" Rocking forward, Cass stood up. "It's supposed to be the season for peace on earth. You're anything but peaceful."

"Well, excuse me," snapped Tabitha. "I guess my life isn't as perfect as yours."

Cass, on her way to the kitchen to get something to drink, halted and spun around to fix her with a steely stare. "Yeah, my life's one laugh after another. Jan keeps writing to me about her crummy home life. Rianne's mad at me because I won't quit bugging her about her weight. Last but not least, out of all the guys who left for college, the only one who isn't home for Christmas is Logan. Yup, I can see how you'd think I have it good."

Tabitha had the grace to blush. "Sorry. I guess I wasn't thinking."

"That's okay." Cass smiled her acceptance of Tabitha's apology and continued across the floor to the refrigerator. "We all have a lot on our minds."

Unfolding her legs, Tabitha planted her feet on the floor and motioned to Kira. "Let's go to my room. I know you don't mind listening to me complain."

As she followed Tabitha out of the room, Kira made a quick detour to whisper to Cass, "That's because I've had years of practice."

"I heard that," Tabitha huffed from halfway down the hall.

Cass and Kira covered their mouths to stifle their giggles.

CHAPTER 23

"Cass." Two days into the new year, Mom shook Cass awake. "Sweetie, you have a phone call."

"What time is it?" Cass mumbled from the depths of her pillow.

"Almost 7:00."

"In the morning?" Cass' tone was horrified. "Who in their right mind calls someone this early?"

"Janette." When Cass didn't respond, Mom added, "From Tennessee."

"Oh, for pity's sake!" Flinging off the covers, Cass sat up and reached for the phone Mom held out to her. "You don't have to remind me who Jan is. I'm not senile, you know."

"Maybe not, but you are a grouch." Mom affectionately rumpled Cass' hair before leaving.

Cass quickly ran her tongue over her teeth before rasping, "Jan? Is it really you?"

"Live and almost in person," came Janette's glum reply. "How's it going?"

"Not bad." Cass scooted back a few inches to lean against the headboard. "Happy New Year."

"Yeah? What's so happy about it?" Jan asked darkly.

"I'll be coming to Tennessee in three weeks. Plus, Dad announced the other day that he and I are going to make a weekend trip to New York so I can see Logan." Cass shivered with excitement. "That makes it a good year, as far as I'm concerned."

"Well, aren't you the lucky one?" Jan drawled.

Cass barely managed to hold onto her temper. "Did you call just to give me grief? Because if you did, you're wasting your time. I'll hang up and go back to sleep."

To Cass' surprise, Janette laughed instead of taking offense. "I have to hand it to you, you're the same old Cass. Some things—or, in your case, people—never change." She paused then added softly, "I'm really looking forward to seeing you."

Thinking about their rocky relationship, Cass couldn't help commenting, "That's quite a switch from last year when you hardly made any time for me."

"I know," Jan grudgingly admitted. "Things have changed."

"Starting with your mother's marriage." It was a statement, not a question. "How's it going with your stepfather?"

Janette's snort of derision said it all. "You mean Billy the Caveman? If anything, it's gotten worse. I can't imagine what my mother sees in him. He's loud. He's obnoxious. He thinks belching is hysterical so he does it every chance he gets. It's like living with a sixth-grade boy."

"He sounds charming," Cass said sarcastically. "I can't wait to meet him."

"That's why I called. I wanted to check what day you're arriving. Hold on a sec," Jan requested when a male voice said something in the background. After a brief, muffled conversation, she came back on the phone. "That was Billy, telling me to get off because he's waiting on a call. I'd better go. I don't want to make him mad. My mother's not here to stick up for me. Tell me quick when you'll be here."

Cass did then echoed Janette's hasty good-bye before her friend hung up. Pressing the off button, she lay the phone on the nightstand and snuggled back under the covers. The thought of meeting Jan's stepfather gave her the creeps. He sounded like a real jerk, and she pitied Jan for having been saddled with him.

"Lord," she whispered, gazing up at the ceiling, "thank You for bringing Dad into my life." She thought back to the last week and a half, filled with Christmas services and activities. Being able to celebrate the birth of Christ, the Savior, with her whole family had been wonderful. "I don't know what I'd have done if Mom had married somebody like Billy." She smiled to herself. "Of course, Mom has better sense than to do something like that. Anyway, show me how I can help Janette deal with her situation when I get back to Tennessee. Please give me the right words to say to her. In Jesus' name, amen."

Over the course of the next several days, Tabitha and Cass returned to school, and life resumed its normal routine. Micah, who'd competed with Sam throughout Christmas break for Tabitha's attention, was forced to back off during school hours. Sam remarked on the change the first morning he came by to escort Tabitha to school.

"I halfway expected Micah to be here when I rode up," he joked when Tabitha brought her bike out from behind the house to join him on the road.

"What would you have done if he had shown up?" After

stowing her backpack in the handlebar basket, Tabitha pointed the bike in the direction of the school.

"Left, I guess," Sam admitted with a shrug.

Tabitha shot him an annoyed look. "When are you going to give up this stupid inferiority complex of yours?"

"As soon as I grow another six inches and develop Arnold Schwarzeneggar-size muscles," Sam replied cheerfully.

"Do you realize how ridiculous you're being?" Tabitha demanded. "In a weird way, I think it would make you happy if I dumped you for Micah."

Sam's expression instantly sobered. "It would kill me if you did. I joke about you preferring Micah because, if it turns out you really do, maybe it won't hurt so much if I've prepared myself."

"How many times do I have to tell you it's not going to happen?"

"I'll do better once Micah goes back to college," Sam assured her.

"Yeah, but then what?" Tabitha persisted. "I mean, what about when we go off to school? How do you expect us to maintain a relationship if you're convinced you're not good enough for me?" Realizing what she'd said, she grew flustered and began to stammer, "Uh ... not that I assume you and I ... I mean ... you might not want to ..."

The face Sam turned to her was a study in amazement. "You've actually thought about us staying friends after we go off to college?"

Ducking her head in embarrassment, Tabitha nodded. "Well ... sure. Haven't you?"

Please say you have, she silently implored. *Otherwise, I'll die of humiliation right here in the middle of the street.*

"Absolutely, but I figured I was the only one." Sam's face glowed with his smile. "Wow! I'm totally blown away that you want to stay friends."

"Of course I do. You didn't think I'd let you get away that easily, did you?" Tabitha gave him a teasing glance. "It brings us back to my question, though. How can we have a future if you're going to worry all the time that I'm on the verge of dumping you?"

"Hey, this gives me major incentive to stop," Sam breezily assured her. Shaking his head, he said almost to himself, "She actually wants to stay friends. Will wonders never cease?"

Tabitha's expression was skeptical. "That's all it takes? You decide you'll quit worrying, and that's it?"

"Okay," Sam conceded, "maybe it'll require a bit more effort. But you have my word I'm going to work on it. I promise I won't be putting myself down anymore. At least not when you're around to hear me," he added with a mischievous grin.

"You're hopeless," Tabitha chided good-naturedly.

"On the contrary." He grinned at her. "You've given me more hope in the past couple of minutes than I've had in years."

While Sam and Tabitha continued on to school, Cass pedaled around the side of the house to discover Alex waiting for her. Braking, she straddled her bike and leaned on the handlebars to gaze at him with a steady regard.

"To what do I owe the honor?" she drawled. "I hardly saw you over the break. Now, all of a sudden, you show up again? Pardon me if I'm suspicious."

Instead of responding in kind, Alex hung his head and scuffed the toe of his sandal in the dirt bordering the road. "I didn't get out much during the holidays."

Cass arched an eyebrow at him. "Not even with Kendra?"

Alex's head shot up, and his face darkened. "No. I basically holed up in my room."

"Why?" With a wave, Cass urged him to begin the ride to school.

"I called your house a few times, but you were always out." Alex pulled alongside Cass, and the pair headed down the street. "I guess you didn't get my messages because you never called back."

"Everyone in my house is very good about taking messages," Cass defended her family. "If I didn't get your messages, it's because you didn't leave any. Besides," she went on when Alex opened his mouth to protest, "don't try to lay a guilt trip on me because you didn't socialize over break. It's not my job to schedule activities for you."

"Are you always this argumentative?" Alex's question was half-jest, half-serious.

"No, most of the time I'm even worse. You, of all people, should know that." Cass rode in silence for several seconds then turned to look curiously at Alex. "What's the real reason you stayed in during the break? Were you sick?"

The teasing light in his eyes was replaced by despair. "Define sick. If you mean physically, the answer is no. Being sick at heart, now that's another matter."

Taken aback by his response, Cass didn't say anything for a few moments. "Did something happen? Did your family get bad news or something?"

Clenching his jaw, Alex stared straight ahead. Just as Cass decided he wasn't going to reply, he spoke so softly that she had to strain to hear him.

"I couldn't stop thinking about the ... you know ... the baby."

What baby? Cass wondered blankly. The only baby she could think of was Hannah, but why would Alex be thinking about her? Then it dawned on her, and she inhaled sharply. *Of course. The baby Alison aborted. Jesus, please help me here. I don't want to say the wrong thing.*

"You mean your and Alison's baby, don't you?" Cass ascertained.

Alex nodded.

"What did you think about?" Cass felt as if she were walking through a minefield. One false move, and everything could explode sky-high.

"That it would've been the kid's first Christmas," Alex forced the words out in a strangled voice. "I wondered what I would have gotten it. How it would've reacted to the lights and stuff."

"I see." Cass stalled for time, searching frantically for what to say next. "I guess it upset you to think about him, huh?"

Alex glanced sharply at her. "Why do you call it a him?"

"Because he wasn't an it. He was an unborn baby. The least we can do is refer to him in human terms." *Don't start lecturing,* Cass reminded herself. *Alex is reaching out to you. He doesn't need a sermon. He needs a friend.* "Does it bother you that I say him?" she asked quietly.

"It makes him real." Alex took a deep, shuddering breath. "I don't want him to be real. It—"

"Hey, you two!" a familiar voice hollered from behind them. "Wait up."

Glancing over her shoulder, Cass saw Rianne pedaling madly to catch up with them. She smiled wanly at Alex.

"Looks like we have company," she murmured. "We'll have to continue this discussion later."

A look of relief passed across Alex's face. "That's okay. I probably shouldn't have said anything, anyway." He started to speed up. "I'll see you at school."

"Alex," Cass called urgently, "I really do want to talk to you. Can we get together after school?"

His only response was to lift a hand in farewell and take off down the road at breakneck speed. Rianne took over the spot he'd vacated.

"Whoa, he got out of here in a hurry," she observed. "Is he that scared of me?"

"Has anybody ever told you that you have rotten timing?" Cass grumbled in reply.

"Me?" Rianne pressed a hand to her chest. "What did I do?"

"Alex had just started talking about his and Alison's baby when you showed up." Cass glanced in the direction Alex had taken. He was a speck in the distance. "I had the feeling he was about to admit the abortion was wrong. But you sent him scurrying away like a rabbit being chased by a hound dog."

"How was I supposed to know what you two were discussing?" Rianne said hotly. "Excuse me for being friendly."

Realizing she had a point, Cass relented. "Forget it. Hopefully Alex and I will get another chance to talk."

"There are more than four months left until we graduate," Rianne pointed out. "I'm sure you'll manage to squeeze in a conversation between now and then."

"Do I detect a note of sarcasm in your voice?" Cass glanced over at her friend then glanced back, narrowing her eyes to study the other girl. "You seem different today. You look like you have a secret or something."

Rianne shook her head in admiration. "You're good. I am feeling more upbeat than usual. I wanted to catch up with you before school so I could tell you about the discussion Randy and I had with the folks last night."

"Did you finally talk to them about school?" It was the only possibility Cass could think of that would have lifted Rianne's spirits.

"We didn't just talk. We talked for three hours. I was pooped by the time we were done, but I felt really good about how it went." Rianne wiggled the front tire of her bike a couple of times to show how pleased she was. "Randy was amazing. He went to bat for me just like he promised. He told my parents they weren't being fair to me, that he and I are two entirely different people, and I should be allowed to pursue my dreams the same way they're letting him pursue his. Every time they brought up an argument against me going to a Christian college, he shot it down. He'd really done his homework so he was able to prove to them that a Christian college degree would do just as well for the work I want to go into as a regular school's degree would. He showed them how they could afford to send me to a private college. Best of all, he talked a long time about our faith and what it means to us. After awhile, my parents just sat there and listened because they didn't have anything to say."

"So they agreed to let you go to a Christian college?" Cass asked excitedly.

"Not yet," Rianne had to admit. "But, thanks to Randy, I'm sure they will. It's only a matter of time. I can't wait to visit the guidance office and start looking through catalogues for the right college."

I probably shouldn't ask this, Cass thought, *but I'm going to, anyway. I hope Rianne doesn't jump all over me.*

"Does this mean you're going to start eating again?" she inquired.

Rianne's mood immediately went from elated to irritated. Flashing Cass a sour look, she griped, "Way to ruin things. I should have known better than to think you'd be happy for me. All you care about is my so-called eating disorder. It's like you're obsessed with it. You do your best to work it into every conversation."

"Don't you think you're exaggerating just a tad?" Cass slowed to make the turn onto school property. "I don't bring it up all the time, only when it's appropriate. I figured, since your parents are being reasonable about college, you might not so stressed anymore and you'll go back to your normal eating."

"What I eat, or don't eat, is none of your business." Rianne followed Cass to the bike racks and braked. "You're the only one still getting on me about it. Even Randy's backed off."

Cass turned a troubled face to her. "He has? He told me he was going to keep after you until your appetite picked back up."

"Are you calling me a liar?" Rianne slammed her bike into a slot with more force than was necessary. "You can ask him yourself if you think I'm not telling the truth."

"I will." Cass parked her bike with almost as much force as Rianne. "The problem with you is you'll keep refusing to get help until you finally admit you have anorexia. Which means I'm going to go on being scared out of my wits on your account." Reaching over, she grabbed her friend's wrist. "For pity's sake, look at yourself. You have no meat left on your bones. A stiff wind could pick you up and blow you away."

Rianne snatched back her arm and glared at Cass. "Leave me alone!" she hissed. "If I want your advice, I'll ask for it. Otherwise, starting right now, any talk about my weight is off-limits. If you insist on bringing the matter up, you can kiss our friendship good-bye."

"I ... you ..." Cass sputtered, her mouth opening and closing several times, making her look like a fish out of water. She clamped it shut. "Fine," she muttered through gritted teeth. "You're the boss." *A really skinny boss,* she added silently. *But when it comes to this topic, definitely the boss.*

At her words, Rianne relaxed and even managed to smile at Cass. "Are you ready for another semester?"

Despite her lingering misgivings, Cass forced herself to respond in kind. "As ready as I'll ever be, I suppose. I forget. What's your schedule this time around?"

Comparing classes, they made their way to their lockers. Cass quickly scanned the hallway for Alex, but didn't see him. She told herself to remember to set up another time for them to talk as soon as possible.

CHAPTER 24

As it turned out, the opportunity never presented itself. Alex did a good job of avoiding her the rest of the day. The few times she encountered him, he pretended to be in a hurry and slipped away before she could talk to him. It was a frustrated Cass who climbed on her bike after school to head to the Thayer house to talk to Randy.

"Why are you looking so crabby?" Tabitha asked as she wheeled her bike up behind Cass'.

"Alex is giving me the cold shoulder, and it's bugging me." Jostled by another student, Cass whipped around to scowl at him. "I can't get him to stay in one place long enough to talk to him."

"Oh, well. Small loss." Tabitha dismissed the situation with a careless wave. "You have any plans this afternoon?"

"Rianne's staying after to talk to the guidance counselor about colleges so I'm running over to her house to ask Randy something." Cass lifted a leg over the bike to straddle it. "What about you?"

"I'm going straight home." Tabitha made a face. "The teachers obviously don't care we just got off vacation because they piled on the homework. It'll probably take me till midnight to get it all done."

"Save the history until I get home so we can do it together," Cass suggested. "Two heads are always better than one."

"Especially when it comes to ancient history," Tabitha agreed with a long-suffering groan. "I mean, who cares about the Greeks and Romans? What did they ever contribute to society except togas and all those stupid gods and goddesses?"

"I can see it's going to be a long night." Placing her feet on the pedals, Cass slowly started to ride away. "Tell Mom I'll be home shortly. I don't plan to stay long at the Thayers'."

Randy was heading out the door when Cass rode up. Spotting her, he broke into a grin and wheeled his chair across the lawn to where she'd stopped by the side of the road.

"How was school?" he greeted her. "I thought about you toiling away while I lazed in bed half the morning."

"Funny, I thought about you too." Cass assumed a ferocious glower. "Only you don't want to know what I was thinking. It wasn't very nice."

"Aw, you're just jealous because I'm in college and get longer vacations." Randy didn't seem the least bit apologetic about the fact.

"So what's your point?" Cass aimed a playful punch at his shoulder. "Of course I'm jealous, you nitwit. I'd appreciate it if you didn't rub it in though." Changing the subject, she asked, "Where are you off to?"

"Running an errand for my mother. She likes having me here to run to the store for her." Randy gazed up at Cass. "Did you come by to see me or are you waiting for Rianne?"

Recalling her reason for being there, Cass explained, "I need to ask you a question. Rianne said you've quit bugging her about her eating. Is that true?"

"Not exactly." Randy's mouth twisted with irritation. "I try to talk to her about it, but she either changes the subject or leaves. After watching her the past few weeks, I'm convinced she does have a problem. It might not be full-blown anorexia yet, but everything you said about the not eating and the over-exercising is right on the money. We had a good talk with the folks about college last night, and I'm hoping that'll help. If she doesn't have to worry about school anymore, maybe she'll begin eating normally again."

"That's what I told her." Cass sniffed as she recalled Rianne's reaction. "As usual, she jumped on me for mentioning her weight. This time, though, she added the threat of breaking off our friendship if I say one more word on the subject."

Randy's eyes widened in surprise. "You're kidding." He frowned. "That's it. When she gets home, I'm going to make her listen to me, even if it takes all night. Somebody has to talk some sense into her. I leave to go back to school on Saturday, so it's now or never."

"You're a good brother." Cass squeezed his arm. "Call me if you need back-up. I have a ton of homework so I won't be going anywhere."

That settled, she took off for home, thinking, *One down, one to go. I'll call Alex as soon as I get home. With any luck, we'll be able to finish our talk on the phone, and I'll wind up batting a thousand for the day.*

A few seconds after walking into the kitchen, however, Alex was the furthest thing from Cass' mind. She met Tabitha on her way out.

"Hey." Cass treated her to a broad smile. "Don't tell me you've given up on your homework already."

"Uh ... no." Tabitha's gaze shifted uneasily away from Cass. "Micah called. I'm meeting him at the pool."

Propping her hands on her hips, Cass frowned at Tabitha. "Why?"

"Because he asked me to." Tabitha attempted to move past Cass, but Cass wouldn't budge. "Besides, he'll be leaving this weekend so it's not like I'll have that many more chances to spend time with him."

"I don't understand why in the world you want to." Cass backed up to stand in the doorway leading to the porch and folded her arms. "Every time you come in from a date, all you do is complain about the way he hogged the conversation and how he pressured you to kiss and stuff. Why do you keep putting yourself through this?"

Tabitha's expression was genuinely puzzled as she lifted her shoulders in a bewildered shrug. "I don't know. I guess I keep hoping it'll change, that things will go back to the way they used to be before he left for school."

"How many rotten dates do you have to go on before you finally accept the fact that nothing's going to change?" Cass demanded. "Sam is the guy for you, not Micah. It was nice while it lasted with Micah, but it's over." She snapped her fingers under Tabitha's nose. "Wake up and smell the coffee, girl. Maybe it's possible for you and Micah to be friends, but that's it. Why won't you admit he makes a lousy boyfriend?"

"Probably because there's something wrong with me." Tabitha threw her hands up in frustration. "I let people walk all over me. It's the same with my mother. I can't seem to find the courage to tell people off."

"In other words, when Micah and Beth tell you to jump,

you ask how high." The moment the sarcastic words were out of her mouth, Cass regretted them.

Tabitha stared at her as if she'd been slapped. Angry red spots mottled her cheeks, and her breath came in short gasps.

"I'm sorry," Cass began. "I shouldn't have—"

"Don't talk to me," Tabitha ordered, pointing a shaky finger at her. Tears shimmered in her eyes. "In fact, do me a huge favor, and don't ever talk to me again."

This time, when she tried to leave, Cass didn't stop her. Feeling like the lowest, slimiest form of life on earth, Cass stepped aside and watched helplessly as Tabitha stormed out of the house.

Jesus, she prayed as she slunk back into the kitchen, *You're going to have to fix this one because I really blew it big time. Show me how to apologize so Tabitha will listen to me. I'll do anything—eat crow, crawl on my hands and knees across broken glass—anything. Just please make it right.*

Feeling horrible, Cass passed up her usual snack and headed straight for her room. After checking on Mom and Hannah and finding them asleep, she sat down at her desk and started her Spanish homework. She vowed not to get up until every assignment was completed. A sorry excuse for a human being like herself didn't deserve to take a break.

Cass was thoroughly engrossed in translating a paragraph from Spanish into English when she felt a hand descend on her shoulder. The pencil flew out of her hand as she leaped several inches off the chair. Whirling around, she discovered Tabitha grinning down at her.

"For pity's sake!" Cass pressed a hand to her chest where her heart galloped at approximately the same speed as a horse thundering toward the finish line at the Kentucky Derby. "You scared the living daylights out of me."

"Serves you right for being mean to me before I left." Tabitha stuck out her tongue then hoisted herself onto the desk.

"Speaking of that—" Cass leaned back in the chair to peer up at Tabitha, "what are you doing back so soon? Did Micah the Magnificent stand you up?"

"You wish. That would give you another reason to dislike him." Looking pleased with herself, Tabitha crossed her legs. "Actually, I decided on the way to the pool that you might have a point about me kowtowing to Micah and my mother. He snapped his fingers and I went running, completely forgetting about the plans I'd made to get my homework done. When he showed up I told him I shouldn't have agreed to meet him, that I really needed to hit the books."

"No kidding." Cass was impressed, and it showed in her expression. "What did he say to that?"

"At first, I thought he was going to leave without saying anything. You should have seen his face. He was furious." Tabitha chuckled at the memory. "He hates not getting his way. Anyway, he finally asked me if I was sure and if there was some way he could talk me into staying. When I said no, he told me he'd see me around, and he left."

"He didn't even walk you home?" Cass was indignant on her sister's behalf. "What's happened to his manners?"

"I guess he left them in Hawaii, along with that girl Kira says he calls practically every night." Tabitha picked up the paper Cass had been writing her translation on. "You're doing your Spanish assignment? You haven't already done the history homework, have you?"

"I haven't even started it." Cass accepted the paper Tabitha handed back to her. "I'm with you. Ancient history isn't my favorite subject. Give me the Civil War any day. Now that's interesting."

"Spoken like a true southerner." Tabitha patted Cass' head then slid off the desk. "I'm going to my room to work on my French. Holler when you're ready to tackle history."

"Will do." Having already turned her attention back to the complexities of the Spanish language, Cass sent her off with a distracted wave.

Peace reigned in the house for another 30 minutes until Hannah woke up from her nap and shattered it with an ear-splitting wail. From the adjoining room, Cass heard a loud groan and frowned. Tabitha still hadn't adjusted to Hannah's presence. Cass knew Tabitha loved their baby sister, but something about her obviously rubbed Tabitha the wrong way.

Oh, well, Cass thought with a shrug. *It's not my concern. Tabitha will figure it out sooner or later. Meanwhile, I have more important things to worry about. Like why did I translate the last sentence to read, "My angry fish is in the barn with the shoes"?*

Shortly before 5:00, Mom knocked on Cass' door to ask her to entertain Hannah while she made supper. Grateful for the interruption, Cass followed Mom out of the room to the kitchen where Hannah sat in her bouncy seat on the counter.

"Come here, you little cutie," Cass cooed, unbuckling the baby and lifting her out of the seat. "You and I are going to spend some quality time together."

Cradling her sister in her arms, Cass walked out to the living room. About to sit down in the rocking chair, she remained on her feet when Tabitha called to her from the bedroom.

"Hey, Cass! Are you ready to work on the history assignment?"

"No, I'm busy," she shouted back, causing Hannah to wrinkle her forehead in protest.

"Doing what?" The door to Tabitha's room opened, and she appeared in the hallway. "Oh," she said flatly when she spotted Cass with Hannah. "You were roped into baby-sitting. Better you than me."

"Don't say that." Cass covered Hannah's ears. "You'll hurt her little feelings."

"You'll also hurt mine," Mom chimed in from the kitchen. "I didn't realize you considered watching your sister such a burden."

"I really don't." Coming into the living room, Tabitha hung her head in shame. "I don't know why I said that. I guess I was trying to be funny." She flashed Cass a warning look. "Don't say it. I don't want to hear your lecture on you being the funny one and me being the pretty one."

"It didn't even occur to me to mention it," Cass lied, hating that Tabitha knew her so well.

"Are you sure taking care of Hannah doesn't bother you?" Mom leaned over the counter to ask Tabitha. "I don't want you feeling like I'm taking advantage of you."

"Honest, I'm fine with—"

Tabitha's response was cut short by Dad's arrival. Whistling as he walked into the kitchen, he caught Mom around the waist and gave her a resounding kiss that left Cass and Tabitha rolling their eyes at each other.

"Hello, gorgeous. How's your day been?"

"Not bad." Mom patted Dad's cheek and grinned. "It just got a lot better though."

"Aw, I bet you say that to all the guys," Dad teased.

"Only the good-looking ones," Mom shot back, making him laugh.

Moving into the living room, he hugged Tabitha, smiled at Cass, and held out his arms to take Hannah. "Come to

Daddy." He settled her in the crook of his arm and lightly tapped her nose. "Where have you been all my life, you sweet little girl?"

Tabitha immediately bristled and glared at him, even though he didn't notice. Cass did, however, and shot her a curious glance.

"What's with you?" she murmured.

Darting a nervous look at Dad, Tabitha moved closer to Cass and whispered, "Don't you ever get tired of the 'Daddy's little girl' routine?

Cass smiled fondly at Dad and Hannah. "Not really. I think it's sweet. It makes me hope my father treated me the same way when I was a baby."

Tabitha sniffed then pretended to cough when Dad glanced at her. "It's easy for you to think it's sweet," she muttered. "You don't have to watch your father fawning over some other kid."

Cass' eyebrows disappeared under her bangs. "Mom doesn't exactly ignore Hannah, you know."

"Yeah, but you know Mom loves you," Tabitha retorted. "Plus, she remembers stuff from when you were a baby. With Dad, it's like Hannah's the first baby he ever had."

"What are you two whispering about out there?" Mom looked up from the hamburgers she was frying at the stove.

"Nothing." Tabitha waved airily. "Just girl talk. Uh ... can I help you fix supper?"

"Now that you ask, yes, you can." Mom gestured over her shoulder at the sink. "Would you peel the potatoes?" She grinned mischievously at Cass. "And what would you like to do, Sweetie?"

"Now that you ask," Cass mimicked her, "nothing." She walked to the recliner and sat down, raising the footrest. "I'm quite happy to just sit here and watch you and Tabitha work."

"A girl after my own heart," Dad observed. "Why pitch in when there are already more than enough hands willing to do the work?"

"Exactly," Cass agreed. "It's so nice to be understood."

CHAPTER 25

The next three weeks flew by in a flurry of activity. Randy and Micah returned to school, and Cass and family began preparing for the trip to Tennessee.

Cass had every intention of talking to Alex before she left, but never got around to it. Of course, it didn't help that he continued to avoid her, but she had to admit she could have made more of an effort to seek him out. She said as much to Tabitha as they settled themselves in their plane seats on the morning of their departure for the mainland.

"Don't worry about it," Tabitha advised, buckling her seatbelt. "He'll talk when he's ready to talk. It's not your responsibility to drag it out of him."

"I guess you're right." Cass sighed and made a face. "I still wish Rianne hadn't interrupted us that day. I truly believe Alex was ready to admit Alison's abortion was wrong."

"Maybe, maybe not. There's no way to know for sure. Speaking of Rianne," Tabitha went on, "I think she's turned the corner on the anorexia thing. She doesn't seem to be losing any more weight."

"I don't want to get my hopes up yet," Cass replied cautiously. "But it does look like her weight has stabilized. Maybe the combination of all of us getting on to her did the trick. It bothers me, though, that she won't 'fess up about what she's been doing. She keeps insisting we over-reacted."

"That is a worry," Tabitha agreed. "Denial is almost as bad as the disease itself."

Cass sighed, then smoothed the cover of the magazine lying in her lap. "But it was nice of Kira and Rianne to come out to see us off, and to give us something to read on the flight."

Tabitha glanced down at her own magazine. "They're good friends. I hate to think about never seeing them again after graduation."

"The same way you hate to think about not seeing Sam?" Cass arched an eyebrow at her.

"Sam." Tabitha's sigh was blissful. "He's one terrific guy, that's for sure."

"So spending time with Micah didn't confuse you about your feelings for Sam?" Cass checked.

"I'll always have a special place in my heart for Micah." Tabitha watched the flight attendant close and lock the hatch before continuing, "There's a part of me that wishes we could have a fairytale ending to our story."

"Even if it means Sam would be out of the picture?" Cass tried to keep the disapproval out of her voice.

Tabitha hesitated then made a gesture halfway between a nod and a shrug. "It gets really confusing sometimes. I know how good I have it with Sam, but then there's this ... attraction to Micah that just won't go away. I'm hoping, now that Micah's back in school, things will settle down, and I won't feel so torn."

"You haven't heard from Micah since he left, have you?" Although Cass knew the answer to her question, she wanted to remind Tabitha of his behavior.

"No, but I didn't expect to." Tabitha raised her voice to be heard above the revving of the engines. "I figure he's busy with the girl he kept calling while he was here."

"And it doesn't bug the daylights out of you to know he was calling her all the while he was hitting on you?" Cass shook her head. "I can't figure you out sometimes."

"Join the club." Tabitha leaned her head against the seat and shut her eyes. "I'm going to take a nap. Wake me up when they serve breakfast."

About to protest, Cass clamped her mouth shut instead. She wouldn't mind having a little time to herself to think about seeing Logan again. A fluttery feeling bubbled in her stomach. In less than a week, she and Dad were scheduled to drive to New York. At the end of the 12-hour drive would be Logan.

As the plane gathered speed for take-off, Cass closed her eyes and prayed, *Lord, please give us a safe trip to Tennessee. Help Hannah not to cry too much. Keep Logan safe and healthy until we see each other again. In Jesus' name, amen.*

With that taken care of, she shifted this way and that until she found a more comfortable position. Opening the magazine Kira had given her, she stared at the table of contents while thoughts of what she and Logan would do in the 48 hours they'd have together danced through her head. Despite her best intentions, she was asleep within 15 minutes of the plane being airborne.

"Sweetie, wake up."

Dad's voice penetrated Cass' slumber, and, blinking, she struggled to sit upright. "What?"

"They'll be bringing breakfast in a few minutes." Dad stood in the aisle, holding Hannah. "Do me a favor and wake Tabitha, please."

Cass jostled Tabitha's arm then pointed to Hannah. "How's she doing?" she asked Dad.

He nuzzled the baby's neck. "So far, so good. Of course,

we have a whole day of flying ahead of us. But we'll just take it one step at a time."

Yawning and stretching, Tabitha slowly opened her eyes. As they focused on Dad and Hannah, the corners of her mouth turned down in a grimace. "Has she been driving the passengers crazy with her crying?"

"No, she's been a perfect angel." Dad protectively cradled the baby's head against his chest. "Why do you always assume the worst when it comes to Hannah?"

"Maybe because you always assume the best." With a flounce, Tabitha rearranged her position. "As far as you're concerned, she can do no wrong."

Dad laughed. "Give her a break, will you? She's not even 2 months old. How much wrong can she do at this point?"

"Plenty," Tabitha muttered darkly. "She can keep people up half the night with her screeching. She can monopolize parents so they don't have time for their other children. Basically, she can disrupt an entire household."

"Sweetie, you're being—"

Dad was interrupted by the arrival of a crewmember carrying two breakfast trays. "Excuse me, sir. I need to set these down."

He moved out of her way and waited while Cass and Tabitha accepted the food with thanks. As the crewmember hurried away, Dad said to Tabitha, "We'll finish our discussion later. I need to get back to my seat so I can eat."

Tabitha nodded that she'd heard him, but didn't look up from fussing with her napkin and utensils.

"Brr," Cass joked as soon as Dad left. "Talk about giving someone the cold shoulder. The temperature must have dropped at least 30 degrees just now."

Tabitha shot her an exasperated look. "He makes me so mad, the way he fusses over Hannah all the time. You'd think he'd never had a kid before."

"Is that what you have against our baby sister?"

"Hannah's really not the problem. She's okay, for a sleeping, eating, pooping machine. Plus, she's pretty darn cute when she's not crying." Tabitha began spreading cream cheese on her bagel. "Dad's the one who gets on my nerves. I've said it before, but ever since Hannah arrived, it's like I don't exist. He lives and breathes for Hannah. Every now and then, he realizes I'm still hanging around so he pays me a teeny bit of attention. But then he goes right back to fawning all over the baby."

"My advice remains the same. Talk to him about it." Taking a bite of scrambled eggs, Cass rolled her eyes in bliss. "I don't know why people bust on airplane food. I love the stuff."

"You also think a peanut butter and banana sandwich is a gourmet meal," Tabitha drawled. "Face it, you don't have the most sophisticated tastes."

"I like you. Does that fall under the same category?" Cass turned to Tabitha with her most innocent expression, although an impish smile tugged at her lips.

"I sincerely hope Hannah doesn't develop your warped sense of humor," Tabitha said while Cass snickered. "You're so annoying sometimes."

"I know. I like to think of it as one of my charms."

Throughout the rest of the flight, when they weren't napping, their conversation ranged from subject to subject, never lighting long in one place. Logan, however, was a topic that Cass returned to time and time again.

"All right, Spencers—" Dad smiled at Cass, "and Devane, now that we have our luggage, let's move it out."

They had landed at Hickam Air Force Base in Hawaii and needed to get across town to the Honolulu Airport in order to catch the flight to Los Angeles. Loaded down with Hannah and various baby paraphernalia, Mom slumped in a chair while Cass, Tabitha, and Dad rounded up the suitcases. With the luggage assembled around them, the next task was to transport it to the front entrance so it could be piled into the shuttle leaving for the airport in ten minutes.

Hearing the distinction Dad made between her and the rest of the family, Cass frowned as she hefted the two closest suitcases. She knew he didn't mean anything by it, but it bothered her all the same.

I don't like being the only one with a different last name, she realized, shuffling behind Dad toward the entrance. *I don't even share the same name with my own mother and baby sister.*

Caught up in the hassle of getting everyone and the luggage on the same shuttle, Cass quickly forgot the issue. When she collapsed onto the seat beside Dad just as the shuttle pulled away from the sidewalk, sleep was the only thing on her mind.

The next 12 hours were a blur for Cass. Hannah decided to spend much of the flight to California expressing her irritation with the disruption of her normal routine. They took turns trying to soothe her, alternating between walking her up and down the aisle and crooning to her. Tabitha cringed under the glares from the other passengers, while Cass glared right back. In her opinion, if they couldn't put up with a little crying, it was just too bad.

It was a travel-weary group that staggered off the plane at the airport in Knoxville. Some of Cass' fatigue drained away at the sight of her grandparents, waiting for them with huge smiles on their faces. Hannah, having fallen asleep somewhere over Arkansas, didn't stir when Mom passed her to Papaw, who teared up at the sight of her.

"Laws, Sugar—" he kissed Mom's cheek, "I never thought I'd see the day when you'd place another young'un of yours in my arms. The Lord is good, and that's surely the truth."

Mamaw, who'd made the rounds of greeting everyone else, bustled over to Mom and Papaw. "John, quit hogging that child." She gave Mom a quick, hard hug. "I'd like to make my newest granddaughter's acquaintance, if you don't mind."

Papaw reluctantly surrendered Hannah to Mamaw's waiting arms. The moment Mamaw lowered her head to kiss the baby, Hannah's face puckered, and she let loose with a shriek guaranteed to shatter glass. Cass burst into side-splitting laughter.

"Does this kid have good sense or what?" she gasped. "Mamaw, she's not even 2 months, and she already has your number."

"What in the world are you talking about, child?" Mamaw winced as Hannah's wails reached a new decibel. "I'm a sweet, harmless old lady."

"Stop. You're killing me." Cass made a show of slapping her knee. "You're anything but sweet and harmless. But don't worry—" she flung her arm around Mamaw's shoulders and loudly smooched her cheek, "I love you, anyway. And so will Hannah." Frowning as the baby continued to cry, she added, "Maybe someday."

After the baggage had been collected, Papaw ushered them to the van he'd borrowed from Uncle Larry—Mom's brother—for the trip. It was a tight squeeze, but they finally managed to fit everyone in and headed northeast for the two-hour trip to Jonesborough.

Seated next to Cass in the middle row, Tabitha tapped her arm to get her attention. "Isn't it great to be back?"

Cass turned from the scenery flashing by the window. "It's better than great. I can't believe I'll actually be seeing Logan in a few short days. We're in the same time zone and everything." She laughed. "Come to think of it, we're even back on the same day, since we crossed over the International Dateline on the way to Hawaii."

"You'll also be seeing Janette," Tabitha reminded her. "And that won't be nearly as much fun as seeing Logan."

Cass brushed aside the comment. "I know how to deal with Jan. I've been through more crises with her than I care to count." She bumped shoulders with Tabitha. "Don't forget we're also going to be looking at colleges and making up our minds where we want to go."

Tabitha grinned. "Whatever the next two weeks hold, I have a feeling they're going to be very exciting."

"As in maybe even life-changing?" Cass asked in a dramatic voice, teasing her.

Tabitha regarded her with a somber gaze. "I wouldn't be at all surprised if that's the way it turns out. I have a sneaking suspicion God's about to show us a thing or two."

CHAPTER 26

"Cass, when are you coming over to see me?" Janette asked plaintively over the phone line early Sunday afternoon. "You've been in town a whole day, and we haven't gotten together yet."

Refusing to feel guilty, Cass pointed out in a reasonable tone, "If you'd been at church this morning, we could have seen each other then."

There was a long pause on Janette's end before she replied stiffly, "You know I don't go to church anymore. We talked about it when you were here last year."

"I know. I was hoping things had changed though." Stifling a sigh, Cass pushed her hand through her hair and glanced into the dining room where Mamaw had set out enough food to feed a small nation. "Look here's the deal. Mamaw invited the entire family for Sunday dinner, and we're ready to sit down to eat. As soon as we're done, I'll see if someone will let me borrow a car. I'll call you to let you know if I'm coming. If I can't, how about you head over here?"

"I should probably do that anyway," Jan grumbled. "Ever since Billy moved in, I'm embarrassed to invite people to the house. He's nothing but a lazy bum. All he does is watch television, drink beer, and order Mom and me around, usually at the top of his lungs."

"He sounds utterly delightful," Cass drawled. "I can't wait to meet him. If you'd rather come here though, that's fine. It's up to you."

After weighing the two options for a few seconds, Janette decided, "Ask about using a car. I want you to meet Billy so you understand what a total nightmare my life's become since Mom married him."

Cass promised to call the minute dinner was over and hung up. Dread settled in the pit of her stomach, threatening to ruin her appetite. She looked forward to visiting Jan with about as much enthusiasm as she did a trip to the dentist.

"Why so glum, chum?"

Tabitha appeared in the doorway, holding Aunt Linda and Uncle Larry's 4-month-old daughter, Rebecca, in her arms. The baby guzzled a bottle of formula as if it had been weeks, not hours, since she'd last eaten.

Cass made a face. "I just talked to Janette. She wants me to come over after we eat so I can meet her stepfather."

"Ooh, lucky you." Tabitha shifted the baby to her other arm and hastily popped the bottle back into Rebecca's mouth before the baby could voice her protest at having her meal interrupted. "Do you want me to come with you?"

Cass' expression brightened. "Would you?"

Nodding, Tabitha used her pinkie to wipe away a drool of formula that had escaped from the corner of Rebecca's mouth. "After all the horror stories I've heard about Billy, I'm kind of curious to see if he's as bad as Janette says he is."

"Don't let anybody ever tell you that you're not a terrific sister." Cass' voice brimmed with gratitude. "Anyone who'd volunteer to accompany me on a visit like this is all right in my book."

Tabitha laughed. "Gee, it's only taken me—what?—a year and a half to impress you? No one can say our relationship isn't growing by leaps and bounds."

Mamaw bustled into the living room to announce dinner was served. While Larry and Linda's three rambunctious boys made a beeline for the dining room, Cass and Tabitha hung back to follow more sedately with the adults.

"You seem to be enjoying our newest cousin," Cass observed as she and Tabitha brought up the rear of the line.

Tabitha gazed down at the baby whose frantic sucking had subsided to an occasional tug at the bottle. Her face softened with tenderness. "She's a sweetie, all right."

"Not sweeter than Hannah," Cass loyally defended their sister.

"It's not a competition." Tabitha glanced over at Hannah, who was propped up in her infant seat by the couch, fast asleep. "I don't know how to explain it. It's different with Rebecca. I'm not—"

"Jealous of her?" Cass suggested when Tabitha fumbled for the right word.

Tabitha's eyes flashed her irritation. "How many times do I have to tell you Hannah doesn't make me jealous?" she hissed.

"I guess until you finally convince me." Cass sashayed away from Tabitha and found an empty chair at the table.

After returning Rebecca to Aunt Linda, Tabitha sat down next to Cass. Under cover of the various conversations being conducted around the table, she muttered to her sister, "You think you're so smart, but you don't know what you're talking about."

"Oh, don't I?" Cass tossed her head and placed a finger against her lips when Tabitha started to argue. "Hush.

Papaw's about to say the blessing."

His eyes beaming, Papaw asked the family to hold hands while he prayed. Once the circle was complete, he bowed his head. "Heavenly Father, thank You for the food we are about to eat and for the hands that prepared it. Thank You for the rich treasure that is this family. Bless this meal to our nourishment and us to Your service. In Jesus' precious name, amen."

A chorus of "amens" echoed around the table.

Before releasing Tabitha's hand, Cass leaned over to murmur, "Sorry about giving you a hard time. Blame it on jet lag. I'm not myself when my body rhythms are all out of whack."

Tabitha treated her to a look of wide-eyed innocence. "Gee, I didn't notice any difference from the way you usually act."

"Ha-ha. You're so adorable when you're trying to be funny." Cass accepted the bowl of mashed potatoes that her cousin, Andy, seated to her left, handed to her. "Thanks, squirt."

"You'd better watch your step," Tabitha warned, "or you'll find yourself heading over to Jan's by yourself."

Mom looked up from her place across the table. "When are you planning on visiting Janette?"

"After lunch, if that's okay." Cass glanced around the table at her relatives with a pleading expression. "And if somebody will loan me a car."

"Are you sure you remember how to drive?" Uncle Larry joked. "After all, it's been a year since you were behind the wheel."

"Of course I remember. It's like riding a bike. Once you learn, you don't ever forget." Cass fixed her gaze on him, taking his teasing as a good sign. "If I promise to drive five miles under the speed limit, will you let me use the van?"

"Laws, child, don't beg," Mamaw snapped before Uncle Larry could reply. "It's unseemly. Besides, your aunt and uncle will be heading home after we eat. You may borrow our car, if it's all right with your folks."

Cass turned expectantly toward Mom. "Can I?"

"May I?" Mom corrected her.

Cass rolled her eyes. "Okay, may I?"

Mom silently consulted Dad, who nodded. "That will be fine." Her brows arched. "You and Tabitha will both be going? Janette doesn't have a problem with that?"

"She doesn't know yet," Cass blithely informed her mother. "I'll tell her when I call her back."

Beside her, Tabitha giggled. "I'd like to see her face when she hears I'll be tagging along. Of course, it's only fair that you share your friends here with me since I had to include you in all my activities with my friends when you first moved to Kwaj."

"Aren't you over that yet?" Cass grinned to let Tabitha know she was kidding. "Boy, you sure know how to hold a grudge."

Before Tabitha could respond, Mom laughed and jeered good-naturedly, "Look who's talking. You, my dear Cassandra, are a champion grudge-holder."

After the others shared a good laugh, the conversation moved on to different topics. All too soon, the last bite of apple pie had been eaten, and it was time for Uncle Larry and Aunt Linda to leave so they could put their two youngest children down for naps. After waving good-bye from the porch, Cass headed straight to the phone and dialed Jan's number. Her friend picked up on the first ring.

"Yeah?" came her surly greeting.

"What kind of way is that to answer the phone?" Cass chided.

"Sorry," Janette sullenly apologized. "Billy and I had

another fight. He thinks, just because he married my mother, he can tell me what to do."

"Is now not a good time to come over then?" There was a part of Cass that hoped Jan would postpone the visit.

"Nah, it's fine." Jan emitted a short, humorless laugh. "If you wait for a good time to visit, you'll never come. Billy and I are always fighting. We can't be in the same room together without somebody getting mad."

"Jan, I'm sorry. It sounds awful," Cass said, honestly sympathetic.

"Awful is putting it mildly. It's way worse than that." Janette's tone was bitter. "But you'll see for yourself in a few minutes. I take it you managed to talk somebody into lending you a car."

"Mamaw offered me theirs. Uh—" Cass hesitated, knowing Janette wouldn't be pleased with what she was about to say, "Tabitha's coming with me. She asked if she could, and I didn't have the heart to turn her down."

Cass squirmed at the guilt that stabbed her conscience. Technically, she'd told the truth, but she'd deliberately misrepresented the discussion so it sounded like she didn't want Tabitha to accompany her.

"Yuck! Does she have to?" Janette whined. "I was hoping we'd have some time to ourselves."

"We will," Cass assured her. "Except for the trip up to West Point, I'll be here another 12 days. We'll have lots of chances to get together."

"Okay," Janette said grudgingly. "I guess I can put up with her for an hour or so. I mean, you have to live with her 365 days a year so who am I to complain?"

Cass decided to let her comment pass. It was true that, in the beginning, she'd griped to Jan about Tabitha. Apparently, her friend hadn't noticed her relationship with Tabitha had improved 100 percent from those early days.

"Great. We'll be there in about 10 minutes."

"I can't wait to see you."

Hanging up, Cass mused about the difference a year made. When she'd left to return to Kwajalein last February, she and Jan had barely been on speaking terms. Now her friend was looking forward to seeing her.

Go figure, she thought as she went in search of Tabitha to tell her to get ready to go.

Fifteen minutes later, Cass and Tabitha stood on the front step of the Foster house, waiting for someone to answer the doorbell. Just as she about to ring again, the door was yanked open by a man Cass assumed was the infamous Billy.

"Who are you and what do you want?" he growled.

Cass gulped and forced herself to look up into his unshaven face. She wrinkled her nose at the smell of beer emanating from him. "We're here to see Jan."

Turning away from the door, Billy bellowed over his shoulder. "Janette! Get your lazy butt down here."

Behind Cass, Tabitha made a sound of distaste. Cass hoped Billy hadn't heard her. She wasn't at all eager to have him turn his ill temper on them.

A moment later, Janette appeared in the hallway and muscled her way past Billy, who snorted and stomped away. Jan waited until he was out of earshot before speaking.

"Isn't he a sweetheart?" she muttered.

"An absolute prince of a guy," Cass agreed, her voice dripping with sarcasm.

Stepping aside, Janette motioned for the sisters to enter. "Come on in. My mother is dying to say hello to you."

Cass and Tabitha exchanged wary glances. Neither of them looked forward to another encounter with Billy.

As if reading their minds, Jan assured them, "I'll take

you straight back to the kitchen where Mom is, then right up to my room. With any luck, we won't run into Billy."

"All right." Cass walked into the house, followed closely by Tabitha.

Jan ushered them down the hall to the kitchen where her mother sat at the table, reading the Sunday paper. She jumped up when she spotted Cass and hurried to her with open arms.

"Let me hug you, you sweet thing! Long time, no see. I've missed having you around the house."

Cass enthusiastically returned her hug. "I've missed you too, Mrs. Foster. Uh ... I mean ..." For the life of her, she couldn't remember Billy's last name.

"It's Mrs. Clark now." Releasing Cass, she patted her cheek then turned to Tabitha. "And this must be your stepsister. I didn't go to your mother's wedding so I never got a chance to meet her."

Tabitha awkwardly shook hands with Janette's mother.

"Why don't you girls sit down and—" Mrs. Clark began.

"Hey, what's going on?" Billy barged into the kitchen, in search of another beer. "You gals fixin' to throw yourselves a hen party?" He cackled at his own humor.

Mrs. Clark flushed a bright red. "Cass, Tabitha, have you met my husband?"

"He ... uh ... answered the door." Cass kept a nervous eye on Billy as he shuffled to the refrigerator. Tabitha moved closer to her side.

"Yeah, and they're about as impressed with him as I am," Janette sneered.

If Cass could have vanished into thin air, she would have, taking Tabitha with her. "We didn't ... I mean ... we never said ..."

"Stupid kids." Billy slammed the refrigerator door so hard that the tinkling of bottles from within could be heard. Twisting the cap off the bottle of beer in his hand, he stalked to the door leading back to the living room. "I don't give a rip what y'all think of me."

While Mrs. Clark groaned and hung her head in her hands, the girls escaped to Jan's room. The moment the door closed behind them, Cass whirled to face her friend.

"Why in the world would you say something like that?" she blazed. "Now Billy thinks we don't like him."

"Do you?" Jan asked coolly.

"Of course not," Cass huffed. "But that's beside the point. You didn't have any right to put words in our mouth."

"So sue me." Pulling out her desk chair, Janette sat down and scowled up at Cass.

After several seconds of a tense stand-off, Cass decided to let the matter drop. "Forget it. The damage has already been done." She forced herself to smile. "I definitely see why you're less than thrilled to have Billy as a stepfather. He's so crude he makes a gorilla look like a perfect gentleman."

"Yeah, I didn't luck out like you did with Steve." Jan glanced in Tabitha's direction and nodded curtly. "By the way, hi. Nice to see you again."

Tabitha managed a wan smile. "Same here."

Janette shot her a "yeah, right" smirk before turning her attention back to Cass. "I guess now you understand why I'm counting the days until I graduate and can move out."

Cass crossed the room to the bed and sat down beside Tabitha. "Is your mother happy with him?"

Jan shrugged. "As far as I can tell. No accounting for taste, huh?"

"How are you coping with the situation?" Cass asked. "Have you talked to a guidance counselor? Or maybe Pastor Wilson?"

Jan's snort was all the answer Cass needed. "Like I'm going to spill my guts to a guidance counselor. Get real."

"What about Pastor Wilson?" Cass persisted.

"How many times do I have to tell you I don't go to church anymore?" Janette glanced down at her hands. "I know church is important to you, but it doesn't work for me. I guess I've outgrown it."

"But, Jan—" Cass leaned forward to peer earnestly at her friend, "Christ is the only one you can count on to get you through stuff like this. I guarantee you that praying and relying on God for—"

Jan held up her hand to ward off any more conversation on the subject. "Look, I appreciate your concern. I really do. But the only thing guaranteed to change the situation is time. Graduation is a little over four months away. There's nothing I can do until then. But the minute I walk across the stage and get my diploma, I'm out of here. *Sayonara. Arrivaderci.*"

"Where are you planning to go?" Cass studied her friend with worried eyes. She doubted Janette had thought it through.

"Lauren and I are getting an apartment." Janette's smug smile indicated she was pleased with herself. "Lauren already has a job, and I'm going to start looking for one this week. Between us, we'll make enough to get a nice place."

"What about college?" Tabitha couldn't resist asking.

"It's not high up on our priority list at the moment." Janette dismissed her query with a breezy wave. "All we're interested in for now is moving out so we get to call our own shots. We've had it up to here—" she slashed a hand across her neck, "with parents telling us what to do. We're ready to bust loose."

The longer Jan talked, the lower Cass' heart sank. It seemed that the gulf separating them widened with each word. She had a difficult time recalling how close they once were.

It's amazing what different paths our lives have taken, she mused as Jan droned on and on about her plans for the future. *As usual, Lord, You knew what You were doing when you had me move away. Our friendship would have broken up anyway. At least, this way, I wasn't around to watch it fall apart. When am I going to get it through my thick head that You always know what's best?*

Cass and Tabitha spent an uncomfortable hour with Janette before finally making an excuse to leave. As they hurried across the lawn to the car, Tabitha pretended to mop her brow in relief.

"Whew! I'm glad that's over."

"You and me both, Sis." Cass opened the driver's door and slid in behind the wheel. "She's one mixed-up chick."

Nodding vigorously, Tabitha buckled her seatbelt. "I don't even like her, and I feel sorry for her because she's so messed up." She waited until Cass started the car and pulled away from the curb before asking, "Are you going to see her again?"

Cass sighed. "I guess I'll have to. The thought doesn't exactly thrill me though. We have nothing in common anymore. I'll keep trying to talk her into going back to church, but I doubt I'll have much success."

"Good luck," Tabitha muttered pessimistically. "Remind me to be busy any time the two of you plan to get together. Even watching Dad dote on Hannah is better than spending time with Jan."

Over the course of the next few days Cass, Tabitha, and Dad toured the several colleges within an hour's driving time of Jonesborough. The more campuses they visited, the more excited Cass and Tabitha grew about the prospect of going to college. By the time they checked out the fourth school, they'd reached at least one decision. They were determined to go to the same college.

"That's wonderful," Mom approved when Tabitha made the announcement at dinner one night. "I'm glad you girls enjoy each other's company so much that you want to stay together."

Cass grinned at Mom from across the table. "Hard to believe, isn't it? Who says God doesn't work miracles anymore?"

After the family laughed, Papaw asked, "Are you ladies leaning toward any particular school yet?"

Tabitha exchanged a smile with Cass, whose nod said it was okay to answer. "Milligan's at the top of the list, but we still have two more colleges to check out."

"I vote for Milligan," Mamaw said. "It's a Christian school. It has an excellent academic reputation. Best of all, it's only a hop, skip, and a jump away. I'd get to see you whenever I wanted."

"There's one huge strike against Milligan," Cass quipped, earning herself a snort from Mamaw. "Dad, how about we start looking at places a little farther away? Say, four or five hours?"

"I propose y'all take a day off from touring colleges tomorrow," Mom said. "Mamaw and I want to take you girls clothes shopping. Tabitha, I thought we'd buy you a dress for the Valentine formal."

Tabitha grinned. "Really? I thought we'd decided I'd wear the dress I wore last year since Sam hasn't seen it."

"We did," Mom said. "But I got to thinking that we're here, and it would be fun to look for a store-bought, rather than homemade, gown. What do you say?"

"I say, why wait until tomorrow?" Tabitha bounced excitedly in her chair. "Let's go after supper. How late does the mall stay open?"

Mom glanced at Mamaw, who shrugged. "Until 9:00. I suppose we could head over there tonight. I'll feed Hannah, and she should be okay for a couple of hours."

Cass frowned. "Hello? What about me? I'm not going to the dance, and you know how much I hate shopping for clothes. Surely you don't expect me to tag along while Tabitha tries on formals, do you?"

"Of course you're coming," Mamaw replied before Mom could. "Your mother and I want to spend some time with you girls. If you don't want to watch Tabitha try on dresses, we can check out the new sneakers at that sports store you like so well."

Cass couldn't help laughing. "What do you know about sneakers?"

"Nothing," Mamaw shot back with a twinkle in her eyes. "You can show me what to look for. I'm not to old to learn."

"You're not too old, period." Cass smiled fondly. "You're as sassy as a teenager."

"See what a bad influence you are on me?" Mamaw reached for the jam to spread on a biscuit. "Do I take it you've decided to grace us with your presence?"

"I'd be crazy to pass up the chance to watch you try on a pair of Nikes." Cass spooned up a hefty helping of beef stew. "Count me in."

Their trip to the mall stretched to almost three hours. In that time, they managed to find a gown for Tabitha, a new outfit for Cass to wear when she visited Logan, and ice cream at the food court. When they returned home, they were worn out, but even Cass was pleased with what they'd accomplished.

Slipping into bed that night, Cass shivered in anticipation. *Only two more days until I see Logan. Father, I don't want to wish time away, but I can't wait to leave. Friday morning can't come fast enough for me.*

The next day, Tabitha and Dad headed across town to visit with his parents. Busy packing for the trip to New York, Cass begged off, as did Mom, who was concerned that Hannah was coming down with a cold.

To Tabitha's disgust, the baby's fussiness had kept the household up half the night. Recalling Hannah's piercing wails, Tabitha heaved a long-suffering sigh. Dad glanced across the seat at her.

"What was that for?" he queried.

"I was remembering how annoying Hannah was last night." Her mouth twisting into a grimace, Tabitha stared out the car window at the bleak winter scenery. "Honestly! I don't know why people have kids. They're nothing but trouble."

"Aw, Hannah's not that bad. I think she's been a real trouper about the trip." Dad turned left at the traffic light.

"Of course you do." Tabitha couldn't keep the bitterness out of her voice. "You're always sticking up for her. Meanwhile, I'm stuck here with her crying and carrying on while you and Cass go traipsing off to New York."

"Actually, I was going to talk to you about that." Dad pulled into the driveway of his parents' house, shut off the car, and turned to Tabitha. "Mom and I discussed it last night, and I'd love to have you join us on the trip to West Point."

"Me?" Tabitha's curious look changed to one of suspicion. "Why? I don't have anyone at the Academy."

"Because—" Dad playfully tweaked her nose, "I'd appreciate your company. Cass will be spending every waking moment with Logan. What am I supposed to do on my own for two days?"

"Are you sure you want to bring me?" Tabitha sniffed, unbuckling her seatbelt. "Wouldn't you rather take Hannah?"

"Absolutely not," Dad assured her with a wink. "You're a much better conversationalist than she is."

Opening the door, Tabitha shot him a saucy look over her shoulder. "I need to think about it. I'll let you know tonight."

Before she could climb out of the car, Dad reached over to take her hand. "All kidding aside, Toots, I'd really like you to come. We haven't spent much time together since Hannah arrived."

"And whose fault is that?" Tabitha slid her hand out of Dad's and stood up. "Like I said, I'll get back to you."

Her answer turned out to be yes, and, for the rest of the evening, she tried to figure out what to pack. Thrilled with the news that Tabitha would be accompanying them, Cass offered to do whatever she could to help Tabitha get ready. Without a single complaint, she did a load of laundry for Tabitha and helped her choose what clothes to bring. Exhausted, Tabitha and Cass finally fell into bed at midnight.

Four hours later, Cass woke to Dad shaking her awake. Since he wanted to be on the road by 5:00, she and Tabitha hurried through their showers and, still half-asleep, spooned cereal into their mouths like a couple of robots. After kissing Mom good-bye, they stumbled to the car, and Dad pulled out of the driveway at exactly two minutes to five.

While Tabitha stretched out in the backseat, Cass, too keyed-up to sleep, sat straight as an arrow in the passenger seat beside Dad. Her gaze restlessly scanned the countryside flashing by the window.

"I can't believe we're actually on our way," she breathed. "In a little over 12 hours, I'll see Logan for the first time in seven months." She smiled as excitement tingled up her spine. "I really, really appreciate you doing this."

"Aw, what are dads for?" Dad flashed her a boyish grin. "I was young once. I remember what it was like."

Cass' eyes twinkled with mischief. "You mean, way back in the Dark Ages when you dated Mom in high school?"

"Yup, years and years and years ago. As a matter of fact, I believe it was right after high schools were invented," Dad returned the teasing. "Our class dreamed up the whole prom idea. And senior skip day?" He polished his knuckles on his sweatshirt. "We thought that up too."

"Wow, I'm impressed," Cass drawled. "Generations of teens since then thank you."

"It was the least we could do." Dad fiddled with a couple of knobs on the dashboard. "Are you warm enough? Would you like me to turn the heat up?"

"I'm fine." Yawning, Cass stuffed her hands in her jacket pockets. "So tell me what it was like to date Mom. I've heard her version of events. It'd be fun to hear yours."

For the next hour, Cass was entertained by Dad's stroll down memory lane. He recalled his first date with Mom, the first time they held hands, and their first kiss. Just as he was getting to their break-up, Tabitha woke up in the back seat.

Pretending to be a cranky 5-year-old, she whined, "Are we there yet? How much longer?"

Dad smiled at her in the rearview mirror. "Only another 10 hours or so." At her groan, he offered, "Would you like me to pull off at the next fast food restaurant and get you a sausage biscuit?"

"You'd do that for little ol' me?" Tabitha pressed a hand to her chest and fluttered her lashes. "Why, Daddy dearest, a sausage biscuit would be positively divine."

"Don't pull that southern belle act on me," he good-naturedly growled. "Don't forget, I grew up down here. I'm immune to it."

Glancing over her shoulder, Cass shared an amused smile with Tabitha. "Yeah, right. Mom uses it all the time, and it always works. You may talk tough, but you're a big pushover."

"Maybe with your mother," Dad stubbornly insisted. "But nobody else gets away with it."

"Whatever." Cass rolled her eyes then pointed to a sign coming up on the right. "Look, there's a McDonald's at the next exit. They make great sausage biscuits. Hint, hint." She nudged Dad and winked broadly.

Laughing, he switched on the blinker.

They spent the rest of the trip in idle conversation, punctuated by frequent catnaps on the part of Cass and Tabitha. All thought of sleep was abandoned, however, the moment Dad crossed the state line from New Jersey into New York. Cass, who'd traded places with Tabitha, let out a whoop in the back seat.

"It won't be long now," she said with a grin. "I'm supposed to meet Logan in Grant Hall at 7:00."

"That'll give us enough time to check in at the Thayer Hotel and get something to eat. It'll also give us enough time to find out exactly where Grant Hall is." Tilting his head first to one side then the other, Dad eased the cramped muscles in his neck and shoulders. "I'm looking forward to seeing West Point. The place is brimming with history."

"It's also brimming with guys." Cass poked Tabitha in the back. "What do you say? You want me to ask Logan to set you up with one of his friends?"

"No, thanks." Laughing ruefully, Tabitha shook her head. "I'm having a hard enough time, trying to juggle two guys. Adding another one to the mix would probably do me in."

By the time Dad pulled into the parking lot of the Thayer Hotel on the grounds of the Military Academy, night had fallen. Climbing slowly out of the car, Cass gasped at the gust of icy wind that hit her full in the face.

"Brr." She pulled the collar up on her jacket and lowered her head into its meager protection. "Logan warned me it was cold, but this is ridiculous. How do people survive up here?"

"They don't stand around outside complaining about the weather," Dad cheerfully informed her. "They're smart enough to get inside as quickly as possible."

"Well, duh. Silly me." Cass hit her forehead with the palm of her hand. "Thanks for the advice. Otherwise, I might have stayed out here so long I turned into an icicle."

They grabbed their bags and jogged across the parking lot to the hotel. The billow of warm air that enveloped them as they entered the lobby brought sighs of relief from Cass and Tabitha.

"At least the place is heated." Tabitha shivered, despite her coat, scarf, and gloves. "Remind me never to live north of the Mason-Dixon line."

While Cass and Tabitha tried not to stare at the cadets milling about the lobby waiting for their dates, Dad checked in. When he was finished, he ushered them to the nearest elevator and held the doors so they could enter. The moment the doors whooshed shut, Cass and Tabitha collapsed against the wall.

"Did you see those guys?" Tabitha fanned herself. "Do they look gorgeous in their uniforms or what?"

"Just think. If all goes according to plan, Sam will be wearing one come July." Cass bumped shoulders with

Tabitha. "You could have your very own cadet."

"Oh, brother." Feigning disgust, Dad made a face. "I wish your mother were here. I'm not up to speed on how to handle girlish infatuations."

"What's there to handle?" Cass waved aside his concern. "All we plan to do is look and drool."

The elevator dinged their floor, and the doors slid open to reveal a dimly-lit hallway. After a brief hesitation, Dad turned left and led the girls to the third room on the right. Once inside, Cass immediately crossed the floor to peer out the window.

"Hey, cool! The room overlooks the Hudson River." She squinted through the glass. "I can't tell if it's frozen or not. Logan wrote that it's been known to freeze solid. Can you imagine it getting cold enough to freeze an entire river?"

"Around here?" Tabitha dropped her suitcase on the bed closer to the window and moved to the radiator to bask in its heat. "Absolutely."

Since it was already after 5:00, Cass claimed the bathroom first so she could shower and dress. She'd just stepped out of the tub and wrapped a towel around herself when there was a knock at the door.

"Oh, Cassandra," Tabitha singsonged, "there's somebody on the phone for you."

She was instantly reduced to a mass of quivering jelly. It took all the will power she could muster not to yank open the door and race to the phone.

"Tell him to hold on a sec." Cass shrugged into her robe and tied the belt, not caring that she was still wet. "Okay—" she opened the door "here I am."

The phone sat on the table between the two beds. Taking a deep breath, Cass picked up the receiver. "Logan?"

"Of course. Who else do you know up here?" came his teasing response. "I've been calling every 15 minutes to see if you'd checked in yet. I can't tell you how great it is to hear your voice and know you're just down the road."

"You don't have to. I know exactly how you feel." Cass pressed a shaky hand to her throat. "Are we still on for 7:00?"

"Actually, it turns out I can meet you at 6:00. Can you make it by then?"

"Wild horses couldn't keep me away." Cass whipped the towel off her head and began finger-combing her wet hair. "Here, talk to Dad and tell him how to get to Grant Hall."

Without saying good-bye, she handed the phone to Dad and dashed to the bathroom, determined to be ready to leave in a half hour.

When Cass emerged from the bathroom 25 minutes later, Dad wolf-whistled while Tabitha enthusiastically applauded.

"You look lovely." Retrieving Cass' jacket from where she'd tossed it on the bed, Dad held it for her as she put it on. "Logan won't believe his eyes."

Too impatient to wait for the elevator, Cass insisted they take the stairs down to the lobby. If anything, the outside temperature had dropped another 10 degrees, but Cass didn't care. All that mattered was that she'd be seeing Logan in just a few minutes.

Dad drove past a row of stately brick houses on the left. To the right was a sidewalk, bordered by a stone wall. Gray granite buildings loomed ahead. Cass sat tensely in the back seat, silently taking it all in.

So this is Logan's home for the next three-and-a-half years, she mused. *This place has become as familiar to him as Kwaj is to me.* She shook her head. *Weird.*

Following Logan's directions, Dad parked the car in a lot beneath one of the gray buildings and steered the girls up and across the street to another building with massive wooden doors. Tall windows lined the length of the building, spilling light onto the sidewalk. Carved above the doors were the words, *Grant Hall*.

Cass' heart executed a double flip, then a reverse cartwheel in her chest. Logan was somewhere behind those doors. *Wait a minute! No, he wasn't.* A cadet detached himself from the shadows and hurried toward the family with a broad grin.

"You made it!" Logan's voice rang with joy. Although he nodded to Dad and Tabitha, he had eyes only for Cass. "It's great to see you."

Recalling West Point's ban on public displays of affection, Cass refrained from throwing herself into Logan's arms, as she longed to do. Instead, she drank in the sight of him, marveling at how mature he looked. He was no longer the boy who'd left Kwajalein seven months earlier.

"You look—" she fumbled for the right word to express her feelings, "incredible. No, even better than incredible. You're—"

"A hunk," Tabitha completed the sentence for her. Propping her hands on hips, she studied Logan for a full five seconds then gave a satisfied nod. "Yup, it's definite. You've become a genuine, full-fledged hunk. Way to go, buddy."

Her teasing produced laughs all around. Logan held open the door for them and escorted them into Grant Hall. Scattered about the large room were several cadets and their dates, conversing quietly as they sat on leather chairs and couches.

Cass' dazzled eyes took in the scene then returned to Logan. He looked even better in the light.

"So—" she tried to get her foggy brain to start working properly, but all she could do was gawk at Logan, "what are the plans for the evening?"

"Captain Howell—that's my sponsor—and his wife

invited us to dinner. He said to call whenever we're ready, and he'll come pick us up. Then I thought we might go to a movie. Or flick," Logan added with a smile, "as they call it around here." He suddenly appeared anxious. "If that's okay with you."

"We could do nothing, and I'd be perfectly happy," Cass assured him. "As long as I'm with you, I don't care what we do."

Dad cleared his throat and tugged on Tabitha's sleeve. "I believe that's our cue to take off. Unless you're of a mind to stay and listen to these two lovebirds coo at each other."

Tabitha pretended to gag. "Please, get me out of here. They're so sweet my teeth are starting to ache." She waggled her fingers at the couple. "Have fun, you two."

"Before we go—" placing a hand on Tabitha's arm, Dad turned to Logan, "what time do I need to be back here to get Cass?"

"I have to be in at 11:00. Let's say we meet you out front at 10:45." Logan grinned at Cass. "I don't want to waste a single minute of our time together."

"I agree with you 100 percent." Her grin matched his for brilliance.

Snorting, Tabitha motioned to Dad. "We'd better get out of here before they start making goo-goo eyes at one another. That's not an image I want in my head."

With a wave, Dad and Tabitha left. Alone for the first time in seven months, Cass and Logan exchanged longing stares.

"I'd like nothing better right now than to give you a good, long hug," Logan murmured.

Cass drew a shaky breath. "The feeling's mutual. But just seeing you is almost good enough."

"I don't know how I'm going to let you leave Sunday." Logan ran his hand over his buzz-cut hair. "It's going to be—"

"Shh." Cass shook her head. "Don't talk about it. Let's make the most of the time we have. We'll worry about Sunday when it comes."

"You're right." Logan visibly relaxed. "As usual." He nodded at the phone on a nearby table. "I guess I should call Captain Howell." Leaning down, he placed his mouth close to Cass' ear. "Maybe we can figure out how to hold hands in the car without getting caught."

Cass batted her eyelashes at him. "My, my, Cadet Russell," she purred, "aren't you the sneaky one? I like that in a guy."

CHAPTER 27

Leaving Grant Hall, Dad and Tabitha headed to the town of Highland Falls. A couple of hundred yards outside the main gate, Dad spotted a sign for Schades Delicatessen and pulled into an empty parking space across the street.

"What do you say we try some real New York food?" he suggested to Tabitha.

She shrugged. "At this point, food is food. My stomach's been rumbling so loud, I thought they were shooting off cannons back on the post."

Once inside the deli, the tantalizing aromas emanating from the kitchen elicited another round of growls from Tabitha's stomach. Catching Dad's eye, she giggled.

"Sorry to be such an embarrassment."

"Don't worry about it." Dad guided her to a booth at the other end of the crowded restaurant. "If you could hear my stomach, you'd know it echoed your sentiments."

After studying the menu for several minutes, Dad decided to order a pastrami sandwich on rye while Tabitha opted for a calzone. When the waiter delivered their drinks, Dad lifted his glass in a toast. Tabitha followed suit, touching her glass to his with a faint clink.

"Here's to a safe trip and the fun of being together." Dad

smiled over the rim of his glass before taking a long swallow.

"It has been a long time since we've done anything together. Just the two of us, I mean." Tabitha sipped her Coke, then set it down on the red-and-white checkered tablecloth.

Dad shot her a wary glance. "I suppose you hold Hannah responsible for that."

"Well, naturally." Tabitha sounded more matter-of-fact than upset. "Everything changed when she showed up."

"I take it you mean for the worse." Dad toyed with the wrapper Tabitha had taken off her straw, coiling it around his finger.

"In some ways, yes." Tabitha realized if she were going to be honest, it was now or never.

"Such as?" Dad inquired softly.

Inhaling deeply, Tabitha blurted in a rush all the grievances she'd bottled up for the past two months. "Such as you spending all your time with her and practically ignoring me. Plus, you don't remember a single thing from when I was a baby. Mom compares Hannah and Cass all the time. But it's like you blanked everything out from my early childhood. I can't decide if it's because you didn't help Beth out the way you do Mom or because you—" she hesitated, choking on the words, "you love Hannah more than you loved me."

Dad slowly removed the straw wrapper from his finger and took his time flattening it on the table. "Whew." He expelled a long whoosh of pent-up breath. "That's quite a list of complaints. I'm not sure where to start. First off, I'm sorry I've been neglecting you. I'd forgotten how much time and energy one tiny baby requires. I probably have gone a little overboard though. I promise I'll try to do better at remembering I have two daughters."

Tabitha made a show of looking around then leaning across the table to warn in a whisper, "You'd better not let Cass hear you say that. She'd remind you loud and clear that you have three —count 'em, three—daughters."

Nodding solemnly, Dad agreed, "You're right. Thanks for the heads up. Anyway, on to your second concern. I haven't reminisced about your early childhood because I didn't want to upset you. I thought it might stir up painful memories of Beth abandoning you, especially if you compared her behavior to Mom's complete devotion to Hannah."

"Actually, it had the opposite effect." Using her straw, Tabitha swirled the ice in her soda. "Between Beth taking a hike and you acting like you'd blocked out everything about my early years, I started to think there must have been something really wrong with me. I figured I must have been one rotten kid to have caused so much trauma."

"Oh, sweetie, no." Dad reached across the table to place his hand over Tabitha's. "Nothing could be further from the truth. You were a terrific baby. In a lot of ways, you were much easier than Hannah. I have wonderful memories of you, and I'll prove it by telling you every last one of them before the weekend is over."

"Really?" The corners of Tabitha's mouth slowly curved into a smile. "Does that mean you don't love Hannah more because she's the baby you had with Mom?" She ducked her head as she admitted gruffly, "That's been my deepest, darkest fear. That maybe you don't love me as much because of Beth."

"Believe me—" Dad squeezed Tabitha's hand for emphasis, "I love you and Hannah exactly the same. I thank God everyday for blessing Mom and me with Hannah. I also thank Him everyday for blessing me with you. You're my first child. You're the one who made me a father. For that reason alone, you hold a very special place in my heart.

Add to that all the other reasons why I love you, and you've got yourself a whole truckload of love."

A relieved giggle escaped Tabitha's lips. "In other words, I should quit worrying about Hannah replacing me in your affections."

"Precisely." Dad released her hand and sat back in his chair. "Our relationship—" he pointed first to himself then to Tabitha, "is in a different season than Hannah's and mine, but different doesn't mean bad. Mom and I have been discussing the passage in Ecclesiastes which talks about the fact that there's a time for everything and a season for every activity under the sun. I believe it's true of relationships, as well. It would be mighty strange if you and I had the same relationship now as we did when you were little."

Laughing, Tabitha nodded her agreement. "I hadn't thought of it like that, but you're right." Her eyes lit up as a waiter approached the table with their orders. "Speaking of there being a time for everything, I do believe the time has come for me to find out what a calzone tastes like."

Dad waited until the waiter had set down the food and left before quipping, "One of the verses in Ecclesiastes says there's a time to mourn and a time to dance. Once you sink your teeth into the calzone, I think you'll agree it's time to dance."

"In that case—" picking up her knife and fork, Tabitha pretended she was ready to dig in, "hurry up and say the blessing. I can't wait to break into a jig."

CHAPTER 28

While Dad spent Saturday showing Tabitha West Point and telling her stories from her early childhood, Cass and Logan alternated between savoring their time together and dreading the upcoming separation the next day.

Early in the afternoon, they decided to brave the cold and walk to Trophy Point, overlooking the Hudson. Cass longed to take Logan's hand and rest her head on his shoulder as they gazed down at the river, but contented herself with tucking her arm through his. Logan glanced down at her when she sighed.

"Are you cold?" he asked. "Do you want to head back to Grant Hall?"

"I'm okay." Cass allowed herself a short chuckle. "Although I will admit it is a bit nippy for someone who's used to temperatures in the 80s. No," she went on, "I sighed because I was wondering when I'd get to see you again. I guess it won't be until the summer, and then only for a short while. West Point sure doesn't give you a lot of time off."

"That's because they're afraid we'll come to our senses and not return," Logan joked. He pressed Cass' arm close to his side. "Which leads me to something I've been thinking about lately, but especially since last night. Seeing you again has made me realize how much I care for you. In a way, it's easier to be apart while you're on Kwaj because there's no chance of us getting together. But come the summer, it's going to drive me crazy knowing you're down in Tennessee. What's that phrase? So near and yet so far? Something like that. Anyway," he continued, "even though you'll be within driving distance, I still won't be allowed to come see you, and that'll make it worse somehow."

"I'll come see you as often as I can," Cass assured him.

"Realistically, that won't be very often." Logan stared down at the river. "You'll be busy with school. Plus, it costs money to drive up here and spend the weekend, money that most college students don't have to spare."

"So you're saying it's hopeless?" Cass didn't like thinking the prospects for their getting together on a regular basis were as bleak as he made them out to be.

"No. That's where what I've been thinking about comes in." Logan guided Cass to a nearby bench, and they sat down. "Hear me out before you say anything, okay?" When she nodded, he went on, "I've gone on-line and collected information about colleges in East Tennessee. The state schools are pretty reasonable. I figure I could quit the Academy this summer and transfer to one of them. That way, we can go to schools within a few miles of each other."

Although Cass' imagination began to race at the possibility of the two of them being together, her practical nature asserted itself. "How would you afford a regular college? You came to West Point because your family didn't have the money to send you to school."

"I've been looking into scholarships and student loans," Logan explained. "Between that and working, I think I could swing it. I'll be honest. It wouldn't be easy, but it sure would be worth it, if it meant we'd be together." He peered eagerly at Cass. "So, what do you think?"

"It's a wonderful idea," she replied, hardly daring to hope it might actually come to pass. "I can't think of anything I'd like better than to have you close enough that we could see each other every day."

Logan expelled a pent-up breath, causing a cloud to billow around his head in the frigid air. "That's what I hoped you'd say. I don't want us to be apart one second longer than we have to."

Cass' forehead puckered in a frown. "What will your folks say? Or have you already talked it over with them?"

Logan shook his head. "Not yet. I wanted to see what you thought about the idea first." He rubbed his hand along the side of his gray wool trousers. "They probably won't like it at first. They're proud of me being here. But, ultimately, it's my decision. I won't be asking them for money, plus I'll be 19, so they can't forbid me to quit."

A shiver of excitement tingled up Cass' spine, and she turned to Logan with shining eyes. "Just think, we could be living in the same town by the fall."

"I know." A broad grin stretched across Logan's face. "It makes me want to get right to work on choosing a college and finding enough funds to go there."

"I'm supposed to meet Dad and Tabitha at the hotel at 4:00," Cass reminded him. "Maybe you could go on-line for awhile before Dad drops me off at Eisenhower Hall at 5:30."

"I could do that." Logan's expression became thoughtful. "Uh ... are you going to tell your dad about this?"

"Sure. Why not?" The wind picked up, and Cass burrowed deeper into her jacket, shoving her hands into the pockets.

"What if he talks to my folks before I do?" Logan worried.

"He won't, especially if I ask him not to." Cass' face lit

up. "Actually, it might be a good idea if we talked to him together. He might be able to help you track down scholarships and stuff."

"That's not a bad idea." Warming to the suggestion, Logan thought out loud, "There's a snack bar downstairs in Ike Hall. I could meet you and your dad there at 5:00, and we could eat supper while we discuss what I should do."

Cass reminded herself not to throw her arms around Logan's neck. "I love it! The sooner you start putting your plan into action, the better your chances of getting the money you need. Except," she added, frowning, "we probably shouldn't leave Tabitha out. She wouldn't like being stuck alone in the room while the three of us get together."

"Then invite her too. The more, the merrier." Logan stood up and began pacing as he continued to talk. "In fact, why don't we ask her to tag along with us to the dance? She'd have a blast. I guarantee the guys'll swarm all over her."

Cass grinned. "Let's see. Spend another boring night with Dad or go to a dance where the guys outnumber the girls ten to one. Unless I don't know Tabitha as well as I think I do, I predict she'll choose the dance."

Cass and Logan spent the remainder of their time together discussing how he could best make the transition from West Point to a civilian school. She was chilled to the bone but floating on air when she walked into the hotel room shortly after four. Tabitha, sprawled on the bed, smirked at her.

"If you looked any happier, you'd be positively glowing," she teased.

Hugging herself, Cass twirled across the room before collapsing on the bed next to Tabitha. "I can't tell you how wonderful it is to be with Logan again. He is absolutely, without a doubt, the best guy in the whole world."

"Hey," Dad protested, looking up from the chair where

he sat reading the paper.

"Yeah, hey," Tabitha chimed in. "What about Sam?"

"Okay." Cass shrugged agreeably. "Logan's the best guy in the world for me. Sam's the best guy in the world for you. And Dad—" she blew him a kiss when he looked up from the newspaper, "you're the best father in the entire universe."

"Absolutely, without a doubt?" he ascertained.

"Absolutely, positively."

Dad gave a satisfied nod. "Thank you. It's nice to know quality is still recognized and appreciated."

Standing, Cass slipped off her coat and tossed it on the other bed. "As a matter of fact, Logan appreciates you so much that he wants you to have supper with us at Eisenhower Hall. He was wondering if we could meet him at 5:00."

"Really?" Dad folded the newspaper and laid it on the arm of the chair. "Does he have a particular reason why he wants to get together?"

Cass abruptly bent down to untie her sneakers, neatly avoiding Dad's penetrating gaze. "Well ... yes" she mumbled from her awkward position. "But he doesn't want me to tell you what it is. He wants to tell you himself."

Tabitha shot up to a sitting position, grabbed Cass' sleeve, and forced her up and around so she could see her face. "Is Logan planning to ask Dad for permission to marry you?"

"What?!" Cass snapped, feeling her cheeks flush hot pink. "You know Logan and I haven't even talked about love yet. Doesn't it seem a little farfetched to think we'd skip right over that and go straight to discussing marriage?" Before Tabitha could reply, she hastily continued, "By the way, you're invited to supper too. Logan also said to ask you if you'd like to go to the dance with us. He said you'd be quite a hit with the cadets."

Her ploy worked. Tabitha immediately dropped all talk of marriage. "You wouldn't mind me tagging along?" When Cass assured her she wouldn't, Tabitha bounced off the bed and hurried to the closet. "Do you think the dress I brought to wear to church would look okay?" She retrieved it from the closet and held it in front of her.

"It better," Dad warned good-naturedly, "because I'm not buying you another one."

"You look like a million bucks in that dress," Cass replied without a trace of envy.

Glancing at the clock, Tabitha let out a little shriek. "If we're supposed to meet Logan at 5:00, I'd better get a move on. I need to shower and do my hair and—" Her voice trailed off as she hustled into the bathroom.

Dad and Cass exchanged amused glances.

"I'd say she's excited about the dance, wouldn't you?" Dad drawled.

"I'd say she's way past excited," Cass countered. "She's practically beside herself. Which," she added with a saucy grin, "is the last thing I need. One Tabitha is all I can handle, thank you very much. Two would be a nightmare."

Tabitha got ready in record time, and the trio left the room at 4:45. After they climbed the steps from the parking lot, they blew through the doors into the lobby of Eisenhower Hall on an arctic blast of wind off the river. Spotting them, Logan rose from a couch and waved to get their attention. As they crossed the floor, Cass noticed the cadet who'd gotten up to stand beside Logan, and her steps slowed.

"Uh-oh," she muttered.

"What?" Tabitha turned to her with a curious expression.

"Don't look now," Cass hissed. "But I do believe that's the girl Logan's told me about. You know, Shiloh."

Taking care not to be caught, the sisters studied the

other girl. She was almost as tall as Logan, with a sturdy build and a confident air. Her dark hair was neatly braided, and she had a smile that could light up a room.

The moment the trio reached Logan, he moved to Cass' side, which bolstered her faltering spirits. They soared when he took her arm and slipped it in his.

"Cass, I'd like you to meet Shiloh McNally. Shiloh, this is Cass Devane."

"I'd have known you anywhere," Shiloh said to Cass, shooting Logan a mischievous grin. "Your boyfriend's made me look at your pictures so many times that your image is burned into my brain."

Despite her plan to dislike Shiloh on sight, Cass discovered she couldn't. Put at ease by the girl's teasing remark, she instantly relaxed. "I'm so sorry. He does have a tendency to be a little obsessive at times. I've tried to break him of it, but I haven't had much luck so far."

"I've heard there's medication to correct the problem," Shiloh played along, adding in a stage whisper, "You might suggest he check into it before people start avoiding him. There's already talk in the company about what a pain he is."

"You two are a riot," Logan sniffed. "You ought to consider taking your act on the road."

"Is that a hint to leave, do you think?" Shiloh arched an eyebrow at Cass.

"If it is, I'm ignoring it," Cass shot back. "What about you?"

"Ignoring what?" Shiloh pretended to look past Logan. "I didn't hear anything except an annoying buzz."

Logan threw his free hand up in disgust. "Just what I need, two comedians. As if you—" he bumped shoulders with Cass, "weren't bad enough." He continued before she could think of a snappy comeback, "Anyway, Shiloh, this is Cass' father, Mr. Spencer, and her sister, Tabitha Spencer."

Cass frowned. For the second time in recent days, she was reminded that she had a different last name from the rest of the family.

After a few minutes of small talk, Shiloh excused herself and joined a group of cadets on the far side of the lobby. Logan offered his other arm to Tabitha, who giggled and took it.

Puffing out his chest in a show of mock pride, Logan crowed, "Have I got it made or what? I'll be the envy of every guy in the snack bar, escorting the two of you."

"I'll try to walk far enough behind so they don't realize you're also escorting their father," Dad said dryly.

"Way to ruin my fun." Logan flashed Dad a grin over his shoulder.

"As I always tell the girls, that's what fathers are for." Dad poked him in the back.

They descended the steps to the snack bar where they all chose cheeseburgers with the works. Carrying the food-laden trays, Dad and Logan followed Cass and Tabitha to a booth in a relatively quiet corner of the room. After Logan said a blessing, they tucked into the meal with relish.

"This cold weather is wreaking havoc with my appetite," Cass observed, about to pop four French fries into her mouth at one time. "I've been starving ever since we arrived."

"I know what you mean." Tabitha washed down a bite of cheeseburger with a long drink of Coke. "Maybe we should all chip in and fly Rianne up here. She'd fatten back up in no time."

Logan, who knew about Rianne's weight loss, asked how she was doing. By the time Cass had caught him up on the latest details, nothing remained of their food but a few crumbs.

Stacking the trays one atop the other, Dad set them in the middle of the table then turned his attention to Logan.

"Cass tells me you have something on your mind. I'm all ears if you're ready to chat."

Inhaling deeply, Logan folded his hands on the table. Beside him, Cass tensed as she waited for him to begin. She leaned closer, hoping he sensed her support.

After a halting start, Logan outlined for Dad his plan to leave West Point and enroll in a college in Tennessee. Dad listened quietly, his expression revealing nothing of what he thought as Logan explained his reasons and shared the information he'd collected so far about possible sources of funding.

When Logan finished, Dad regarded him with a steady gaze for several seconds. Then, to Cass' surprise, he asked just one question.

"Have you prayed about this, Son?"

Logan blinked and stammered, "Uh ... well ... not really."

"For something this important, why aren't you asking God to reveal what He would have you do?" Dad let the question hang in the air for a few moments before going on, "The strange thing is, since last night, Tabitha and I have had a couple of conversations about God's timing. We've talked about Ecclesiastes and the idea that there's a time for everything. The question you have to prayerfully consider is whether or not it's your time for leave. If it is, I'll do everything I can to help you find the money to go to school someplace else. If it's not—if you're operating out of your own time schedule because you want to be near Cass, and not God's timing for your life—you need to own up to that."

"In which case you won't help me?" Logan asked quietly.

"I can't support someone who's going against God's timing." Dad's expression was affectionate. "I know how much you care for my daughter. I'm glad you do because you're a fine young man. I also realize how difficult it is for you two to be apart. But you're going to have to continue trusting God with your relationship. He's brought you this far. He won't let you down."

"So your advice is that I pray before I make up mind about staying or leaving the Academy?" Logan asked.

"Not just you," Dad replied. "Cass needs to pray too. Between the two of you, I believe you'll come to the right decision."

Logan turned to Cass with a wry smile. "It looks like we're facing some serious knee-time, pal."

Making a comical face, she wrinkled her nose. "Can we hold off on the praying for a few more hours? Otherwise, we're going to look pretty silly kneeling in the middle of the dance floor."

"Yes, please postpone the prayer compaign," Tabitha fervently implored. "I'd hate to have to pretend I don't know you, especially since I'm counting on you introducing me to your good-looking friends, Logan."

"There you go—" Cass shook her head in mock disgust, "always thinking of yourself."

"No, I'm not," Tabitha protested with a toss of her golden curls. "I'm thinking of all the cadets who shouldn't be deprived of the pleasure of making my acquaintance."

"Whoa!" Dad made a show of lifting his feet. "Is it me or is it getting rather deep in here?"

Following a few more minutes of lighthearted conversation, Dad arranged when and where to pick Cass and Tabitha up, then took his leave. He'd barely left the table when Tabitha rounded on Logan with an eager expression.

"Okay, I'm ready." She rubbed her hands with relish. "Show me where they keep the cutest guys."

"You're awful," Cass chided. "What about poor Sam?"

Tabitha immediately dropped the boy-crazy act. "Sam has nothing to worry about. I'm just playing around," she defended herself. "Ever since we got here, all I've done is think about Sam. Not that I wasn't thinking about him anyway, but there's something about the cadets that reminds me of him." She grinned at Logan. "You guys are special. Ordinary guys can't hold a candle to you."

Instead of responding with a witty comeback, Logan shyly ducked his head to acknowledge the compliment.

Cass was the one who spoke up. "Does that mean Micah doesn't measure up to Sam?"

Tabitha met her gaze straight on. "Yes, it does. I've done a lot of thinking the past couple of days. I've had it with being a pushover. The time has come for me to make some changes in my life, beginning with my relationships with Micah and my mother."

"Hey, this sounds interesting." Propping her elbow on the table, Cass leaned her chin on her hand. "What kind of changes are you talking about?"

"Number one, I'm going to quit thinking things might work out with Micah. They're not going to, and that's that." Tabitha flashed Cass a wry smile. "You were right awhile back when you said Micah's a better friend than boyfriend. I'd been thinking about calling him to come out to the airport since we have that long layover in Honolulu, but now I'm not going to. What would be the point? When all is said and done, I really don't want to see him."

"Wow." Cass sat back in the booth, her eyes wide with amazement. "Talk about a major change. What have you decided about your mother?"

"As soon as we get back to Tennessee, I'm going to do what I should have done the first time she got back in touch with me." Tabitha's expression was as determined as her tone. "I'm going to call her and tell her I won't be coming to Oregon this summer. The time may come when I want to pursue a relationship, but I'm definitely not interested, either at the moment or for the foreseeable future."

"You go, girl," Cass cheered. Beside her, Logan gave Tabitha a thumbs-up. "I like the new, improved you." She lowered her voice and subtly pointed to the right. "Apparently so does the guy over there. He's been trying to get your attention for the past five minutes."

Tabitha oh-so-casually glanced around the snack bar. The moment she caught the cadet's eye, he waved and got up from his table.

"Don't look now—" Cass giggled at the blush that instantly bloomed on Tabitha's cheeks, "but he's making a beeline for you."

When the cadet arrived and introduced himself as Vince Bertelli, it turned out to be the start of a fun evening. Cass, Logan, Tabitha, and Vince wound up playing pool for an hour or so before heading to the dance.

By the time Dad picked Cass and Tabitha up at 11:30, they were exhausted, but in high spirits. After bidding Logan and Vince goodnight, the girls climbed into the back seat of the car and collapsed in a fit of giggles.

Dad eyed them in the rearview mirror. "I don't even want to know what you're laughing about."

Tabitha made a face at him in the mirror. "Good, because we weren't going to tell you anyway."

Dad pulled away from the curb. "You're not planning on staying up all night and talking, are you?" he asked plaintively.

"It's a distinct possibility," Cass said.

"Great." Dad heaved a gusty sigh. "I wonder what the chances are of me getting another room."

CHAPTER 29

Sunday, the day Cass had been dreading, dawned bright and clear and slightly warmer. She dressed for church with a sick feeling in the pit of her stomach. They'd be heading back to Tennessee right after the service, and it would be another six months before she saw Logan again. Sensing her mood, Tabitha pulled her close for a hug.

"Hang in there," she said encouragingly. "You'll get through this. Dad and I are praying for you."

Cass clung to Tabitha, grateful for her understanding. "You'd better be. That's the only thing I'm counting on to keep me from dissolving in a puddle of tears."

Logan met Cass, Tabitha, and Dad outside the immense doors of the Gothic-style cathedral that was the Cadet Chapel. As he escorted them into the church, Cass' mouth dropped open in astonishment.

"This is where you go to church every Sunday?" she asked in an awed whisper. When Logan nodded, she murmured, "Wow."

"My feeling exactly," Tabitha agreed.

Cass' eyes moved across the soaring ceiling, past the dozens of stained glass windows, and finally came to rest on the enormous pipe organ behind the altar. Logan laughed at her expression.

"Kind of impressive, huh?"

Cass snorted softly. "That's like calling the Grand Canyon a measly little hole in the ground."

With their heels clicking on the stone floor, they walked three-quarters of the way down the aisle to a pew on the right. Dad went in first, followed by Tabitha, Cass, and Logan. Sitting down, Cass bowed her head to pray, acutely aware of Logan's arm pressing against hers. She shivered with the joy of worshipping together again after such a long time.

All too quickly, the service was over, and the time to leave had come. Dad and Tabitha said good-bye to Logan outside the chapel and went on ahead to the car to wait for Cass. She turned to him, tears shimmering in her eyes.

"I guess this is it."

Logan looked as miserable as she felt. "I guess so." A muscle clenched and unclenched in his jaw as he fought for control. "It's been great seeing you. But I'm sure going to miss you, even more than before. Letting you go is the hardest thing I've ever done."

"I wish—" Cass shook herself. "Never mind what I wish. It doesn't do any good. Wishing is for children." She stared up at Logan, memorizing every feature on his dear face. "What I should say is I'll be praying. I know what I want you to do, but it's up to God. It's like Dad said. He's brought us this far. He won't let us down."

Logan nodded. "I believe that. I want you to know something though." His voice became hoarse with emotion. "I know beyond a shadow of a doubt that you're the one for me. If you'll have me, someday I'm going to ... uh—" his courage momentarily faltered, and he took a deep breath before finishing in a rush, "ask you to marry me."

"Oh, my." Cass' hand fluttered to her throat, and she repeated, "Oh, my."

Logan's laugh broke the tension. "Wow, I don't think I've ever seen you when you didn't know what to say. Score one for me."

On that lighthearted note, Logan walked Cass to the car then stood in the street as Dad drove away. The last view Cass had of Logan was of his hand lifted to the azure sky, his index finger pointing to heaven. Torn between weeping and smiling, she leaned her head on Tabitha's shoulder.

"Are you okay?" Tabitha took Cass' hand in a comforting grip.

To her surprise, Cass found herself nodding. "I don't get it, but I am." She placed her mouth near Tabitha's ear. "He said I'm the one for him, and that he's going to ask me to marry him someday."

Tabitha's squeal brought a sharp glance from Dad. She smiled innocently as if she had no idea why she'd done it. The moment he turned his attention back to the road, she hissed, "You're kidding! He actually said that?"

"He actually did," Cass confirmed. "It won't be for a long time, of course. But just think, he cares about me that much. Is that an incredible thought or what?"

"It's not so incredible. After all—" Tabitha's eyes sparkled with mischief, "you can be very likable when you put your mind to it."

Despite Cass' fears, the journey back to Tennessee wasn't nearly as bad as she'd thought it would be. Every time she felt like crying, she'd remember Logan's last words and her heart would burst into song again. She also realized she was looking forward to seeing Mom and Hannah. She missed her sweet baby sister, and she had so much to tell Mom.

The remaining time in Jonesborough flew by. Cass spent as much time with Janette as she could stand, coming away from every get-together with an increasingly unsettled feeling. Jan was adamant about not returning to church, while Cass continued to argue how helpful it would be, given her current situation. When they parted for the last time, Cass couldn't shake the feeling that their paths wouldn't be crossing again.

Oh, well, she mentally shrugged as she descended the steps from Janette's house and walked to Papaw's car parked in the driveway. *It's in God's hands. If He wants our relationship to continue, it will. If He doesn't, nothing in heaven or on earth can make it happen.*

When the family walked into the Kwajalein terminal on the following Saturday afternoon, they were greeted by a welcoming committee of three. Grinning from ear-to-ear and waving madly, Kira and Rianne seemed as happy to see Cass and Tabitha as they were to be back. Standing off to one side, but smiling just as broadly, was Alex. Cass' eyebrows disappeared under her bangs when she spotted him.

"What are you doing here?" she asked, once she'd hugged Rianne and Kira then Rianne again, noting with concern that her friend appeared to have lost a couple of pounds.

"We brought him," Rianne announced, laughing at Cass' startled expression.

"Since when can you stand being in the same room with him?" she demanded.

"Excuse me." Alex raised his hand to get their attention. "Would you mind not talking about me as if I weren't here?"

"Okay," Cass accommodated him. "When did you and Rianne start being able to stand the sight of each other?"

Sharing an amused glance with Rianne, Alex furrowed his brow and scratched his chin. "I guess that would be—let me think—last week when we sat together in church."

"I was there too," Kira put in as Cass and Tabitha gaped at each other in stunned silence.

"You ... you ..." Tabitha stammered.

"Went to church?" Cass finished for her. "On purpose?"

"I have a lot to tell you," Alex replied, in what had to be the understatement of the year.

"No joke!" Cass exploded. "When I left two weeks ago, we hadn't really talked in nearly a month. Now you're here to welcome me home, and, on top of that, you've been to church. This isn't some parallel universe, is it?"

Alex laughed. "Nope. It's the real thing."

Before he could continue, Dad and Mom approached the group, nodding weary hellos. Ed Nishihara stood behind them, holding Hannah.

"Ed's here with a car to take us home," Dad explained. "Do you want to come with us or walk with your friends?"

Without hesitation, the girls answered in unison, "Walk with our friends."

"See you later then." Trailed by Ed, Dad ushered Mom to the door.

"All right, give," Cass ordered, whirling on Alex. "I can't wait one second longer to know what's going on."

"Why don't you and Cass walk together so you can fill her in on the details?" Kira suggested to Alex. "And we'll do the same thing with Tabitha."

With that decided, they all headed for the door. Stepping out into the blinding sunlight and tropical heat, Cass lifted her face to the sky.

"It's good to be home," she exulted.

"You can say that again," Tabitha agreed. She winked at Cass before settling her sunglasses on her nose. "I'll see you at the house. This should be interesting."

While the girls took the road, Cass and Alex opted to walk on the beach. Climbing down from the rocks, Cass flung off her sandals and buried her toes in the sand.

"You have no idea how good this feels." She gave a small moan of pleasure. "My feet felt like blocks of ice the entire time we were gone."

"Sort of the way my heart felt all those months after Alison's abortion," Alex remarked quietly. "Then, little by little, God used you to chip the ice away and make me face what we did. We created a life we had no right to create, then ended a life we had no right to end."

Cass stopped dead in her tracks and stared at him. "Oh, Alex." Overcome by emotion, all she could do was reach out and take his hand. "Thank God you realize the truth."

"It's taken me a long time to admit to myself how angry and guilty and yes, sad, I've been since Alison called to tell me she'd had the abortion." He dropped Cass' hand and shrugged. "But seeing things now for the way they really are—well, I'm not the person I was when you left."

"But ... how ... why ..." Cass still couldn't quite get her mind around Alex's remarkable transformation.

"You remember our first day back to school after Christmas break? We were riding to school and Rianne interrupted us." When Cass nodded, Alex continued, "You referred to the baby that morning as a *he*. You said it was because he wasn't an *it*. He was a person. That hit me like a ton of bricks. Right up until you left for the mainland, I did my best not to think about what you said. Then one night I couldn't run away from the truth anymore."

He lowered his head and spoke so softly that Cass had to strain to hear him. "I broke down and cried when I realized what Alison and I had done. It made me sick to my stomach. The only thing I knew to do was beg God to forgive me. Since you weren't here, I called Rianne and told her what had happened. She came right over with an extra Bible and told me to keep it as long as I needed to. Over the next few days, I read about Jesus, and how He died and rose again—all that stuff I used to bother you about. But it suddenly hit me that He died for me—to forgive me. Last Sunday I went to church for the first time in years, and it felt like God was really there, welcoming *me*. I couldn't wait for you to come home to tell you."

Tears were running down Cass' cheeks by the time Alex finished, and she threw her arms around his neck. "I don't know what to say. This is the most wonderful news I've heard in a long time."

"The next thing I plan to do is write to Alison, but I wanted to wait until you could help me with the letter." Taking Cass' hands, Alex held her at arm's length. "I want her to know what we did was wrong, but that God has forgiven me and He forgives her too. I'll ask her to seek his pardon, so he can have the same peace I do."

"Wow, this just keeps getting better and better." Tilting her head to the side, Cass regarded Alex with a humorous look. "Who'd have thought you'd ever write to Alison to witness to her?"

Alex laughed. "Not me, for sure. But God definitely knew." His mood abruptly sobered, and he placed a hand over his chest. "Alison's and my baby will always have a place in my heart. I even gave him a name." He swallowed hard then rasped, "I decided on James Franklin, after my grandfathers."

"That's a good name," Cass whispered around the lump in her throat. "I'm very glad he won't be forgotten."

"He won't," Alex vowed. "Not as long as I'm alive."

"Whew." Cass passed a hand across her eyes. "Talk about an emotional homecoming." She managed a wan smile. "You might warn a person before you spring something like this on her."

"What, and ruin the surprise?" Alex dismissed her complaint with a wave. Releasing Cass' other hand, he gestured down the beach. "Maybe we ought to get going before your folks send out a search party."

"They can be overprotective at times." Cass fell into step with Alex, savoring the feel of the sand between her toes. "I'll probably be the same way when I have kids."

"If I'm ever blessed with more kids, I definitely will," Alex declared. "I don't want them growing up to be like me."

Cass butted her shoulder against his. "Aw, you're not so bad. Now anyway," she added, making Alex laugh.

That night, the family sat down to a supper of soup and sandwiches, the only thing anyone had the energy to fix. With a cooing Hannah lying in her bassinet beside the table, the others reminisced about the trip, citing their favorite memories.

As the conversation gradually wound down, Cass flicked her fingers against her glass to get everyone's attention. "I have something I want to say." She waited until all eyes were on her before continuing, "I've decided I'm tired of being the only Devane in this family. Nothing against my birth father—I'm sure he was a good man. But everyone else in this room is a Spencer, and I want to be one too. Would it be okay if I changed my name?"

"Would it be okay?" Emotion thickened Dad's voice. "Sweetie, it would be fantastic. Nothing would make me prouder than for you to officially become a Spencer." He hesitated. "You're sure you've thought it through though? It's a big step." At Cass' vigorous nod, he looked over at Mom. "Do you have any objections?"

Mom's eyes glistened with tears as she gazed lovingly at Cass. "I never let myself hope the day would come when you'd want to change your name. This means more to me than you'll ever know. It symbolizes us truly coming together as a family."

"Cassandra Aileen Spencer." Tabitha tried out the name then grinned. "I like it. Of course, it's not as good as Tabitha Joi Spencer or Hannah Elizabeth Spencer, but it's not bad. How soon are you going to do it?"

Cass shrugged and glanced at Dad. "As soon as I can."

"I'll talk to a lawyer first thing Monday morning," he promised. "Now, Mom and I have an announcement we'd like to make."

"Uh-oh." Tabitha's mouth rounded into a perfect circle. "Don't tell us you're having another baby. I just got used to having Hannah around."

"Don't worry," Mom reassured her. "The only new Spencer around here for awhile is going to be Cass. What Dad and I want to tell you is that we're seriously considering moving back to Tennessee when you girls go to college. We realized we're not ready to split up as a family yet. You'd be gone before Hannah had the chance to get to know you."

"Yes!" Cass pumped her fist in the air. "The thought of being so far away has been bugging me too." She frowned at Dad. "But what would you do in Tennessee?"

"Uncle Larry and I talked about the possibility of going into business together," Dad replied. "In case that doesn't work out, I'm going to put together a resume, and start sending it out. Who knows? Jonesborough might be in desperate need of a first-rate deejay."

"Then you're their man," Tabitha loyally declared. She smiled across the table at Cass. "Didn't I tell you God had a couple of interesting weeks planned for us back on the mainland?"

"Yes, you did." Cass returned her smile, an impish twinkle dancing in her eyes. "Do you have any predictions about what the next few months hold for the *Spencer* family?"

"Now that you mention it, I have the strangest feeling we haven't seen anything yet. I do believe God has a few more surprises up His sleeve."

"For some reason, He does seem to enjoy keeping us on our toes," Cass agreed, rolling her eyes in comic fashion.

The laughter from around the table startled Hannah, and she added her voice to the happy noise.